ASHLEY R. KING

A VAMPIRE REALITY SHOW NOVEL

NIGHT RACE

MYSTIC OWL

AN IMPRINT OF CITY OWL PRESS

NIGHT RACE
Vampire Reality Show, Book 2

MYSTIC OWL
A City Owl Press Imprint
www.cityowlpress.com

Cover Design by MiblArt. All stock photos licensed appropriately.

Edited by Heather McCorkle.

For information on subsidiary rights, please contact the publisher at info@cityowlpress.com.

Print Edition ISBN: 978-1-64898-203-3

Digital Edition ISBN: 978-1-64898-202-6

Printed in the United States of America

PRAISE FOR ASHLEY R. KING

"King debuts with a delightful, character-driven rom-com, *Painting the Lines* about two underdogs working toward redemption... an expert at balancing chemistry and tension to create a couple readers will root for. Fans of slow-burn romance will be swept away."
— *Publisher's Weekly*

"*Forever After* is SUCH a fun read-the perfect blend of paranormal and contemporary romance with a side of mystery. The unique premise of a vampire reality show hooked me instantly, and the descriptions and details from the confessional booth to the coffin beds kept me absorbed in the fantastical world that Ms. King created."
– *Kat Turner, author of Hex, Love, and Rock and Roll*

"*Painting the Lines* is a fast-paced, chemistry-filled, feel good sports romance! Who knew tennis could be so sexy? Game. Set. Match. You'll fall for Amalie and Julian in straight sets, guaranteed."
— *USA Today Bestselling Author Natasha Boyd*

"Lovely characters, smart dialogues and a great romance! Both characters were lovable, and I couldn't get enough of them!"
— *Read More Sleep Less*

"The characters in *The Wilde Card* are so sweet and their connection is so so genuine. I cried and I laughed, and I laughed until I cried. My heart is so connected to this story, and I'm honestly blown away."
— *Colby Bettley, author of Christmas at the Grotto*

"I really cannot wait to see what Ashley comes up with next! There was absolutely no hesitation in deciding to rate this book five stars, it's truly well deserved!"
– *Naomi, This Ginger Loves Books Blog*

"I love Autumn. I love Oliver. I love the whole concept of this book. I loved it all so much I got a paperback so I can read it all over again. If you want to read a paranormal romance with memorable characters, a clever premise, and a compelling mystery, you *need* to read *Forever After*!"
– *Gabrielle Ash, author of The Family Cross and For the Murder*

For each and every incredible bookstagrammer out there. Thank you for all you do for us authors. It means the world, and you are so appreciated. Thank you from the bottom of my heart.

1

THEODORA

Theodora Nash leaned over the edge of the Rio Grande Gorge Bridge, drawing in a deep breath as her emotions finally quieted. The drop was nearly seven hundred feet and, in her opinion, still wasn't quite high enough.

Light from the bridge illuminated the night, and she took a step backward, releasing part of her bungee cord so it pooled at her feet. Stars dotted the navy sky like freckles, and it *should've* been beautiful. The sight *should've* poked at Theo's heart, begging her to immerse herself in the experience, but she wasn't here for that. Yet again, she chased the same thing that she had for the past three hundred and thirty years, and she'd never found it. Probably never would.

Even after all that time, she still thought about her old life. About Jonathan, too handsome for his own good, especially with that smile and laugh. Theo shook her head, suppressing a grin at the memory.

Would it ever *not* hurt? Would she ever find a way to calm the incessant buzz of guilt and regret that seemed to smother her from day to day? Or was she doomed to live out her immortal days like this? One adrenaline-soaked adventure after the other?

"We're still waiting for a few more people, and then we'll get started," Syd, the jump organizer, called from the entry point of the bridge, his hands cupped around his mouth.

Theo held up a thumb. It didn't matter. She had all night to wait. And then she'd hunt for the next biggest drop or maybe race a car along the Autobahn. The world was her oyster and all that.

A poof behind her, signaling a vampire changing from bat form to human form, startled the humans scattered nearby. They were still clearly not used to vampires, even though her kind had made themselves known to society about three years ago. At least there had been one thing that surprised her in the endless monotony.

Theo didn't have to turn around to know who the other vampire was, catching a hint of the familiar scent of leather and spice. She fought the urge to hang her head, instead standing up straighter, keeping her eyes ahead on the sea of lights in the distance.

"Bored, huh?" she asked.

"Guess you could say that. Although worried is more appropriate. What the hell are you doing out here? Isn't this the fifth jump you've done this week?" Andreas moved into her view. He looked formidable and handsome in his designer coat and classic Andreas scowl, his rich umber skin forever frozen at thirty. Copper eyes bore into hers as he ran a hand over his short curls before moving to his neatly trimmed black beard.

"I thought we've been over this, Andreas. I don't need a keeper. I'm a vampire. You of all people know that." She shrugged off his concern as she toed the edge of the bridge again.

Andreas blew out a breath. The poor guy had appointed himself as her vampire dad and watcher ever since he turned her on that fateful night in 1692.

"I worry about you, Theodora. It's been a while since you've been home, and we miss you." He shoved his hands into the pockets of the perfectly tapered onyx trousers fitting his tall frame like a glove.

Obviously, there had never been anything romantic between

them. One, Theo couldn't fathom loving anyone aside from Jonathan, no matter how much time passed. Sure, she'd heard lots of talk about a mate bond, the type of bond signaling two beings were, in fact, soul mates. Yet she'd gone so long without finding that, which further proved Jonathan was her one and only. Two, Andreas found his mate not long after he'd turned Theo. Davina was part of the "we" he spoke of. The truth was she missed Andreas and Davina, but being around them served as a reminder of what she lost that last summer of her human life.

She clenched her fists at the memory, anger still surging through her veins after all this time. "I miss you both, but I've got to do this. You know why."

Andreas helped facilitate her revenge right after she'd been turned. It was something Theo could never thank him enough for. As a matter of fact, that was the one moment in this whole long, miserable life that she never regretted. Those assholes had it coming to them, and if given the chance, she'd do it all over again. In a heartbeat.

Her oldest friend placed a hand on her shoulder, causing her to meet his eyes. His dark brows were furrowed in concern. She hated that she put that look on his face.

"Theo, this isn't healthy. We can help you if you come home." His lips twisted to the side in thought. "There are plenty of other hobbies, like...drums or drawing. You could even go back to your roots and maybe open up a midwifery or revisit the healing arts."

Yeah, because that would go over well. Blood and all.

She tucked her black hair painted with a rich silver ombre behind her ear, steeling herself for the admission coming forth from her lips. Andreas knew what she actually sought all this time and thought it pointless. After all, he'd been around since, well, forever. He hadn't actually told her an exact year, but he gave off the vibe of a powerful and ancient vampire—yet he had never heard of anything that could help her plight. She tried to arrange her face into a placid expression but felt her nose crinkle regardless.

When she spoke, her words were hushed, as if said too loudly, they might not be true. She met his stare head on. "I found it, Andreas."

He froze, which said a lot since vampires were preternaturally very still. He dropped his hand from her shoulder and ran it over his curly hair, a ragged breath drawn from his lips.

"How?"

Theodora tugged at the bungee rope for something to do with her hands. A scoff escaped her lips because she had a feeling he wouldn't believe her answer. She squinted as she turned to face him again.

"A reality TV show."

A disbelieving smile curved his mouth as he shook his head. "No way."

"Yep. It's called *Night Race*. It's like that original race reality show, you know, but for vampires only."

Night Race was brand-new and boasted that contestants would race across the world in the hopes of locating a spelled chalice. Normally Theo would snicker and move on, but this particular artifact could be the answer to all her problems.

Andreas lifted his chin. "And the prize, tell me about it."

"It's a magical goblet that has the power to be used once. The holder can choose to turn into a vampire or a human."

And with those words, it felt like the air had been sucked out of the ether surrounding them.

Her old friend adjusted his jacket, shock still written across the sharp planes of his face. "Are you for sure on the show?"

She kicked the bungee rope. "No. I'm awaiting a call any moment now. But if I make it on there, you know I'll do whatever it takes to get what I want."

Anyone who ever crossed paths with Theodora knew that much.

Andreas opened his mouth to say...what? To disapprove or

support? She couldn't tell by his expression. She knew he struggled because he'd "made" her, and he didn't do that lightly.

Before he could say anything, Theo's phone rang inside her zippered jacket, and she stepped back from the edge of the bridge, holding up a finger to him. "Hello?"

A male voice came through the line, thick with an Australian accent. "Theodora Nash?"

"It depends on who's calling." She propped a hand on her hip and tapped her foot, impatient that this entire outing was becoming drawn out. She should've already jumped and turned into a bat, just to freak out the organizer. The idea made her lips curl, her fangs poking out.

The voice on the other end of the phone spoke again. "This is Max Wilson, the director of *Night Race*."

She straightened, swinging a wide-eyed glance at Andreas, who observed her carefully. Max had also recently directed a hit vampire dating show, *Forever After*, which garnered a lot of press. There were allegations of murders on location, of contestants being paid off for their silence, things like that. Things that made her suspicious of the director and producers, but it didn't matter in the long run because this could be her chance if Max was calling about what she so hoped.

"In that case, yes, this is Theodora."

"I'm calling to congratulate you on making it onto the show. I've heard a lot about you through my colleagues, and I think you'd be a fantastic addition. Your entry video was well done."

It wasn't. It was straightforward and to the point. But then again, maybe that's what Max wanted. Her heart fluttered in her throat at the idea of what she so desperately sought all these years to be within her grasp. *So close.* Even so, she never liked to appear eager. It was all part of the *I don't give a shit* persona she'd perfected so well over the years. One that had kept her heart safe, locked away cold and unfeeling, but safe.

"If I say yes, when do we start? I'm currently in New Mexico, and I have things to do." She had nothing to do, but he didn't need to know that.

Max didn't miss a beat. "The last Friday of October. Our plan is to take a chunk of November to film since the days will be shorter, giving us more time out and about."

A reality show filled with vampires definitely had its limitations. She didn't say anything, and Max filled in the silence like she figured he would.

"We'd meet at the airport in Jacksonville, Florida. If you agree, I'll forward all the details to the email address you provided on your application." He paused. "Can I count on you to join the show?"

She knew her answer the moment she picked up the phone, but she wasn't one to make anything easy on someone like him—the Hollywood director type who only cared about ratings and money instead of the lives of the people on his show.

"Hmmm," she drawled out, enjoying the serpentine smile that cracked her lips. She heard Max shift on the other end of the phone, and that made her grin grow even wider, made her happy for the first time in a long time. "I suppose so."

The director chuckled. "I had a feeling you'd say that, even if you're playing hard to get. It's not a secret that you've been after what we're offering for centuries. I'll be in touch soon."

And then the line went dead.

Lovely.

She tucked her phone into her jacket and turned to Andreas. "I'm on the show."

He looked pained, but even still, he was her friend, so he managed a smile for her.

"You know how I feel, but more than anything, I want you to be happy, so I support you." He took her hands in his and squeezed them once before dropping them. "But be careful."

Theo nodded. "Of course. Careful's my middle name."

Andreas snorted and gestured toward the bungee rope at her feet, causing her to laugh too.

She shrugged. "Okay, maybe not. But what do you say we jump and change midway? Give these humans something to really freak out about?"

He shook his head, a smile still on his lips. Even so, he got sorted with the jump organizer, who didn't mind another jumper.

"The more, the merrier," Syd had said with a grin as he accepted Andreas's money.

"Ready?" Andreas asked as they lined up on the edge of the bridge.

It felt as if that question was twofold. Ready for the jump? Ready to find the chalice that could change *everything*?

"I am. I feel like everything's led to this moment, Andreas."

He released a beleaguered sigh. "I hope you're right, Theo."

From behind them came Syd's voice. "All right, everyone, on my count, we jump. Remember everything we discussed in our practices..."

Theo already tuned him out, feeling a little lighter with a plan in place. The instructor finally began to count down, and on three, Theo and Andreas jumped. Wind whipped Theo's hair back from her face, taking her breath with it. Dizzying adrenaline pumped through her, bringing her to life, making her *feel* for a precious moment. Midway through, she and Andreas transformed into bats, their veined wings flapping in the cool evening air, reveling in the freedom as the bungee cords fell away.

As they flew into the night to a series of surprised shrieks from the bridge, Theo grinned.

Night Race, indeed.

2

AIDEN

THE END CREDITS BEGAN TO ROLL FOR *FRIGHT NIGHT*, THE ORIGINAL 1985 one, although Aiden enjoyed the 2011 version too. He ran a hand over his bleary, sleep-deprived eyes as he clicked it off and finished getting ready for his day. Sleep deprivation had become a constant, horrible friend these last three years. He usually went for a horror film when it happened since those were his favorites, but even better were vampire films. Maybe then he could glean a way to... He shook his head, trying not to go down that path. He knew it was a dead end, anyway.

He ran a hand through his dark-brown hair, his fingers brushing the rough skin of the scar that cut through his left brow. Doctors said he was lucky he didn't lose his eye. A few more inches down, and he would've.

His gaze flicked to the framed picture on his nightstand. Cassidy held her hand up to the camera, showing off her engagement ring with an exaggerated smile, her brown eyes bright. Aiden's arms were wrapped around her, his forest-green eyes alight with love for the woman he'd just asked to be his wife. Grief expanded in his chest, and he sighed, going through the motions to get ready for work.

As he slid into his car, he thought about the ornery cat waiting for him at his veterinary clinic. He was pretty sure he'd figured out her issue and was excited to help the animal feel better. On his short commute to work, he tried instead to focus on those things, on the good. He loved his job and knew not everyone could say the same, so at least he had that.

By the time he stepped into the clinic, he felt more like himself again, something that usually took a cup—or three—of coffee to do.

"Dr. Archer!" Monica, his receptionist who was a good friend of his mom's, waved.

Aiden offered her a grin as he sorted through his stack of patient files for the day. "Good morning. It looks like we have a busy day today."

Her expression shifted into one of exasperation. "We do and your sister is in your office. She knows you have a neutering in an hour."

He suppressed a smile at that because if Aurora was in his office, that meant *he* was the one about to be neutered. Or worse, she'd found out what he'd done. He fought a cringe at that.

"Thanks, Monica."

As he headed toward his office, he could almost hear the ominous music playing with each footstep. Aurora Archer-Fredericks wasn't someone people pissed off willingly. And she was ridiculously protective of him, being the amazing older sister that she was.

"Aurora, you know there are these things called phones, right?" he said by way of greeting as he opened the door to his office.

Aurora *tsked* at him like she was a thousand years old and pulled him into a hug. When she drew back, she had a sad look in her eye.

"You kind of go AWOL when it gets close to the anniversary, so I wanted to check on you, see how you're doing."

This he could manage. So his mom hadn't told her what he'd

signed up for. He moved around the desk and sat in his chair, motioning for his sister to do the same across from him.

"I'm okay, Ror. I'm thirty-four years old—I got this." He cleared his throat. "It's been three years, and I'm...I'm working on getting on with my life." Why did those words taste so sour? Probably because they were lies, and he *hated* lying.

Aurora had a bullshit detector that rivaled none other. She tilted her head, scrunched up her blond brow, and skewered him with the Archer green eyes.

"You are so full of it, Aiden. All you do is bury yourself in work and movies. You're still that happy-go-lucky kid I knew, but there's a shade over you now, and..." She winced, pursing her lips. "I'm not saying you need to be happy all the time. That came out wrong. What I'm trying to say is, it's okay to be sad, to grieve, to be angry. But at some point, you have to move on. She would want you to."

"I know that, Aurora. I know, and I'm trying. I really am." He paused and scratched his neck, weighing out his next move. "Maybe this will cheer you up?" He gripped the edge of his desk. Was he really about to do this?

His sister perked up, a mischievous smile playing across her mouth. "Oooh, I sense dirt. Tell me!"

He grinned in earnest. "I sent in a video to audition for a spot on *Night Race*."

Silence descended as Aurora stared at him, her smile falling, her eyes shuttering. "No," she finally breathed.

Aiden anticipated that she wouldn't be happy. Hell, his mom had a conniption fit, but it was something he had to do whether they understood it or not. "Yes."

Aurora brought her hands to her temples, her eyes wide as she shook her head. "No, Aiden. I mean it. That show will have vampires on it. *Vampires.*"

"I thought we discussed that not all vampires are bad."

His sister's face reddened as she shot him a pointed stare. "No, they're not. But the ones who killed my brother's fiancée and nearly killed my brother are."

"Aurora—" Aiden began, his voice cracking because whether she meant it or not, her words were a punch to the gut.

Aurora's eyes went glassy as she leaned forward, clearly not done yet. "I don't get it. What could possibly have possessed you to even *want* to go on that show? What's the prize, Aiden?"

If she had a problem with him possibly getting on the show, then Aurora would most definitely flip out at the prize. "A magical chalice."

"Oh, okay. So like some King Arthur and the round table bullshit? Really? That's what you're risking your life for?" She scoffed and sat back in her seat, still massaging her temples, likely feeling a migraine coming on.

Aiden cleared his throat. "Actually, it's not like that. The cup gives the winner a choice."

She straightened, her fingers dropping to clutch the chair arms. "So help me, God, Aiden, if what I think is about to come out of your mouth..."

"The choice is to become a vampire or human." He paused, meeting his sister's glare head on. "And I want to become a vampire."

"You want to become the very creature that ruined your life? *Why?*"

"You weren't there, Ror. You weren't there when I was helpless to protect Cassidy. If I'm a vampire, I can *always* protect my loved ones—no matter what." His jaw tightened. "What happened that night will never happen again because *I'll* be the one stalking the night. And then I'll find *him*. I'll hunt him down, and I'll tear him apart. That's the only way I stand a chance against him. There are no Van Helsings or Peter Vincents. It's just me and this boiling rage that simmers here"—he pressed a fist over his chest—"and I have to do this. I have to at least try."

Aurora stared at him for what felt like an eternity before

scooting to the edge of her chair. "I don't agree with this at all. I don't think it's a good idea because who'll run your clinic? How will you hang out with your family when we're all in bed by nine and your day's just getting started? But maybe I've jumped the gun here. Maybe I don't even need to worry because who knows if you'll get on the show in the first place?" A sliver of hope threaded those words.

Aiden's phone rang. His sister's jaw dropped open, and she quickly recovered, muttering, "I swear that better not be the freaking show, Aiden."

He gave her a bland smile before clicking the speakerphone button. "Hello?"

"Dr. Archer, you have a call from Lola Mitchell, Max Wilson's assistant," Monica said.

He pulled in a breath. Could this really be what he'd hoped for?

"Put her through, please."

There was a click, and a woman's voice came through the line. "Hello, Dr. Archer. I'm Lola, assistant to the director of *Night Race*."

Aiden winced, wishing maybe he hadn't put the call on speaker after all.

Aurora's searing gaze burned into him as he spoke. "Hi, Lola."

"I'm calling to tell you that should you want it, you have a spot on *Night Race*. We loved your video and think you'll do well."

Aiden met his sister's eyes. While she might not completely agree, she knew he had to do this, so after rubbing a hand over her face, she gave him a shaky thumbs-up.

"Right. I would love to be involved."

Lola sounded pleased and then went through the details, including that Aiden would need to be prepared to show up at the Jacksonville International Airport next Friday, October twenty-ninth, at 7:00 p.m. She closed out the conversation by reminding him that the winner not only received the chalice, but also a large cash prize.

"Wonderful talking with you, Aiden. See you soon." And then the line went dead.

Aiden shot Aurora a sheepish look. While he felt a bit guilty for dropping such a bomb on her and making her worry, he wouldn't be swayed. This was his chance to get some kind of life back, to have a purpose that mattered, to protect what remained of his family. He had to do this.

She pressed her fingertips to her eyes as she leaned back far enough to look at the ceiling. "Well, I guess that's that."

Yeah. Looks like it.

3

THEO

THEO SIGNED ALL THE NECESSARY DOCUMENTS HANDED TO HER BY Max's assistant, Lola, not blinking at the mention of possible death if she didn't make it to the safe house locations before sunrise. She knew the risks when she agreed to the show.

What did make her snicker, albeit evilly, was the mention of not eating her teammate. Now that was unexpected and hilarious because, well, first of all, this would be a free-for-all, meaning there would be no teammate. That was one of the things that drew her to the show to begin with. The auditions claimed it would be every person for themselves, and given how she lived, it was perfect. Secondly, she found out last minute that humans were included as contestants too, which didn't worry her. She had her blood-drinking under control enough that she didn't go off and eat people around her, much less people she knew.

She laid the documents down on the airport terminal seat next to Lola. Not a single regular passenger could be seen since the show had commandeered an entire terminal at the international airport. A camera crew milled around, not filming yet, but checking out the best places for footage.

Several contestants were settled throughout. Some stood in

clumps by the floor-to-ceiling windows that showcased planes taking off into the night sky. Others sat alone, playing on their phones. A few vampires chatted with humans, and while Theo thought about joining them, she wanted a minute to gather her thoughts.

She'd been stuck at thirty-two for three hundred and thirty years, although her human memories still remained fresh, as if they took place only yesterday. Running a hand over one of the rips in her jeans, Theo tried to ignore the unbidden images—images of gathering medicinal herbs with her best friend, Elizabeth, making poultices and tending to the sick, of falling into bed with Jonathan after a long and fulfilling day, of helping him run his shipping company during a time when that was unheard of.

Lola stood up, her heels clacking along the shiny floor as she took center stage in the wide aisle between the rows of seats. She whistled between her fingers, an impressive shrill sound immediately garnering everyone's attention.

"I'm Lola, Max's assistant. Should you need anything at all, call the number on the card you each received when you signed in. I'm human, so that means I'm available to help at all hours. Our last contestant just arrived, so we're ready to start, but a few ground rules before we turn on the cameras for filming." She paused and scanned the room, moving her long, stick-straight red hair off her tanned shoulders. "First, you will have a two-person audio and video crew with you at all times. They stay with you and only you, so needless to say, you'll get to know each other very well. We'll introduce you all soon. You will need to have your mics on unless otherwise specified. Times when you don't need to mic up are when you're sleeping, using the bathroom, bathing, etc. You get the gist, right?"

Everyone nodded and murmured their agreement.

"Before we start, I want to introduce you to the director of this brilliant brainchild, Max Wilson himself." Lola gestured to the side, and Max stepped up.

Theodora raised a brow because he was handsome, that was for sure. Some of his inky black pompadour had escaped and curled over his eye like an evil villain. He pushed it from his pale face before addressing everyone with a broad smile, showing off his very pointy fangs.

"Thank you all for being here. Remember, this is *not* a live broadcast. This show is filmed first and will then be aired later on. Most importantly, I want you to all have fun and be safe. We're going to get started now by introducing you to your host, Daniel Vasquez-Larson. He has a few things to share, not to mention a last-minute twist."

Of course there was. Theo had watched a couple of episodes of Max's first vampire reality show, *Forever After*, and had heard about all the contestant deaths he faked just for the sake of ratings. She fought the urge to roll her eyes at whatever Max had concocted.

A smattering of applause filled the terminal as Max stepped back and Daniel moved forward. Daniel stood taller than the director but was most definitely a human in his early thirties. His black hair was styled effortlessly in a quiff haircut, dimples popping in his warm brown skin, his rich hazel eyes alight with all sorts of mischief. *Da-yum.* He was gorgeous. He straightened the cuffs of his white dress shirt beneath his navy blazer, which hung over matching tailored dress pants with shiny brown shoes.

Daniel went into host mode quickly, and Theo could vouch that he was infinitely better and appeared much nicer than Kerrie, the host of last year's *Forever After*.

"Turn your mics on, please," he began.

Theo reached down to her pack and clicked the button, trying to ignore the wave of nerves that raced through her body. She welcomed the sensation because their appearance caused all the other emotions to dampen, and she'd gladly take that any day.

Daniel continued once everyone was miced up and ready. "Welcome to *Night Race*. I'm Daniel Vasquez-Larson, and I'll be your host." He began to walk in front of all the contestants so the cameras could capture everyone. Theo ignored them and instead focused on the host. "As you know, you all are in a race to complete a series of challenges in order to be the winner of the Solis Occasum chalice. This cup is spelled and has the power to turn one person into a vampire or one person into a human. The magic takes a thousand years to recharge after each use, so if you're a vampire, you'll have to wait quite some time for the chance again."

Theo's chest constricted at that thought.

"It's imperative that you know it is your responsibility to take care of yourself and your safety. Every contestant here has signed a waiver, and *Night Race* cannot guarantee all vampires will make it to their safe house location before dawn each day. We also cannot guarantee that some of the tasks won't endanger humans. Our crew will be looked after, but otherwise, that's the name of the game. If anyone is worried, I highly suggest you leave at this time, please."

Wow, this guy even made "Get out of here" sound pleasant. No one moved.

Daniel looked pleased. "Perfect. Now let's see if any of you leave after hearing the twist." He paused theatrically, and Theo could almost imagine a swell of dramatic music being inserted once edited for TV. "We plan to be the first reality show to team up vampires and humans."

There was another pause as murmurs filtered through the room, Theo's brow furrowing as she questioned whether she heard Daniel correctly.

Seemingly delighted with the bomb drop, he went on. "That's right. Each vampire will be teamed up with a human for a total of eight teams competing to find the chalice. If this is a problem, now's the time to leave." He folded his hands in front of his body as he waited.

Theo shifted in her seat, uneasy. The last thing she wanted to do was work with a human. They'd only slow her down and, well, be fragile.

While no one walked, one contestant, a vampire, raised his

hand. "The chalice only grants *one* change, though, correct? So if a team of two wins..." He cocked a brow, allowing Daniel to elaborate.

The host's slow-forming smile was downright diabolical, those two dimples of his on full display. "You're on the right path of thinking. If a team of two wins, they have to decide who gets the cup because it only works once."

More hushed whispers spread through the terminal. Worry knotted and wound itself tightly in Theo's stomach. This sounded like a recipe for disaster. How would that even encourage working together? Maybe she'd go rogue and do things her way.

Daniel appeared almost smug now. "And before you get any ideas, know that you are *required* to work with your partner, or you're disqualified. The winning team will not only win the chalice, but will also split the cash prize of one million dollars." He paused, letting that sink in. "Now let's get into our first challenge, which will lead to how teams are picked. After that, I'll give you more detailed instructions regarding how *Night Race* will play out." Daniel clapped his hands together and rubbed them eagerly like that popular meme Theodora always saw on social media. "Is everyone ready?"

Various excited hoots and hollers surrounded her, but she remained silent. *Night Race* might be a game to some, but it was *everything* to her. She would win. She'd do whatever she could to make sure of it.

No mercy.

"The first task is for everyone to race to concourse A, Gate A3. But it's not as simple as it sounds. You'll pick up a card and will have to do each step found on it—with your luggage in tow." Daniel did a slow scan.

Theo cringed as she noted some people brought suitcases that weren't backpacks or the rolling types. That should be interesting.

"You'll have a few obstacles in your way, and once you make it to the gate, you'll wait for everyone else to join. From there, partners will be chosen, and let's just say, I can't wait to see how that all goes down. Now, on my count of three, you'll race to pick up your cards, which are placed behind that curtain. Lola, if you please."

Lola pulled a curtain down from one of the windows, something Theo had just thought was part of the decor. Sixteen cards were affixed to the glass, spaced decently apart. Adrenaline coursed through Theo's veins as she grabbed the straps of her backpack, making sure it was settled tightly between her shoulders.

Daniel continued. "On your mark, get set, go!"

Then the madness began.

Theo made it to the front of the window, thanks to her sharp elbows, and grabbed a card.

Take the jet bridge from Gate C7 to the stairs. Below, find a car—the key is in the ignition already. The airport is now shut down just for us. No need to worry about being reckless, so race to the blue lights.

Not worrying about the rest, Theodora hurried through the bridge and down the stairs with a singular focus. She was in the lead as she slid into a souped-up car with purple lights beneath it. For a terrifying moment, she feared it might not start due to some trick played by the show, but it did. Tires squealed as she took off.

Behind her, other cars revved to life and started flying all over the place. In the middle of it all was one car driving at the speed of a turtle's crawl. It had to be a human behind the wheel. No vampire she knew would drive so slowly. She shook her head. Whoever it was driving that car, she did *not* want to be paired up with them. Scoffing, she pushed her foot down on the accelerator, barreling toward the blue light.

This would be a piece of cake.

4

AIDEN

A<small>IDEN KEPT REPEATING A MANTRA HIS DAD USED TO SAY</small>, "S<small>LOW AND</small> steady wins the race," in his head.

Okay, sure, he was driving the slowest of everyone, but some of them were stalling out, and some had already spun their cars off the runway. One lone car with purple lights flashed ahead in the distance, and he fought down admiration for the beautiful raven-and-silver-haired vampire. It'd been a while since anyone had caused him to stumble. But she was his competition, or at least at this point she was. It was highly unlikely he'd get paired up with her.

He screeched to a halt at the blue light, which was outside what he assumed to be Concourse A. Only one other car had made it ahead of him, which meant he had managed to remain in good standing so far. The card directed him to take the stairway leading to another jet bridge. Shooting out of the vehicle, he raced up the stairs and through the tunnel, stepping out at Gate A3. Cameras followed him as he set off to complete the next task on the card: to locate the Shula Burger restaurant and find a puzzle.

It didn't take long for him to find the restaurant, and there along the tabletops sat various bags of puzzle pieces. The lovely vampire with pale skin he'd glimpsed traveling at warp speed was the only one in the place aside from camera and sound crews. Her head was down as she worked frantically at putting a jigsaw puzzle together. She turned as Aiden approached, narrowed her kohl-lined eyes, and hissed at him. After a pause, she did it again before returning her attention to her puzzle.

Yep. She actually hissed at him.

While every instinct in him screamed to grab a weapon, he repressed the urge. This was no time to show weakness. For all the other contestants knew, he wanted to be a vampire for the whole "eternal life" crap. And for now, it was best they thought that.

So what did he do? He offered her a big ole smile as he grabbed his bag and took up the spot at the table adjacent to hers. If he was going to do this, he had to show the vampires he wasn't afraid of them. But then again, not all were aggressive or even semi-aggressive. He knew that. Despite what had happened, he didn't hate them all, just the ones who had ruined his life. Vampires weren't all alike any more than humans were.

"Really? Out of *all* the tables, here?" she snarled, even as she kept her focus on the task in front of her. She was pretty close to finishing it, too, revealing what he assumed to be the Solis Occasum.

Aiden began to piece his puzzle together quickly, thankful for all the ones his mom made him do every time he went over to visit. How most parents framed their kids' artwork, his mom made her kids do puzzles and framed those instead.

He shot the vampire a look, still unable to keep from smiling because she was *so* put out by him. And it didn't hurt that she was really pretty, the kind of pretty that made people feel off-balance.

"Oh, I'm sorry. I didn't know you had a claim on all the tables," he said with a chuckle.

The outer edges were already complete.

"Shhhh! I need to focus and can't with all that human noise."

Camera people buzzed around them like flies.

"So would you rather I hiss, then? Maybe snarl or growl? Would that help you focus better? Because I can totally do that too. Whatever your highness deigns most appropriate."

Putting the final piece in the puzzle, the vampire looked at him again, even as other contestants finally made their way in and were rushing to start the task.

"Stay out of my way." Baring her fangs, she called for Daniel to come over.

"Theodora 'Theo' Nash is our first-place winner for the vampires," Daniel boomed.

Theodora. He liked that name. For some reason, it fit her.

The host gestured for her to wait outside the restaurant, but before she did, she turned around and gave Aiden a feline smile.

"Suck it," she snapped.

"Actually, I think that's what you do since you're the vampire. But I mean, hey, whatever," Aiden volleyed back with a shrug.

Theo huffed before turning on her heel to wait outside the restaurant. He could feel her searing stare the entire time he worked on finishing the puzzle. His sister would tell him not to poke the bear, but he couldn't help it, especially when Theo started it. Kill them with kindness was another platitude his family liked to repeat over and over again. Still, he also wanted to let anyone competing know he refused to be a doormat. He might be nice, but there was a line, and once crossed, things got real.

Shaking fingers snapped the last piece in place, relief settling in Aiden's bones. He threw his hand into the air to grab Daniel's attention.

The man raced over and quickly proclaimed, "Aiden Archer, first place for the humans!"

He wasn't entirely sure, but it sounded as if Theo muttered, "Damn it" under her breath. It didn't matter. This meant he was one step closer to his goal—to revenge and peace. After three long years. The knowledge made him feel lighter as the image of the chalice danced in his mind, a golden cup laced with red and black gemstones that looked more at home in a Tolkien novel than in real life. Then again, who would've ever thought vampires were real? But now, after their coming out, the same year Cassidy died, the entire world had changed.

Cameras buzzed around the other contestants, making sure to get shots of them all working. One even hung around him and Theo as they waited, hoping for more banter probably.

The thing was, Aiden had nothing. He was ready to get this over with. The fact that he'd be given a vampire partner to work with in the first place was nearly enough to send him scattering, but his plan was more important than his comfort. He'd make do.

In the end, there would be an apparent battle—perhaps the rumors of real murders on the set of *Forever After* were true? It felt like they might be because it wasn't explicitly stated, but it seemed like Max had pretty much given them permission to off their partners once they made it to the chalice.

Fine. Aiden had never killed anything or anyone in his life. Still, he could figure it out, especially since his end game included killing the vampire responsible for Cassidy's death and his eyebrow scar. He could handle the scar. It served to remind him every day of that night. But Cassidy? He would never be able to bring her back. He clenched his fists at the thought.

Daniel moved around, declaring contestants finished and putting them in order—humans behind Aiden, vampires behind Theo. The vampire was even more beautiful up close. Jet-black hair colored with silver midway through fell to her shoulders, slightly curled, framing her pale face. Bright-blue eyes, bright like tropical waters rather than the stormy seas he assumed they would be, barely glanced his way. Her legs—clad in black jeans—went on forever, stretching up her tall frame to meet a leather jacket and white T-shirt. Running sneakers laced up tight like she meant business completed the look. Her pink lips seemed to rest in a forever pursed position. Simply put, she was stunning.

Theo leaned in, her scent entirely at odds with her being—she smelled like a warm, sunny day filled with spring flowers. "I feel sorry for whoever ends up with you as their partner," she whispered, even though the camera crew stood right on top of them, no doubt capturing every juicy moment.

Aiden shrugged as he crossed his arms. He might've been a little more than pleased to catch her watching his muscles as he did so. Part of his training to become stronger and better was to spend a lot of time in the gym—it also helped a lot with the trauma he went through. He popped his bicep muscle, biting back a smile as Theo realized she'd been caught checking out the competition.

Her blues eyes skewered him, but he was unaffected. He tilted his head toward his arms. "I think my partner will be pretty lucky. They might even like my arms." And then, just because this was the first time he felt some semblance of not being a zombie sluggishly going through life, he shot her a wink. Aiden Archer was not the kind of guy who winked at the ladies. *Ever.*

He met his fiancée in college, and it took him forever to get up enough nerve to even ask her out. Even with the assurances of his closest friends, who'd done recon work for him on the matter, he still bumbled his way through things with her, disbelieving that a woman like Cassidy would even look at a guy like him.

Theo rolled her eyes and turned back to the action, watching the contestants push and fight their way through the puzzle. If the competition was already this heated, he wondered what it'd be like once they were actually competing for the Solis Occasum.

After the final contestant finished, Daniel drew everyone's attention back to him. All the contenders stood in two lines in the middle of the airport in front of the burger place, eyeing their host expectantly. Glancing at them, Aiden wondered what brought each of them here. A chance at eternal life, to be stronger maybe, or walk in the sun. The last one tugged at his heartstrings, but he couldn't let himself get sucked into sympathy. This was his chance, his prize, and he would not be beaten.

"Excellent job with that challenge, everyone!" Daniel's grin went from easygoing to mischievous, and Aiden instantly felt uncomfortable.

What did the show have up its sleeve? With each passing moment, he was starting to believe all the rumors about the director, Max Wilson.

"So here's the catch. We're pairing you up based on how you finished the last task. If both lines would face each other—that's your partner for the next month."

The camera crew circled them like sharks in the water, desperate to capture everyone's reactions, ranging from excitement to disappointment. Aiden should've felt something akin to dread at having to fight with the disgruntled vampire in front of him, but instead, he felt...glee? Happiness? Anticipation?

"Man, I sure feel sorry for you since you're my partner," he needled, unable to resist throwing her earlier insult back at her.

Her nostrils flared as her lips pulled into a frown, the hint of a fang exposed. When she spoke, her words held a menacing edge. "Best watch your back. I'm winning the chalice for something I've waited entirely too long for, and I won't hesitate to kill you once we find it."

The words hit Aiden like a punch to the gut. This had been his sole focus for the last three years. He'd repeatedly come upon dead end after dead end, and when he heard about *Night Race*, he felt like the universe had finally deigned to answer his cries for help.

He lifted his chin, allowing some of the anger he felt at her threat to seep into his voice. "That's funny because I've been working on sharpening my stake, and I'm not the one who has to hide from the sun each day." He smirked. "Think about all the things I can do that you can't. So when we find the Solis Occasum chalice, because we *will* find it first, I won't hesitate to drive that stake through your slow-beating heart if I have to, and I will do what I've come here to do. Without thinking twice. Don't underestimate me."

Theo snarled and looked as though she had an impressive

rejoinder winding up on her tongue, but was interrupted by the host.

"Now that everyone has had a chance to meet, I want to remind you that you *must* work with your partner. You can't do solo missions, or you'll be disqualified. Your two-person camera crew will check in with us daily, and if we don't hear from them, we'll disqualify you, if you're catching my drift. Once you reach the chalice, you may do as you wish, but only one victor may drink from it. I'm to reiterate that *Night Race* is not responsible for any injuries or death occurring along the way. Are we clear?"

The contestants all grumbled their assent, Aiden among them.

"Good. Now onto our first official task. On my mark, you'll go back the way you came. You'll race down the jet bridge to one of the cars you drove here and make your way to Gate C. Once you climb those stairs, instead of going through and heading back into the gate, you'll board the plane. As you board, the flight attendant will hand you your travel packet detailing your destination and task upon arrival." Daniel gave a dramatic pause, folding his hands in front of him as he eyed everyone. "Vampires, you needn't worry. Anytime air travel is involved, all contestants will fly VampJet."

A few vampires released a sigh of relief. Aiden peeked at his new partner from the corner of his eye to see her tapping her foot impatiently, her face etched in a scowl as she rocked forward on the toes of her sneakers, gaze fixed on the entrance to the jet bridge. At least he knew they had this in the bag if she drove.

"But...that's not all."

Of course it wasn't. It was beginning to sound like an infomercial gone wrong.

"There's only room for five teams on the first VampJet. If you don't make it on that one, you'll have to wait to board the second one, which will take off in three hours, putting you at a disadvantage. Another incentive for getting on that first jet is that you will be released for the next challenge in the order in which you board. Now when I say go, you're on your own until we meet again at our first destination."

Theo finally looked at Aiden, determination practically vibrating off her skin. That look basically said, "Don't screw this up for me."

Well, it wasn't as if he was super thrilled to be working with her either, but he'd make do until he had to stake her. Honestly, the animosity between them would make that part easier.

Daniel cleared his throat before stepping out of the way. "On your mark—" Everyone moved into position. "Get set—" Aiden feared his heart might race out of his chest, the sound roaring in his ears. "Go!"

"Get moving, imbecile!" Theo shouted, even though Aiden wasn't *that* far behind her.

This is going to be fun.

5

THEO

AIDEN WAS A FOOL AND WOULD ONLY SLOW HER DOWN. WELL, TO BE fair, any of the humans would, which was decidedly ironic considering she was going through all of this to become one again.

Theo slid into her car, Aiden slamming the door shut behind him, and both members of the camera crew tucked in. She sped off so fast the car fishtailed, and Aiden smacked his head against the window.

"Shit," he growled before grabbing the overhead handle, aptly named the "Oh crap" bar.

"Sorry, not all of us drive like we're a thousand, Aiden."

She wasn't sorry at all.

Aiden rubbed his head, casting her a dark glance. "Seriously?"

She made sure her expression was completely innocent, the kind of doe-eyed look that allowed her to feed off so many humans. "What? I'm just trying to give you another scar to match that one on your left. How'd you get that anyway?"

It was something she'd noticed, although she tried not to. The scar made Aiden seem tougher, rugged, more attractive. *Ugh*.

"Oh, so you want to get to know me? *Now*? Of all times."

Blowing out a breath, she shrugged. "You're right. I really don't care."

Pressing the gas, she rocketed them toward the front of the group, barely slinging the car into park before running up the gangplank and making it to the door to board the first VampJet.

"Welcome. Here's your packet," a kind-eyed flight attendant, human, said as she handed Theo the slim portfolio.

It was deceptively heavy in her hand, and she couldn't wait to dive into it and see what was planned. She liked not having to seek out her next adrenaline rush—all of them would be lined up perfectly for her over the course of filming.

She felt Aiden at her back as she moved toward their seat on the plane. The front part of the aircraft held actual seats, much like a regular plane—there were two sections, a middle section spanning five seats with two rows and two side sections that had two seats apiece. Two rows for a total of ten seats on the sides. Twenty seats to hold the teams and their camera crews.

Behind the middle section, there were five coffins, neatly spaced. There was easily capacity for more, but at least they had more room to move about. Sleeping in a coffin that wasn't hers had become commonplace given her nomadic lifestyle, but she anticipated—no, she *hoped* that it would bug some of her fellow contestants. There were rumors that some vampires simply couldn't do it, or they were huge germophobes. Funny, that.

Theo shoved her backpack into an overhead compartment and plopped down in one of the two-seater sections, claiming the window seat, which was actually safe on the VampJet aircrafts. Aiden followed suit before sitting next to her; his scent of bergamot and a beachy amber, reminiscent of the sea, enveloped her. Of course he smelled good.

It was hard, but she managed to fight the urge to roll her eyes at his presence. The man was like a gnat. A handsome gnat, giving off major Ben Barnes vibes with the dark, messy hair, dark brows, and matching scruff dotting a sharp jaw. His green eyes reminded her of a misty forest, mysterious and beautiful at the same time, the kind of eyes that hid secrets well, that protected them at all costs. Beginning over his left brow and slashing through, stopping just below it, was that scar she'd already noticed. It cut deep, leaving a white line in his tan skin. The thing was ridiculously sexy.

She shook her head and began to study Aiden's lovely muscles. He wore clothes that showed them off, a gray V neck clinging to his abs, tapering to narrow hips in dark denim and sneakers. He was beautiful and it was impossible not to notice. After all, she wasn't immune to such things—but he was still a nuisance and would be treated as such.

The camera crew divided up—one to the side and one in front of them. Theo guessed not much would be filmed on the flight because how could they sit like that? Besides, they hadn't even been properly introduced. The human, otherwise known as her partner, might've gotten on her bad side, but the camera crew had not.

"Hi, I'm Theodora, but you can call me Theo. I figure we should know each other's names, huh?" She shot each one a smile.

Aiden stiffened next to her, but she didn't look at him.

"And I'm Aiden," he added.

The woman, clearly a vampire stuck in her early twenties, with warm brown skin, black hair cut into a pixie style, and light-brown eyes, gave them a little wave. "I'm Bridget."

In front of them, the cameraman dipped his head. He appeared to be physically slightly older than Bridget, with pale skin and floppy blond hair that fell into his dark-blue eyes. Before he spoke, he adjusted his flannel shirt, hanging open over a white T-shirt.

"Dylan. Nice to meet you both."

"So are you two gonna kill each other, or can we trust you to behave at least until the final day?" Bridget asked with narrowed eyes.

Theo chuckled. "Of course, we can behave until then. Right, Aiden?"

Aiden's expression was fierce as he raised one dark brow. "Right. Until the final day."

Letting loose a sigh of relief, Bridget mimed wiping imaginary sweat off her forehead. "Good, because I don't think I could handle that."

Dylan gestured to the travel portfolio Theo clutched in her hands. "Why don't you go ahead and open that so we can get filming in, and then we'll let you have the rest of the flight in peace?"

It was already strange having cameras shoved in her face all the time, but at least Theo liked Bridget and Dylan. They could've ended up with awful crew members. She looked down at the black portfolio with the *Night Race* logo on it. This was the first step in the direction of a new life. A new Theo.

"Yeah, sure. Let's do it."

Slowly unzipping it, she pulled out a thick laminated card with the show's logo on one side and on their task list on the other.

She drew in a deep breath before reading it aloud. "When you get here, you'll have to sleep. Humans, you can't make a peep. Once night has fallen, the task begins, the first one to Mirador Base Las Torres wins!" Theo glanced up at Aiden at that.

"We're hiking Patagonia?" A satisfied, excited smile curved his lips upward, changing his entire countenance. Tiny crinkles fanned out from his eyes, endearing this human to Theo just ever so slightly. She blamed it on the crinkles. Jonathan had crinkles like that when he smiled—which had been often.

"Yeah, looks like it. There's more here." She swallowed, willing her fingers to stop trembling at the thoughts of her husband of 1692, and began reading again, thankful her voice remained steadier than her hands. "It's important to remember, contestants, that you must work together on each leg of the race. The sun may rise at any point during a task. Vampires, changing into a bat to reach your location quicker/to avoid sunlight results in immediate disqualification of you and your teammate. Coffins await at the final destination, and there are safe houses along the way, which are marked on the map provided. Humans, several legs present imminent danger or death to you as well. Due to the disclaimer you signed, *Night Race* cannot be held responsible for either. For more information on your task, find the Night Hike brochure in your portfolio."

She flipped through the pages, finding the brochure, and handed it over to Aiden, not wanting to exclude him, although she had no idea why she cared or wanted to be remotely civil... Oh, of course. Aiden was required to reach the end as well, or she was disqualified.

He began to read aloud. "Travel will take at least twenty hours to reach Hotel Las Torres, which is where contestants will stay after the hike—vampires, we have made arrangements suitable for you there as well, so no need to worry. From there, you will depart and hike to Mirador Las Torres, which is an eight-to-ten-hour hike. Backpacks for each contestant filled with all your needs for the hike will be waiting at the welcome center. Get some rest and good luck!"

Theo had never been to Chile, had always swooned over images of Patagonia, but not once in her wildest dreams had she imagined she'd get to hike it. Night hikes were even more dangerous, which put her emotions on lockdown. Usually, everything got too loud for her—not other people's feelings, but her own. Since the race started, things were blissfully quiet in her head, allowing her to feel like she could breathe for the first time in an incredibly long time.

Dylan and Bridget gave them thumbs-ups and turned off their cameras, moving to sit next to each other and whisper as other passengers boarded the plane. Theo didn't really pay many of them much mind, well, except for one team. The way the vampire stared at them as he boarded the flight was slightly unnerving. Probably meant to be that way, really. He towered over everyone, his pale skin almost translucent, along with mousy-brown hair and beady eyes that were so pale they nearly matched the sclera of his eye. His human companion was a woman who looked to be a few years older than Theo's age when she'd been turned at thirty-two. Her blue eyes watched her vampire teammate in an almost hero worship sort of way. Theo made a note to keep an eye on those two, especially the vamp.

"So do you have a familiar?" Aiden's voice interrupted her thoughts.

She scrunched her brows as she turned to face him, ignoring the last team boarding the plane. "What?"

"You know, a familiar? I read that most vampires have those to help them with their day-to-day tasks, to keep an eye out while they're sleeping to make sure they don't get stabbed in their coffins. You know, things like that?"

Theo looked down at the travel portfolio in her lap and started rummaging through it as she answered. "No. I don't employ a familiar, never have, never will. I move too often anyway and I'm capable of taking care of myself."

Through her fumbling, she found that the producers had included money, first aid materials, and a few other small items that fit in the portfolio.

Aiden didn't miss a beat. "Actually, you need my help now. You know, to win the chalice? And I bet that kills you, huh?"

She lifted her head and narrowed her eyes at the human next to her. He looked entirely too gleeful to have pointed that out. So she smiled, ever so slowly and menacingly, allowing her fangs to be on full display. She planned on not being a vampire in a few short weeks, so why not enjoy using all it had to offer while she could?

"It doesn't kill me, but you're awfully sarcastic for someone who's getting shanked once I get the Solis Occasum in my hands. If you don't piss me off too much, I might let you live." She tapped her chin with her black-painted fingernail. "But I doubt it."

Aiden shifted, presumably so he could see her better, completely unfazed by her words or fangs. The man was like a sheet of steel, impenetrable. It irked Theo to no end.

"Look, I don't like you either. You're standing in the way of something I need. But we need to agree to work together at least until we find the Solis Occasum cup. Otherwise, if we don't..." He looked around the plane's cabin as everyone milled about preparing for takeoff.

His eyes were wary, suspicious. "These people will beat us, and then all of this will have been for nothing, and I don't know about you, but..." He drew in a deep breath, his green eyes turning a shade darker with his intensity. "I can't go back to life the way it was before this night. It's miserable, and I...I have to find that chalice. What do you say?" Aiden met her stare head on, and she was able to clock several emotions clouding his face. One was utter agony and grief, the other anger, another hope. An interesting mixture that shouldn't have surprised her because the human was somewhat of an enigma.

Theo allowed her head to fall back on the seat. "Fine. You're right—and don't get too comfortable with me saying that because you'll likely never hear it again." She tapped her nails along the arms of the seat. "You're right, and we'll work together, but then all bets are off. This doesn't mean we have to be friends, and it's probably better that we aren't since one of us will have to...you know." She mimicked drawing a knife across her throat, sticking her tongue out dramatically.

Aiden's expression shifted to a pout, his pretty eyes doing some sort of puppy-dog thing. *Okay.* That move had literally never, ever been used on her once in her vampiric life. It was...interesting.

"Ah, hell. I guess that means I need to throw away the best-friend bracelets I made for us?" His lips twisted to the side.

"Um, what? Best-friend bracelets? No...ah, keep mine in case... you need to tie them together to escape somewhere?" Probably the dumbest thing that had ever come out of her mouth, but she blamed it on the puppy-dog eyes.

Before she could say anything else, Aiden chuckled, the sound smooth and rumbly, vibrating her bones.

"I'm just messing with you. I didn't make us bracelets, although I kind of wish I had now because I'm curious how I'd use them to escape. Tell me, what type of scenario are you thinking I'd escape from? Would I just throw the two bracelets out the window and scale down them like Rapunzel or...?"

He smiled at her, the thing crooked and good-natured, and she had a disturbing thought. It was easy to see how someone could be attracted to this man and his absurdities. But that was something she never had time for. Even after she became a human, she didn't know if she would. The grief over Jonathan was a scabby wound that got torn back a few too many times, never fully healing. And Elizabeth, too...that was a huge part of why she never really had friends. Because she felt like she'd been a terrible friend to her and didn't really deserve another.

The pilot came over the loudspeaker, interrupting any sort of rebuttal Theo could form. "Please prepare for takeoff. Make sure you are buckled in your seat. Thank you."

She decided silence was the best answer and pulled out her headphones. Listening to music was another of her go-to methods of finding solace. There were about ten hours until sunrise before she needed to be safely tucked away in her casket, and she planned to make the most of that time ignoring her handsome and ridiculously endearing seatmate.

6

AIDEN

By the time the first five teams rolled up to Hotel Las Torres in what might be the literal middle of nowhere, everyone was more than a little grouchy. The vampires had only recently risen from their coffins in the back of the plane two hours ago so everyone could pile into shuttles, which Aiden found cool, though it took some getting used to. He tried to remind himself that soon this would be his life. Would he miss the warmth of the sunshine on his skin? *Most definitely.* But did he need to do this? *Absolutely.*

Even in the darkness, he could make out the beauty of the hotel. It sat at the base of the Almirante Nieto Mountain and was the eastern entrance to the Torres del Paine National Park, something that had been on Aiden's bucket list since he was a kid. The wood-front hotel had welcoming lights on, and his body begged him to go and lie down in an actual bed for just two minutes. Too bad they didn't get to stop here for the night.

This going nocturnal thing would definitely take some getting used to, especially when he was an early riser since his first appointment at his vet clinic was usually at eight. He briefly worried about his practice, knowing his patients and staff understood his need to close for the month. Thankfully he was able to pay Monica and Jan, the vet tech, for their time off.

Daniel waited for them outside near a line of fully stuffed backpacks. The cold night air took a second to acclimate to since he was a Southern boy, born and raised in Georgia, and it barely got lower than the 50s during the coldest months there. It couldn't be any more than forty degrees now. He zipped up his jacket, thankful Theo had urged him to bring it.

Hearing the sound of his zipper, she turned, giving him an "I told you so" smirk. That was progress, though, and was much better than their snarling from the night before. This truce had to work. They both had to compartmentalize the here and now—the final day of this race was something they couldn't afford to think about or entertain. If Aiden did, it would tear him apart.

"Thank you," he mouthed to Theo.

She rolled her eyes—her favorite thing to do when it came to him—and faced the show's host.

"Welcome, teams. As you know, you are the first five to arrive. The other three teams are still en route. In a moment, I'll release you in intervals based on the order you made it to the plane. Once your team is released, you and your teammate will both grab a backpack, leaving the original luggage you came here with. Inside this backpack, you'll find supplies for your night hike. The only suggestion I can give is for the humans to put on the headlamps immediately to avoid any dangerous scenarios. The sun may rise since this hike is an eight-to-ten-hour trek. Should that happen, we have placed safe houses along your route for vampire contestants and crew. Remember the rules. The first to base camp at Mirador Las Torres wins. Are you ready?" Daniel did a dramatic scan of their group.

Aiden did the same, mentally calculating who might be a problem for them. Later he and Theo would need to sit down and make a list and talk strategy, but only after they saw how this went, which hopefully would be well.

"All right, teams. On my mark, the first team to go is Theo and Aiden. One—"

A roar filled Aiden's ears, his pulse already reacting to the adrenaline rush.

"Two—"

He took in a deep breath and gave a steady nod to Theo.

"Three!"

Theo and Aiden wasted no time hustling to get their backpacks —who knew how spaced apart the intervals between teams were? They took a moment, moving off to the side to take out a map as Aiden pulled out his headlamp, throwing it on quickly. Their camera crew, Bridget and Dylan, kept up with them, a quiet, steady presence.

"All right, let's get this over with," Theo groused, clutching the map in her hand. "And don't hold me back with your mortality."

Aiden smirked. "Isn't that what you're after, though? My mortality? If you look at me as such a hindrance, why do you even *want* to become human?"

They moved along the path, passing over a few small bridges that only allowed two people to cross at a time. Behind them, they could hear other teams being released, and they picked up their pace.

She flicked a wrist in the air, her tone bored. "I no longer wish to be a vampire, simple as that."

"Right, but that can't be all, can it?"

Theo ignored him and continued walking. In the darkness, the surroundings were stunning and serene. Above them, millions of twinkling diamonds were set in the clear night sky. The mountains cut a beautiful silhouette across the darkness, like giants from stories of old. The thick scent of greenery filled Aiden's nose as he drew in a lungful of the incredibly fresh air.

A gray fox ran across their trail, barking once before disappearing. Accompanying its bark was the symphony of an owl searching for its next meal. The path sloped downward toward a river crossing before heading into the Ascencio Valley. Once they moved into the valley, they began their first slow ascent of the climb. The goal was to make it to Refugio Chileno before sunrise.

According to Aiden's map, it would take about two hours to get to the place that offered dorm-style rooms, showers and bathrooms, and food. Depending on time, they might not take an extended break there, but either way, it was nice to have a goal in mind. That was how he'd gotten through these last three years, singularly focusing on revenge.

He just dreaded that the next eight or ten hours were going to be incredibly boring if they continued to walk in silence. It wasn't as if he could talk to Dylan and Bridget—they'd already said once cameras were rolling, they were basically ghosts. Aiden spent plenty of time in his head as it was, and he didn't always like what he saw. Cassidy's brown eyes forever opened wide in horror flashed into his mind more often than he could tolerate, which was why he overworked himself at the vet clinic.

Clearing his throat, he lifted his head from the wide rocky path momentarily, so he could get a look at Theo's face. As expected, she gave him a pointed glance, a hint of fang poking over her full lips. He hadn't been kidding when he asked about why she wanted to be human again. He really wanted to know.

Swinging his headlamp ahead on the path, he spoke up. "So I think maybe we should talk more to pass the time. We could get to know each other."

If anything, his vampire companion picked up her speed. "I'm not looking to talk right now or ever. I have no interest in learning more about you as it serves no purpose in the end. We work together, and we don't kill each other until the end, okay?"

"You and I both know that sucks. I've done nothing to you—" His words were cut off when his foot slipped off the stony path, sending rocks skittering. He lost his balance and began wavering to the side. The light strapped to his forehead revealed a yawning chasm ending in darkness, waiting to swallow him up. In a flash,

Theo whipped her arms around him, hauling him back to the trail.

She moved her hands to his shoulders, her touch light as if she were checking him for injuries. They weren't too high up, but still high enough that a fall over the edge would seriously injure him. Maybe kill him, depending on how freakishly he fell.

Theo pursed her lips, her voice snapping quick like a whip as she took a step back. "Damn it, Aiden. Be careful."

Aiden's heart thudded forcefully in his throat, his hands shaky as he smoothed them over the athletic clothing he'd changed into on their flight and then scrubbed them through his hair.

"Thanks for the save, Theodora," he managed, although the words felt like cotton in his mouth—not because she saved him, but because that had been terrifying.

For someone who always paid attention to detail, he'd certainly dropped the ball then, all because he got distracted by the beautiful vampire who was his teammate. *Wait.* Beautiful? Why did that have to sneak in again when it came to her? He shook his head in an attempt to shake away the thoughts.

"This doesn't mean I like you."

He snickered as he wrapped his fingers around the strap of his backpack. "Don't worry. I would never deign to think that."

And he wouldn't. Theo just made it clear that she'd save him when she needed him, but he knew if they'd been on the final leg of this race, she wouldn't have hesitated to let him tumble right on over the side.

🦇

After a quick break at the Refugio Chileno, Theo and Aiden were back at it and ready to tackle the steepest part of the hike. Theo kept looking at the sky anxiously, her features drawn taut, Bridget, their vampire crew member, echoing her sentiments.

Aiden glanced at his watch and saw the reason. "We can go

back to the Refugio or..." He looked down at the map he'd kept clutched in one hand. "We can hit the safe house, which is about fifteen minutes from here if you think you both can hang on?"

Sunrise wouldn't be for another forty-five minutes at least, but the closest safe house after that would be thirty minutes away and might be risking it.

Bridget shot him a thumbs-up while Theo nodded wordlessly as she trekked forward, her words resigned as she released a breath that pulled her shoulders uptight. "Let's go to the safe house. I'd rather not bunk with more people than I have to, and those are supposed to be private, I think."

Thankfully, they came across the safe house faster than expected. A series of tiny wooden structures sat off to the side of the trail. They would be big enough for a team of four, but no more. Aiden could tell consideration to the human contestants and crew was the last thing on the director's mind, as there were two coffins sitting in the far corner of the matchbox, and that was literally it. At least he'd enjoyed camping as a kid and wasn't too fussy.

Aiden shut the door behind the camera crew and turned around to crack a joke when he noticed Theo's hands curled tightly around the edge of the primitive wooden coffin, her body swaying slightly. He opened his mouth to say something but realized in the short amount of time spent together, he'd already been able to pick up a tiny bit about her—despite her trying to keep everything locked up tight. She would only snap at him if he asked her if she was all right in front of Bridget and Dylan, who were still quietly filming.

He moved to where she stood, and her eyes flashed open, blue gaze skewering him. "What?" she growled.

Ignoring her aggression, he asked, "Are you okay? Can I get you anything?"

For a moment, Theo studied him, her hands clenching and unclenching the coffin. When she spoke, her voice was low, so low that Aiden had to lean in closer. He tried to ignore the fact she smelled like a walk through a spring garden, and that he could see the little gray specks in her bright-blue eyes.

"They didn't put blood in our backpacks, and I was so stupid." One hand pinched the bridge of her nose.

Slowly he began to pick up on her meaning, and his brows furrowed as he felt the heat from the camera light on his back. Of course their crew wouldn't be able to miss out on this juicy development. It was a reality television show, after all.

"You didn't eat..." He allowed the words to trail off, figuring the less he said, the better.

She shook her head before finally meeting his stare again. "Max tricked us, that dirty bastard."

"What do you mean?"

Still keeping her back to the cameras, Theo straightened, her lips at Aiden's ear, brushing them slightly. Chills skated along his arms, his spine, making him feel...well, *everything*, like an explosion of fireworks. Holy shit. Now it was his turn to have one hand on the coffin, trying to calm the fuck down.

"He told the vampires part of the rules were that we weren't allowed to feed until we got going on the trail. Only crew were allowed to do so since they had a job to perform. He said he included plenty of blood for each vampire contestant—the vampire crew wouldn't need it, since they'd been sated—and now I'm realizing of course he did because he meant that we would need to drink from our human partners." She widened her eyes meaningfully at him.

Well. That killed any sort of sexiness to the moment, causing Aiden to back up quickly.

"What happens if you don't get blood? You're like a million years old, aren't you? Aren't you supposed to go longer without feeding or...?" He kept backing up, not caring if the cameras were filming his very real, very nervous reaction.

Theo crossed her arms over her chest. "I'm not a million years old. I'm three hundred and thirty years old, thank you very much."

Aiden drew a hand over his forehead, pretending to wipe sweat from it, although he was *really* about to be sweating if things took the turn Max expected them to. "Glad you cleared that up."

"And our age has nothing to do with how often we feed. Max set us all up big time. We have to feed every day to keep our strength up, or the longer we go, the weaker we get. The longest I've ever gone was a week, and I was pretty much near death at that point. My skin"—she touched her face—"started to shrivel." She shuddered at the memory. "But it's been since the day before we left. Max asked us not to feed that day and had us checked to make sure we didn't."

Shrugging off his backpack, Aiden cursed Max under his breath. His hands wouldn't stop shaking as he dug through all the stuff packed inside.

"Maybe there's some blood in my backpack?" He knew there wouldn't be—he'd already rummaged through it before they set off on their hike, but he couldn't give her *his* blood, could he? Not after what happened three years ago. Bile rose in his throat as he stood up and ran his hands through his hair, letting out a hissed, "Shit."

Bridget spoke up for the first time since they started filming. "Max wanted us to let you know at this point that we are not allowed to step in and help. If Theo requires blood, it has to come from her partner." She swung her gaze to Aiden, almost apologetic. "From *you*."

The scar on his eyebrow started to throb as the memories he tried to keep at bay flitted across his mind in fragmented, razor-sharp pieces. The vampire had knocked Aiden out so he didn't recall much from the actual fight. But what he did remember was nightmarish enough. When he woke, he found Cassidy lying on the grass in a bloodied heap, her blond hair fanned out around her. He'd hoped it was just a bad dream that he'd wake from, that the throbbing pain in his shoulder wasn't what he thought it was. But he wasn't so lucky. Not only had the bloodsucker killed Cassidy, but he'd drunk from Aiden as well, and he still wore two jagged, rough scars on the slope of his shoulder, usually covered by his shirt. How many times had he wished the vampire had killed him instead of Cassidy? And now he was supposed to *feed* one? To feel that pain again?

"You really can't make it without blood?"

Theo hung her head. "Not as fast as we want if you want to win."

And he wanted victory more than anything. Becoming a vampire would be the only way he had any chance of avenging Cassidy or protecting his family so history didn't repeat itself.

"I do want to win, but I think there's something you should know before..." He paused, swallowing hard as he brought a hand to that curve of his shoulder, where that other reminder of his failure lay. Was he really going to do this? "Before I let you drink from me." He forced the words out.

Theo's countenance changed, became softer. "I understand."

He didn't think she would, not after he explained everything.

7

THEO

THEO KNEW SHE COULD BE COLD AND HARSH AND KNEW SHE'D BEEN exceedingly so to Aiden. But the way he trembled before her, his eyes wild as he ran his hands over a spot beneath his shirt on his shoulder, made her regret it. Just another one to add to the pile.

Of course, offering to feed a vampire wouldn't really be appealing to some people, especially when one didn't know said vampire well, if at all. There needed to be a level of trust built before blood sharing began, although way too many vampires drank during an attack. Not all of them had come around to a more cultured way of existing.

Thankfully Andreas wasn't like that and had trained her to be like him—drinking only enough to sustain. There was a highly guarded secret among vampires, a secret not even most of their species knew. Vampires over three hundred or so could develop a new trait—if they were privy to the knowledge.

They were able to lull humans into a trance, bending them to their will. Theo did this only to make her victims more comfortable before drinking from them. But there was something else equally as dangerous—they also could wipe away memories. There was a reason these secrets were highly guarded by a precious few, by the vampires desperate to retain good standing in the human world.

But she couldn't outright offer to wipe Aiden's memories or put him in a trance. Otherwise, the secret would be out in the open. Seeing as how she planned to be a human herself in a few weeks, having a lot of pissed-off vampires after her didn't exactly sit well.

So there was really nothing she could do to help. Or could she? Before she'd been turned, before she'd been thrown into that rotting jail, she'd been kind, been the one to put Elizabeth's patients at ease during difficult sicknesses. Oh, it'd been so long since she'd put *anyone* at ease. But she could at least try.

"Aiden?" His head snapped up. Theo moved to a different corner of the bleak cabin. She folded herself onto the floor, sitting cross-legged. "Come sit with me for a moment, please. I give you my word that I will not harm you."

He did, albeit slowly, and the cameras followed him doggedly. Theo squinted at them, all but snarling, aware her fangs were on full display, but she couldn't bring herself to care. Not when they were in the middle of a fiasco, the chalice in the balance.

"Do you have to film this? It's pretty raw, and not everything should be put into the world for their consumption."

Dylan shrugged. "Sorry, Theo. Max's orders. We have to shoot until you bed down in that coffin. Then mics are off."

Of course, Theo couldn't help but wonder if Max knew about the trance and for some weird reason was willing to expose it. It seemed like something he'd do, or maybe she was being paranoid? Either way, she didn't have time to question it too deeply with the need to feed burning through her body.

Aiden angled so he wasn't facing the cameras, and a flip in Theo's stomach had her reaching for the floor beneath her to steady herself. She squeezed her eyes shut for a minute to regain her composure. That was strange.

When she opened them, Aiden was staring at her with concern, the scar above his brow standing out in stark relief against his skin.

In the dim light of the safe house, staring at each other felt intimate. Entirely *too* intimate.

Aiden's voice was soft because of course it was. "Hey? You okay?"

Theo leaned her head back, glaring at the wooden ceiling, thankful there were no cracks in it. "I'm fine, Aiden. Just a weird feeling. Anyway, let's talk about you."

Aiden dropped his gaze to his hands, strong hands, she noticed. Nope. No, she did *not* notice. Why was she suddenly paying attention to these things? The starburst flecks in his eyes. The small freckles on his nose. The rise and fall of his muscular chest.

She glanced down at the floor, desperate to look anywhere *but* at him. However, the sound of him drawing in a deep breath that should've sucked all the air from the room made her eyes return to him yet again. Like they couldn't help themselves. What in the world was happening?

Pain etched grooves into his face, around his eyes, bracketing his mouth, holding the lines of his shoulders all too tight. Green eyes became glassy as he spoke. "Three years ago, my fiancée, Cassidy, was killed by a vampire."

Whatever she expected, it certainly hadn't been that. Theo sat up straighter.

Still not meeting her stare, Aiden continued. "He bit me too." He thumped his fingers against the spot on his shoulder that she'd seen him touch earlier. "And that's how I got this." He tapped at his brow. "But both of those are nothing compared to what I carry here." A hand pressed over his heart, anguish painting his countenance.

"Oh, Aiden." She knew grief was a tricky thing. People meant well when they shared their apologies and laments, but no words would ever heal the unhealable wound. Only time could lessen the dagger-esque pierce to the chest. "I'm so sorry. You never should have had to experience that."

Finally, he looked up at her, tears cutting sharp paths down his tanned face. "I would've gladly taken Cassidy's place, but I didn't even get a chance. I was too weak to protect her, and that's why... that's why I hesitate now. It's not because I want you to suffer. I'd *never* want that."

Those words penetrated the well-worn armor Theo had wrapped around herself since the night Jonathan had been executed. Because of *her*. She understood Aiden's pain more than he knew, but also, she'd been nothing but horrible to him, yet here he was feeling remorse over not wanting to offer up his veins because of his painful history. She silently cursed the presence of the cameras again, because now she had a change in plans. She'd put him in the trance after all, anything to make this better for him, to cause the least amount of pain.

She quickly racked her mind for ways to hide was she was about to do, understanding the risk she was dead set on taking.

"Let's change positions," she offered, standing so he could take the spot angled into the corner. Theo plopped down in front of him, hiding him from the cameras and whispered, "Thank you for sharing your past with me."

All the pieces suddenly clicked for her, and she knew why he'd chosen to participate in the *Night Race*. Yet sharing his past didn't change anything, didn't change her plans. And if he stood in the way of her becoming a human at the end, her path wouldn't waver. Her hand would remain steady.

"Are you sure you want to do this, Aiden?"

He trembled again but nodded.

Keeping her eyes on his, she called out to Dylan, avoiding eye contact with Bridget. "Hey, can you look in both of our bags real quick? I'll need something to put over his wound once I finish..." She didn't say the rest because she didn't want to freak Aiden out any more than he already was.

Theo didn't need anything to put over the bite marks. All she had to do was lick them—which shouldn't have given her that weird little thrill in the pit of her stomach—and they'd heal immediately.

Bridget knew this and Theo hoped that the other vampire wouldn't rat her out. While the camerawoman didn't say anything, she also didn't help Dylan as he rustled through the bags, falling for the ruse. She turned back around to Aiden, not wasting a moment. She flicked off both of their mics.

"Would you rather not feel anything as I do this? To be put in a calm state, so you're not afraid?" She wouldn't do it without any sort of consent.

He nodded quickly, and then she narrowed her eyes as she'd so often done, making her stare bewitching so that Aiden couldn't look away. It didn't take long for the trance to take hold.

Her voice was barely a whisper, spoken just loud enough so only Aiden could hear. "This will not hurt. A vampire is drinking from you, but you will not feel pain or fear. Trust that this vampire will not harm you."

Eyes glazing over, Aiden nodded. She held him closely, carefully biting his neck. His blood burst sweet onto her tongue, an explosion of color sparking across her eyelids. Nothing else she'd ever drank compared. It was as if his blood wasn't entirely human... or if it were...there was something unique about him. *Huh. That's odd.*

Before she could think on that more, something extraordinary and strange bloomed in her chest. The languid, slow beat sped up, and she suddenly felt flushed. One hand gripped Aiden tighter as her other flew to her chest...where her heart *raced*. Then the final telltale indicator presented itself—lust pooled in her stomach, something utterly foreign to her in her vampiric state. She'd shut that part of herself down that night in June of 1692.

There was no way...

That feeling, and the light-headedness she'd felt only moments before, her sire had told her about those signs. They meant she'd met her mate. But she had no interest in someone who was destined to be her partner when she was a vampire. The only one who mattered was the one who had been taken from her when she'd been human.

She wanted to laugh hysterically because she was starving, and she'd just met her stupid mate, the very man she'd vowed to kill at the end of this race. Andreas always waxed poetic about finding Davina, his partner, about the feelings associated with it, and how the time frame for finding one's companion was different for each vampire. The connection could be found in a variety of ways—sometimes it was immediate, sometimes it came after a bit of time was spent around said mates, and in some cases even rarer it was discovered once bitten.

Of course this was a rare case.

Of course.

Earlier, she'd thought things were thorny... How wrong she was. Meeting her mate and knowing she had to kill him to get what she wanted... Well, that was beyond complicated and twisty.

She would take this knowledge to her vampiric grave. No one would ever know that Aiden Archer was her mate. Not a single living, breathing soul.

Pushing away those thoughts, she focused on Aiden's hands as he tightened them on her shoulders and then unclenched. She tuned out the irritated curses of Dylan as soon as he realized he was missing the best part of the show, or so Max would've thought. Taking just enough blood to make it to the base camp, she stopped and licked Aiden's neck. His skin tasted like the beach—salt and sea and perfection. Pleasant as it was, she would gladly lick a tree to get the taste out of her mouth.

Instantly, Theo released her hold on the human, his eyes blinking rapidly as the fog cleared.

Bridget arched a brow at her as she lowered the camera. "Turn the mics back on, please."

They both sluggishly followed her directive.

"You okay?" Theo asked, surprised at the tenderness in her

voice. *No.* She could not let any sort of mate emotions get in the way of things—and she wouldn't. Her desire to become a human again long outdated any notions of whatever was at play here.

Aiden scooted backward, moving a hand over his neck—not the ravaged shoulder. Theo had known better than to go for that. He studied his hand as he pulled it away from his skin, flicking his stare at her. His face hardened for a moment before smoothing back out.

"This changes nothing," he croaked. "I still want that chalice."

Theo's lips curled. "That's exactly what I hoped to hear. We'll get the Solis Occasum, Aiden. Don't you worry. Just enjoy the days you have left until we do." She winked at him and made her way to the coffin, the burning in her chest signaling the sun would soon rise, Bridget doing the same.

"Wake me as soon as night falls," Theo called out, and then she hopped inside the casket, pulling the lid over her until it secured properly.

Did she like sleeping in a little hut with virtual strangers? *Hell no.* But did she think anything would happen to her? *No.* At least not at this point because Aiden needed her. With that knowledge, she pressed her arms over her chest and closed her eyes, falling into a heavy sleep where dreams of a certain green-eyed mate dominated.

🦇

The next night, Theo woke feeling much better than she had in days. Actually, she felt better than she ever had, her fists curling with the knowledge that it was due to drinking the blood of her mate. She snarled as she ran a hand over her ratty hair. *Fucking mate.*

Her ire came from so many deep, dark places. First of all, she had to rely on someone in order to survive—which had been against her number one rule since becoming a vampire, since losing Jonathan. She didn't want to rely on *anyone*. It was just better that way.

On top of that, she was most definitely not looking for a mate. Nope. No way. Theo knew this all wasn't necessarily Aiden's fault, but she couldn't help but allow that anger at herself to simmer and boil, eventually extending to him. She had to keep him at arm's length. Coming here with a job to do, a chalice to win, it was the only way to make it.

Aiden didn't look particularly thrilled at being nocturnal, but at least he'd been able to change his clothes. She shuddered at the idea of not getting a shower or a fresh change of clothes.

"What's that?" she asked, noticing he held a creamy square of cardstock between his long fingers. Worrying about clothes and a shower could wait. They had a race to win, she reminded herself as she hopped from the coffin, slinging on her backpack and turning on her mic.

Tapping the card against his thigh, Aiden looked at her with renewed irritation. "A new command from Max since we're almost to the top."

Dread settled in her chest. Max was nothing more than a sadist, and not the fun kind she read about in books either. Aiden slung open the door to the cabin, the moon shining brightly on them through the sparse trees. Quiet as ever, Dylan and Bridget followed, their cameras raised and ready for filming.

Theo arched a brow as she pointed toward the trail. "Well? Are you going to tell me, or are we to play charades to figure out what's on the card?"

Ignoring her, Aiden picked up a piece of rope from the ground.

She wouldn't exactly say she was the worst vampire, but she wasn't the best at it either. Andreas once told her that despite her feeling too much, the fact she wasn't great at being a vampire helped keep the majority of her humanity intact. She was too nice when she drank from her victims, he said. She rarely bared her fangs but had done so more than a few times already with this human.

So when Aiden dangled a hideous, awful rope in front of her, she hissed, standing up tall—the height difference between them wasn't too much, and it nearly reminded her of Jonathan. Blinking away familiar laughing brown eyes, she hid her pain with a growl.

"And what are you planning to do with"—she tilted her head toward the offending rope—"that?"

His voice was dull when he spoke; that almost golden retriever-esque part of him deadened since she'd drank from him. The little pang in her chest at that was unexpected and absolutely unwelcome.

"We have to tie it around our ankles for the remainder of this leg of the competition. It's for"—he held up his fingers to air quote his following words—"'team building.' The only time we can untie is for bathroom purposes."

Fighting the urge to roll her eyes, she groaned, moving to stand next to him. Their shoulders brushed, and even though they'd been hiking, he smelled delicious, like the ocean and something undeniably male. If she lifted her arm and caught a whiff, it would smell like death. *No pun intended...or maybe intended.*

Aiden said nothing as he bent and tied their ankles together. His fingertips brushed against her cool skin, and Theo swore she felt sparks jolt through her bloodstream. She bit down on her lip hard enough to draw blood in order to avoid gasping. When was the last time anyone had touched her so?

Brown eyes again ran through her mind, and she swallowed down any emotion as Aiden straightened.

"Ready?" he asked, looking as thrilled about this as she was.

"Might as well get this over with," she huffed.

Then they were off into the night, an unlikely team.

I guess it could be worse.

8

AIDEN

Just when Aiden thought things couldn't get any worse, they did.

Any headway he and Theo made the night before had been imploded by Max's stunt. He knew Theo couldn't help it, and he'd appreciated her being kind enough to do that trance thing that made him calm when she drank from him. Even so, it'd brought a lot of dark memories to the surface and reminded Aiden exactly why he was here on the show, and it reinforced the lengths he was willing to go to in order to win.

Yet he couldn't seem to stop thinking about Theo biting him. The experience had been completely different from the attack in ways he hadn't expected. He felt something unfurl inside his chest when she did, even under the trance. The feeling still remained as if a fist had opened and took up space within his rib cage. He could ask Theo about it, but then again, it was probably a normal reaction to being consensually bitten by a vampire.

He sighed as he squinted into the night, his headlamp shining on the team ahead of them. That's right, the team *ahead* of them, moving up the hill.

"You should just give up. We're winning this," the Nosferatu look-alike shouted down—Aiden still hadn't caught the vampire's actual name.

Either way, he looked menacing, his eyes sparking red in the dark. Aiden had never seen that before. Did that happen in *Fright Night*? He suddenly couldn't remember.

The guy's partner, a human woman, kept up her pace and seemed just as intent on winning, her face scrunched in determination.

The hill started slanting upward, the ascent pushing Aiden's calves to work harder. The gloom made it difficult to see, even with a headlamp.

And that's when a boulder came rolling toward them, shaking the ground. The sound of tree leaves dancing and whooshing filled the night air.

"Son of a bitch!" Theo hissed as she tried to maneuver.

The rope that tied them together yanked taut, and she fell down, dragging Aiden with her. The thundering of the boulder grew closer and closer. This was not the way Aiden was going out. Not that he wanted to get taken out at all, but still.

He dug his fingers into the gravel and dirt, so hard some of the stone cut into his skin, but he didn't care. He used the rock to pull himself and Theo out of harm's way along the edge of the path. Huffing and straining, Theo helped, using the ground as leverage.

Once they swung themselves back up onto the path, Theo stumbled, something he hadn't seen her do except when hungry— the woman was the epitome of grace. The rope wrapped around their legs tightened, and she tripped forward onto Aiden, falling right on top of him. Thankfully, they landed in the dirt rather than tumbling over the edge.

He wrapped his hands around her waist instinctively, digging into her soft, cool skin as he flipped her beneath him right before the boulder rolled by, violently shaking the earth. After a quick check that Dylan and Bridget were okay, he turned his attention to the vampire he was currently poised protectively on top of, his hand cradled under her head.

That hadn't been an accident because what could've possibly caused a boulder to dislodge and head right toward them? What were the odds?

His suspicions were confirmed when the most definitely evil vampire's laughter echoed through the darkness.

"Are you okay?" Aiden asked in between pants, his heart ricocheting around in his chest as he shone the light on Theo.

She appeared just as stunned as he was by the murderous act. Her breath rose and fell quickly, her chest brushing against his. He needed to put space between them or else she would feel his growing excitement down below. In what he hoped was a smooth move, Aiden rolled off her, jumping to his feet and offering his hand to her.

Grasping it, Theo pulled herself up, furiously dusting off the dirt on her clothes.

Aiden didn't step away from her, which caused her to pause her frantic brushing.

"Here," he said quietly before wiping off some of the dirt smudges on her beautiful face.

Her mouth parted on a gasp, his gaze dipping to her pink lips.

What would it be like to kiss her? Oh, shit. Where had that come from? Most definitely the near-death experience. He cleared his throat and dropped his hand, stepping away.

Gesturing down the hill, where the boulder had disappeared, he spoke. "We can't let that stand. Those bastards..."

Theo's jaw clenched tight as she gave him a nod. "Hell no, we can't. Let's go."

He'd thought they'd been moving quickly before, but now they nearly flew. If Theo could pick him up and carry him in bat mode, he knew she would. As it was, they raced through the remainder of the climb, both brainstorming out loud ways to derail Team

Assholes. Or Team Tried to Kill Us—an act that Max probably approved of for the sake of ratings.

An excited little sound came from Aiden's side where Theo walked. When he turned to her, he found the light illuminating her face, and she bounced on the balls of her feet, her fingers steepled together like an evil genius.

"You know how we can't do anything unless we have our partner? What if we get that vampire's partner?" She blew out a breath, brows raised high. "Because let's be honest, I don't know if I can contend with the Nosferatu wannabe. I'm not nearly as old as he is, so I don't have the strength range, or else I'd pull up a random tree and smack them off the side of the mountain."

Aiden's eyes widened.

Theo's lips twisted to the side as she tapped her chin. "What? Too violent?"

An unbidden laugh, the sound a little sad and rusty, erupted from Aiden.

This apparently did not sit well with Theo. Propping her hands on her hips, she tilted her head to the side. "Are you laughing at me?"

He lifted his hands in mock surrender. "No, not at all. I, uh, I'm laughing at the idea that you were too violent. Seeing as how they nearly killed us, I'm game to knock them out of the running for first place."

A smile curled Theo's lips. "Good. Let's get that human then and no matter what, block me, okay? We can't let..." She trailed off as she canted her head toward their camera crew behind them. "Them see everything."

He gave her a mock salute. "Got it."

At their accelerated pace, it only took a few minutes to get within sight of Team Asshole. They'd paused on the side of the path just around the bend ahead, the human panting, and the vampire with his arms up in the air, ranting about something. The human stood up straight, shooting him the bird before storming off in their direction.

"I'll be right back. I have to pee, and I don't need you to be around when I do it," she called over her shoulder.

Theo rubbed her hands together. "This is perfect. We just need her a little closer..."

Though he wanted to protest with a question—why did they need her closer?—he decided to trust Theo for the moment. She mimed turning off their mics, and they managed to do so without attracting attention from Dylan or Bridget. A good fake yawn complete with a stretch worked wonders for that kind of thing. Then they all but held their breath as they waited. When the human pulled to a stop, Theo was on her in seconds, putting her in a trance before she even had a chance to shriek. Aiden blocked the camera's view, grabbing the microphone hooked to the woman's shirt and sneakily flicking it off.

"You will go into the bushes to go to the bathroom, and you will stay there once you're done. You will not move even when your vampire comes for you. He will have to carry you the rest of the way."

Eyes lost in a glossy haze, the woman nodded.

"All done. Let's get out of here because we'll have to pass that prick before we get to the finish line." Theo straightened her shoulders. She moved a finger toward her mic pack, but Aiden put a hand over hers, stopping her. The coolness of her skin distracted him for a heartbeat.

He leaned in close. "Wait, that guy is older, and he's probably fed off that woman. Can't he just override your trance?" he whispered.

Theo shook her head. "Not since they are at odds with each other."

With a reluctance that surprised him, he let go of her hand. She flicked the mic back on and Aiden did the same.

From behind them came Dylan's breathless voice. "Hey, you

guys keep messing up all our action shots. We need to see both of you in them, okay?"

"Yeah," Aiden answered as Theo said, "Okay, sure."

"Did you get the shot of him holding her hand?" Dylan asked.

"Yep!" Bridget squealed with a gleefulness that set Aiden's teeth on edge.

They picked up their pace. Aiden hooked a thumb to where the human of Team Asshole had gone into the bushes, knowing he could only say so much. "Good work back there."

Theo's answering smile stunned him. "Thanks."

Up ahead around the bend stood the vampire. He hissed at their approach, looking behind them expectantly.

"Where's my partner?" he snarled. It was full of an unspoken accusation, one that basically said, "Why aren't you dead from that boulder?"

"Haven't seen her," Aiden bit out, not taking his eyes off the sneaky bastard.

"Come near us, and I'll make you regret it." Theo raised her chin in defiance.

The vampire wavered for a moment, and Aiden knew he was trying to weigh out what to do.

"She might've fallen off the cliff. You should probably check, but remember, you can't turn into a bat." Aiden shot him a smug smile as he shrugged.

With a string of curses, the vampire took off to where they left the human. She'd awaken from her trance shortly, Aiden understood that, but he also knew they needed to move if they wanted to get first place, or else all this would be for nothing.

As if of one mind, Theo and Aiden both began to jog, knowing they were almost there.

Rounding the corner, Daniel appeared, standing at base camp with a smile on his face. Theo and Aiden came to a limping halt in front of him, ankles still tied together. They'd done it. They'd actually worked together, kicking the evil vampire's ass, albeit momentarily.

"Theo and Aiden, you are the first team to arrive. Congratulations." He gestured behind him. "You may head to base camp and explore, and when you're ready, we'll transport you back to the hotel where you'll be given your prize for first place. You have tonight and tomorrow to rest before departing on to Challenge Two."

"Thank you," Aiden breathed out, at the same time Theo did.

Daniel dipped his head, and then they moved along.

At last, chests heaving with exertion and sweat working down their brows, they could finally take in the beauty of the place. They flipped their microphones off as they turned around, the natural granite towers soaring into the starry night sky, the water of the lake in front of them picturesque, so much so it was almost unreal, especially with the full moon dancing across it, illuminating the landscape around them.

Aiden couldn't believe he was here, that he got to actually see something so incredibly beautiful. Then his gaze slid over to Theo. She looked radiant, blue eyes wide as they took in the scenery, hair wild, blowing around her. *Nope*, he definitely hadn't seen anything so beautiful. Cursing the ways she affected him, he forced his gaze forward.

As he did so, he swore he felt Theo's stare searing into his skin. Had she caught him checking her out? Or was she doing the same? Anticipation slithered around in his stomach and he fought to ignore it with every fiber of his being.

Bridget and Dylan turned off their cameras, lowering them before giving Aiden and Theo both high fives. Damn it. That little moment had been caught on camera.

"Great job, you guys!" Bridget fist pumped as she raised up on her toes. "You crushed it, and as your reward, you get to be free of us for a bit."

"And I need to ice my arm because I'm out of shape, and this camera weighs a ton." Dylan smiled.

After saying their good-byes, the camera crew dipped, meeting up with the other crews just as their new enemy approached, his fangs bared. His human partner raced to keep up with him.

"I see now that we are evenly matched in competition," he hissed. "I had to carry her"—he pointed at the woman beside him —"the whole way here."

Aiden shrugged. "You started that. I'd say she's easily lighter than a boulder." He flashed a cold smile. "Besides, we're here to win, so if you don't like us playing dirty like you, maybe you should quit, Nosferatu."

"My name is Brandt, *not* Nosferatu." He hooked a thumb at his human counterpart. "And this is Paisley." He straightened, red sparking in his gaze again. "And maybe now we know who to keep an eye out for. Who to...take out? It'd be a shame if an accident were to occur, and this time kill you both." He angled his head and pasted on a fake pout. "Consider that first time practice." He didn't give Theo or Aiden a chance to respond before disappearing, his partner trailing him.

"Where are the cameras when you need them?" Theo sighed.

"I don't know, but I think it's safe to say the competition just got real." They shared a smile, and Aiden couldn't help but think something else had just gotten a bit too real as well.

9

THEO

"Well, this is interesting." Theo stepped inside the business room at the hotel, Aiden behind her.

Their camera crew was in tow, as was the show's host. Daniel gave them a TV-worthy grin.

"Our show's director came up with a pretty exciting prize for you two after your win today. He thought you might be interested in your competition since that could give you an advantage over them." He moved to the nearby desk and grabbed a file from it, hefting it into the air. "One team in particular."

Turning to meet Aiden's stare, Theo's brows furrowed. Where was this headed? Aiden lifted a shoulder, seemingly as clueless as she was.

"You'll have twenty minutes to review Brandt and Paisley's file and utilize the computer." He gestured to the ancient desktop behind him. "To do a little light research. Have fun."

With that, he handed Theo the file and disappeared from the room.

"Why does this feel like a trap?" Aiden stood beside her, his arm brushing against her skin. She tamped down a shiver at the slight touch.

From my mate.

Clearing her throat, she pushed that thought down and opened the file folder. "It's most definitely a trap if Max is involved. At least that's the vibe I get." She lifted a picture of Brandt. "Like we're going to believe anything in this folder."

Aiden reached for the picture of the older vampire, flipping it over. "Okay, here it tells us that Brandt has a tendency to sleep for decades and that he's estimated to be five hundred years old, although no one can confirm it."

Theo handed over the folder before dropping into the chair in front of the computer. "That's shockingly helpful. What else does it say?"

"He's made poor investments, and they say he's known for bad decision-making."

Tapping her chin, she nodded. "Definitely a weakness, although not one we can best him at physically, or at least I don't think. Is there anything else?"

He rummaged through the rest of the file and shook his head. "No. Same for Paisley—nothing that'll make a difference. I don't know about you, but I want to find something that can help us beat him, especially after that stunt he pulled with the boulder."

"And Max knows about it. This 'prize' feels more like the middle finger unless the web can help." Theo pulled up the search browser and typed in "how to defeat ancient vampires."

Aiden sat down next to her, their bodies brushing again. Her heart thudded almost painfully at his nearness, his scent, and her mouth watered with the remembrance of what he tasted like. Maybe this was more of a temptation from Max—hang the forbidden fruit in front of her face and see if she'd drink from it again.

"Hey, you good?" Aiden gently nudged her hand.

Blinking several times, she focused on the screen. "Oh, yeah, I'm good. Sorry." She waved him off. "I zoned out there. Let's see if there's a way to defeat an old vampire like Brandt."

And maybe get herself in check in the meantime.

🦇

Theo and Aiden had zero luck in their 'prize' search, just as she suspected they would. Upon heading to her room, she heard a familiar voice.

"Third is hardly considered competition," Brandt, aka Nosferatu wannabe, growled.

She slowed her walk to a stop as she peered around the corner of one of the hallways in the hotel. Brandt and his partner, Paisley, stood toe to toe with the third-place team, Jax and Derek. Jax was a younger vampire with a very cavalier, cocky attitude. His human teammate wasn't much better, with his hands crossed over his chest and face lined with irritation.

"It's the first challenge, man. *The first.* There are five, and we'll dominate the rest. So why don't you do yourself a favor and crawl back into the crypt you came from?" Jax said with a laugh.

Brandt bared ghastly fangs—the things were ancient, yellowed. "You dare mock me?"

"And me by proxy?" Paisley finally spoke up, everything about her brimming with fire.

"You're both taking this a little too seriously. Besides, shouldn't you be focusing on the team that beat you? You know, instead of us?"

There was a reason Theo and Aiden nicknamed Brandt *Nosferatu.* Although he didn't look completely ancient, he reminded her of the character from the 1929 film. Something about him gave her the creeps, which said a lot because she wasn't scared of much.

The older vampire wrung his pale hands, and that was when Theo noticed his long nails. She held her arms over her chest as her eyes widened.

He finally spoke, his voice a low, hypnotic timbre. "Soon. But for now, you'll have to do."

Jax and Derek scoffed, clearly not picking up on the menacing vibes Brandt was laying down. They rolled their eyes and continued to laugh before Jax turned into a bat and flew off, Derek jogging away. They might have been unaffected, but the entire scene left chills dotted along Theo's arms. That had been a threat, right? She took this game seriously, but apparently not as much as Brandt. She and Aiden needed to watch their backs.

Speaking of her teammate/nuisance, they'd agreed not to hang out during the rest of their downtime at the hotel. She had no fear of absence making her heart grow fonder or any of that cliché stuff.

A few hours later, she set off to find a snack of the human variety who most certainly was not Aiden. As she did, one of the crew members appeared and began ushering her toward the path where the contestants met the day before. "We need you down here immediately, please, Miss Nash."

Her brows scrunched as she followed the woman, alarm bells clanging inside her mind. "Why? What's going on?"

"Daniel will fill you in once everyone has arrived." The crew member then swept a hand toward where the other contestants waited in a crooked line, their eyes on Theo as she arrived. Apparently, she was the last one.

The host stood before them, head bowed in thought. Theo caught Aiden's eye, mouthing, "What the hell?"

He shrugged in response.

"Thank you all for coming here on such short notice. As it's our duty to be completely honest with you, I wanted to fill you in on a recent development." He frowned. "As you know, two teams were eliminated following our first task. Tonight, we had another team leave. Jax and Derek decided that the competition was too much, and they would rather bow out gracefully now." Daniel paused, doing a slow scan of the remaining contestants. "So I wanted to ask if anyone else would like to leave tonight? As you know, tomorrow, we will be en route to where the second challenge takes place."

Lies. That one word resounded in Theo's head, an incessant thud telling her not to believe the lies that Daniel, or Max, or the rest of the *Night Race* crew were weaving. No way Derek and Jax chose to leave, especially not after the high they were riding by being in third place...and then the smack talk with Brandt and his partner.

Something foul was afoot...something undoubtedly caused by Brandt.

Theo slowly slid a glance toward the suspect.

Brandt stood tall and proud, a smug grin pulling his lips up, fangs entirely on display as if daring someone to question him. His tongue darted out, moving in a quick swipe over his lips, eyes widening. That was a telltale sign that he'd just tasted blood...so he'd fed recently, but on who?

The blood had to be Derek's and not Jax's, the vampire half of their team. It wasn't exactly typical for vampires to feed on each other unless they were mated. Otherwise, it was kind of looked down upon. So it'd make complete sense for the Nosferatu wannabe to be a vamp drinker. It was said that if a vampire drank from another vampire—nonmate—they would acquire their powers or strength. Like the trance, this was something guarded as a semisecret. That kind of knowledge wouldn't prove to foster the best of relations between vampires.

"All right, since no one else wants to leave, you may continue enjoying your evening. We'll be in touch soon."

When everyone else left, Theo remained frozen in place, her stare tracing Brandt's steps.

"You okay?" Aiden's deep voice rumbled through the starry night.

Theo pursed her lips. "I'm not sure. I think Brandt and Paisley killed that team, though."

It sounded as ridiculous spoken aloud as it did in her head, but with her gut basically screaming the accusation, she owed it to herself, and to Aiden, she supposed, to listen.

Aiden ran a hand through his dark hair, a curl falling over his brow with the movement. He was so incredibly handsome, a thought Theo loathed each time it popped into her head.

"What makes you think that? Besides the fact that guy is scary as hell and tried to kill us with a boulder." His words were spoken without judgment, which made her feel a little better about her theory.

She stepped closer, peering around the front lawn of the hotel, thankful that everyone else had already started making their way in for the night, even the cameras. "I heard those two threaten Jax and Derek. I think they're going to start taking out teams."

A thoughtful look crossed Aiden's face as he tapped his chin. He moved even nearer, bringing that intoxicating smell of his cologne with him. Something about that male-and-spice scent really did a number on her.

"I wish we could've had more time to search for answers on the computer." His mouth twisted to the side. "The thing is, why is Brandt so dead set on it?"

She cast him a look of disbelief, causing him to raise his hands in the air. "I know, I know. We are too, but at least we agreed to wait to start killing people until we got the chalice in our hands."

Theo cringed at that, but Aiden continued. "Speaking of which, I was thinking—"

"Oh, wow. This ought to be interesting then."

"As a matter of fact, it is interesting." He stood even taller. "Why don't you just turn me yourself? Right before you turn yourself into a human, you could do your little..." He mimicked fangs with his fingers, and she had to bite her lip to keep from laughing. This man was utterly ridiculous, and yet she kept finding him more endearing with each passing minute. Which was a huge problem. "Thing with your fangs, suck my blood, you know the whole nine?"

The reality of what he asked settled on her shoulders like a lead weight, but then something sparked in her mind. She arched a brow.

"Okay, but why don't you just get another vampire to turn you?

Actually, why didn't you do that instead of coming on this show and going through all this trouble?"

Aiden glared at her, his face stony. "Given my past with vampires, I didn't think it'd be great to just waltz into a vampire nest and be all, 'Hey guys, who wants to drain me of my blood until I'm *juuuust* about dead and then turn me into a vampire?' No. I need someone I can trust to do this if I can't have the chalice—"

"No." Theo sliced a hand through the air. "You can't have the chalice, either way. It's mine. And I won't turn you. I can't." She paused, swallowing hard. "When I became a vampire, I vowed that I wouldn't do it."

The beautiful man in front of her turned thoughtful again, his green eyes softening, his entire frame releasing a bit of its tension. "Did you not want to become a vampire?"

She hadn't told him a lot of her story, and that had been by design. While she was sure other vampires—of course aside from Andreas and his mate, Davina—knew about her origin story, she didn't feel like relaying it here and now to this almost stranger.

"I wasn't turned against my will if that's what you're asking. I was given a choice, and I willingly accepted my fate. I chose the path of revenge, and when you make decisions based on that and white-hot rage, I don't think they ultimately end up being the best choices." She blew out a breath. "I've sought a way to fix the situation I got myself into, and here we are. So I get the chalice since there's literally not another way to turn a vampire into a human."

Aiden said nothing for a moment as he studied her. The intensity of his stare felt like a caress over her skin, and she folded her arms across her body to suppress a shiver. Did he have to be so attractive in every single way?

"I guess it'll be a fight to the death when that day comes, because I'm not letting you walk away with the chalice if you refuse to turn me." He arched a brow.

Her tone turned flippant. "So be it then. Your funeral. In quite the literal sense."

Suppressing a smile, Aiden pressed his lips together. "Okay then. To switch gears here for a minute, let's revisit my earlier question because I think that could help us." He rubbed the back of his neck. "Why would Brandt want the chalice so badly? He's super old—doesn't he have all the add-ons vampires get when they reach his age?"

Theo nearly choked on her spit, because how could Aiden know about any of that? She gaped at him, her confusion and curiosity no doubt written all over her face.

He shrugged. "What? I watch movies. I figured there had to be something that came with getting older as a vampire."

A breeze lifted Theo's hair, and she longed to feel the sun on her skin. Getting closer to her goal just reinforced her drive to win this thing at any cost.

"There are things such as powers or incredible strength that vampires acquire as they age or hit certain milestones. The older the vampire, the harder they are to kill." She tucked her hair behind her ears. "But you raise a good question: Why would Brandt want it when he's already one of the oldest vampires I've ever seen in real life? And my friend Andreas is pretty old."

Aiden's eyes flared for a brief moment, watching her all too carefully, as if he were attempting to pickpocket her thoughts and stow them away. When he finally spoke, his tone was surprisingly dull. "Andreas? Is that a...love interest?"

Theo tilted her head, trying not to smile. Did he sound...*interested*? Jealous even? Fireworks set off, one after another, like sparkly dominoes in her chest at that. She shouldn't mess with him...she absolutely shouldn't...but she had to.

"Why? Are you volunteering for the part? Got a kink for sexing up someone that you're destined to kill?" Somehow, she'd managed to keep her face expressionless the entire time.

Shockingly, Aiden was utterly unfazed. "I would prefer it without the killing, actually, but you're pretty intent on it, so..."

"Wait. What are you saying?"

Now Aiden canted his head to the side, his gaze dropping to her lips for one heated moment. "What do *you* think I'm saying is the better question?"

"That you're interested in...*me*?" This man, her *mate* was nothing but trouble.

Aiden smirked, and in the moonlight, he looked almost too pretty to be real. Everything about him was sharp edges and carved planes, the type that could cut. The type that was dangerous. Something about him was hypnotic to her, though, something that beckoned, a feeling she wondered could be due to the mate bond, or was it something else? There was no way she could actually kind of, sort of like the guy, right?

"Hey! They got blood bags set up inside!" Rita, one of the vampire members of the crew, called out from the front door of the hotel, startling Theo from pretty much blatantly staring at her partner, competition, mate, nemesis, mortal enemy.

Her stomach growled in response to Rita's words. Theo had been so thirsty, so hungry ever since she fed on Aiden on the mountain. She hadn't taken much out of respect to him and his past. And then there was her worry that no one else's blood would satisfy her cravings—hadn't she heard something like that regarding drinking from a mate?

"Blood bags, huh? I thought you preferred it straight from the vein?" Aiden asked as they started to make their way up the path, walking close enough she could feel the warmth radiating from his body. The interesting thing was the overactive part of her mind, the one filled with guilt and anger, the one only adrenaline could calm...well...it was...quiet.

She shot Aiden a smile and not one of her fake ones either. One of her genuine smiles that hadn't seen the light of the moon since Jonathan kissed her through the prison bars all those years ago.

"I do. Blood bag is code for human, Aiden."

His expression drew a laugh out of her, and she left him with a wave over her shoulder. She needed to feed and build up her strength, because who knew what the second challenge would bring?

10

AIDEN

Aiden zipped up his jacket, shoving his hands in his pockets as he stood next to Theo outside White Point Garden in Charleston, South Carolina. Two nights ago, Daniel had rushed them to board flights to Charleston and then asked everyone to meet here, at a waterfront park supposedly haunted by the ghosts of pirates. The host shifted from foot to foot under a gazebo with everyone else staring up at him from below.

As they waited, a bat delivered a task envelope to each team, and they weren't allowed to open it until instructed to do so. Several contestants freaked out at the arrival of the vampire bat, but having seen *Forever After*, Aiden expected them to make an appearance at some point. Suppressing a laugh, he kept his attention on Theo. She clutched the envelope between her fingertips, tapping it sporadically against her upper thigh, a movement that had him bewitched.

He wanted to know what it would feel like to touch her there, to feel her beneath him. Ah, hell. Honestly, he shouldn't be surprised since the beautiful vampire had him all twisted up inside.

It was undeniable that he felt an inexplicable pull toward Theodora. It wasn't because "she wasn't like other women" or anything like that. After Cassidy, he thought no one would be able to capture his attention again, but he'd been transfixed by Theo from the get-go. He simply liked being around her, liked her spark and fire, the way she went after what she wanted without caring who got in her way. If he'd told her he *was* interested...which he'd been so close to doing, just to see what she'd say and partly... because he wanted to, what would she have said?

He tugged at the collar of his jacket and released a sigh. Those things had nothing to do with the task at hand. He needed to get his big head in the game and stop thinking with his *other* head.

"Okay, on the count of three, you'll tear open your envelopes!" Daniel's voice carried through the park.

Aiden tensed, and so did Theo. Dylan and Bridget hovered so close he was sure they'd gotten a nice close-up of any nose hairs he might have.

Daniel stood up straight, casting a mischievous smile at all the contestants. "One..." He made sure to drag the single syllable into three. Southerners across the world would be impressed. "Two..."

Aiden shifted so close that his shoulder brushed Theo's. He made no effort to move, and neither did she, even as he felt her entire body stringing tight.

"And three!"

Theo tore into the envelope, pulling out a card. She sucked in an audible breath before she began reading it aloud.

"You're about to embark on a challenge that holds three clues. You'll receive lodging information when you complete the final task. Here's your first clue: Find the grave that inspired Edgar Allan Poe's famous poem 'Annabel Lee.' Good luck and run free!"

Other teams started frantically searching on the phones the show gave them, but Theo remained frozen.

Aiden gently bumped her shoulder with his. "Hey, we gotta get moving. Here, I'll start the search." He dug his phone out of his pocket and started typing.

When she didn't say anything, he looked up to find her staring at something over his shoulder. Turning around, he saw that it was none other than Brandt. The vampire gave them a smile that made Aiden's insides shrivel like raisins. Theo even shivered next to him, and then the old ass vampire shot them the bird before taking off with his teammate.

Cringing, he looked to Theo. She mirrored his expression as she reached forward, laying a soft hand on his forearm. Electric jolts, tiny lightning bolts, sparked through him at the touch, nearly taking his breath away. *Focus, Aiden. Focus.*

Theo's voice was soft when she spoke, which worried him because it wasn't exactly normal Theo behavior. "Aiden?"

"Yeah?"

"I think we need to lose this one on purpose, no matter what it is. We need to try to come in third ideally, somewhere right in the middle of the road."

Aiden jerked, which sadly caused Theo's hand to fall from his arm. He blinked a thousand times while, of course, Bridget and Dylan wasted no time zooming in, cameras all up in their faces.

"Why would we do that?"

"Because of what happened to Derek and Jax. Because of Brandt and his minion." She gestured toward where their vampire nemesis had just stood. "You saw how he looked at us. He's been watching us, Aiden. Like creepy-style watching us, and if he thinks we're a threat, then he won't hesitate in killing us to knock us out of the race. We *did* sign death waivers to come on this show, you know." She widened her eyes meaningfully.

"Right, I got that, but I..." He shook his head, unsure of how to say what he wanted to without sounding like a giant dick. "I don't agree with that idea, though. I say we fight like we've been doing, and when Brandt strikes, we deal with it—maybe even try to come up with ways to trip him up or foil his own plans." He knew his face twisted into a grimace with his words.

Theo stared at him blankly as the rest of the contestants were shouting or taking off running. Adrenaline still pumped through

Aiden's veins, his hands twitching at his sides with the innate need to do *something*. Releasing a sigh, he looked down at his phone, his fingers flying as he searched for the answer to the riddle. Cassidy had been a massive fan of Poe. He tried to swallow down those thoughts and focus on something else. But what? How Theo made him feel? Or this ridiculous idea of hers...one that could possibly cost them the chalice.

"I don't mean lose *completely*, of course. We don't want to get eliminated, but let's give them have a head start is all," Theo continued as Aiden scrolled.

"Unitarian Church Graveyard!" he whisper-shouted, a grin curving his lips.

If it was that easy for him to locate the answer, that meant the other teams were already on their way and would probably get the second clue. Damn it.

Aiden typed the location in a map app, figuring it might be faster to run since he didn't see many taxis this late at night. Besides, he was so small town he didn't even begin to have experience with Uber or whatever those companies were, mainly because they didn't have them at all in Harper's Grove, Georgia, where he had been born and raised. It was either take the *one* taxi available or ask a friend for a ride.

He headed toward King Street with Theo following, her feet all but dragging. When he turned around to look at her, reluctance danced across her face, her features pulled down. Her voice trailed in wisps in the wind.

"I'm telling you now, Aiden. I'm not only doing this for me. I'm doing it for you too. You're a human, and you would never survive against someone like Brandt."

"And I'm telling *you* we're a team, Theodora. We have to make decisions *together*." His hand itched to rub his neck, the spot where she had fed on him. There weren't any puncture wounds, not like his shoulder that had been pretty much ravaged. Her feeding on him had been a decision they'd made as a team.

Theo could've just put him in a trance regardless of his consent, but she hadn't done that. She had asked, earning a modicum of his trust. But this shit? This going rogue-style thing she had going on wouldn't work. He'd never get that chalice, and he'd never be able to avenge Cassidy or protect his family, and that was all he wanted.

And Theodora Nash currently stood in the way of that.

"I agree, but when you're being dense, how can we reach any sort of agreement?" She gritted through her teeth.

Aiden stopped walking through downtown Charleston, the streetlights illuminating their argument perfectly for the cameras. He huffed out an agitated breath.

"I don't know you well enough yet, and I know you've got a wall up between us, hell, between you and the world for that matter, but I can tell you that the woman I met back in Jacksonville wasn't scared of anything. She didn't cower—"

Theo straightened, her fangs protruding over her lips. "I am *not* cowering."

"Okay, maybe not, but you are acting scared, and I don't think we have any reason to be right now."

She narrowed her eyes and even in the grip of fury she was the most beautiful person he'd ever seen. "Were you not there on the side of the mountain when that asshole threw a freaking boulder at us? A *boulder*, Aiden. All while he was tied to his partner, while *we* were tied together. And then with Jax and Derek. Those guys are dead, Aiden. I know it." Conviction strung her words together in a tight line, causing Aiden to move so he stood beside her on the street.

Something in his gut clenched at seeing Theo so distraught, but it was hard to fight with the other louder feeling that screamed for him to run, compete, *win*. He gently touched her wrist, her pale skin smooth and cool to the touch. "You really believe it, don't you? That we're in danger?"

When he went to take a step back, Theo grabbed his hand, not threading her fingers through, just a loose hold. He tried to ignore the flicker that ran through him. Theo lifted her gaze to meet his dead-on. "Yes."

He didn't want to go with this idea, but it was clear Theo didn't plan on budging. The one thing Daniel harped on at the beginning of the race was that they had to work together.

Releasing a heavy breath, he ran a hand through his hair as he listened to the sounds of the Charleston night around them—a car driving by slowly, horse hooves and carriages moving at the same leisurely pace, and the sounds of teams finding what they so desperately sought.

"Fine, but I still say we need to pick up the pace, or we'll be dead last and eliminated."

Theo's expression turned incredulous. "That won't happen."

Anger bubbled up inside Aiden at even being put in this position. "And if it does, then maybe you'll reconsider turning me into a vampire."

"No."

Aiden looked down at his phone and gritted his teeth. Just when he thought he'd made progress with Theo, things like this happened. If he responded, he'd do so in anger, so instead, he focused all his attention on the map on his phone.

The Unitarian Church Graveyard entrance was beautifully spooky with its black wrought-iron gate and lantern hanging in the center overhead, the flame inside flickering as if real. The path inside the graveyard was fairly narrow and shrouded in tree cover, hiding the stars from view.

A few teams raced past them, already on their way out of the graveyard, before Brandt and Paisley rounded the corner, nearly barreling into them. Of course, Brandt made sure to bump Aiden's shoulder hard enough to jostle him. In middle school, Aiden dealt with his share of bullies, so he clenched his jaw, biting back any sort of curse or response, knowing that would be precisely what the ancient vampire wanted. Silence would only serve to piss him off more.

"Falling behind, I see," Brandt snarled, his muddy brown brows raising into judgy arches.

"We'll make sure it stays that way...or worse," Paisley tilted her head with a taunting curl of her lips.

Before any response could be spoken, the pair were off, no doubt about to take out whoever had them beat for the moment.

Aiden spun to Theo. "It looks like we have a target on our backs either way, so we might as well actually try to win."

Theo nibbled on her bottom lip, pink and pouty, and Aiden did all he could not to zero in on it. "I suppose for now we can up the ante, but I still don't think we should try our hardest—"

Another team raced by, and Aiden called out to them. One of the teammates slowed, turning around to jog backward and look at him.

"Are there any teams left?" Aiden hooked a thumb toward the path where the pair had just come from.

"Nope. You're last." And with those parting words, they left, hauling all kinds of ass.

Aiden's stomach dropped to his knees, a fist clasped around his heart with the news. He couldn't believe that they might actually lose. Especially not when he'd tried so hard to focus only on the task at hand and not on other things... Other things being Theo and the slight spark he'd imagined there. But with this realization that they could lose it all, that spark fizzled into a sputtering, barely there flame. He didn't know the vampire well enough to give up a chance at everything he'd needed, *wanted*, for the last three years. All of it had led up to this moment. And it was all about to fall apart.

"Damn it," he bit out, and without waiting for Theo, he spun on his heel and ran toward Anna Ravenel's grave. It was rumored she was who Annabel Lee was based on, although there'd been tons of proof that this actually wasn't true. Even so, he knew without a doubt it was Anna's grave they needed to find, and thankfully the other teams had saved them some time in searching the entire graveyard for it.

Footsteps crunching fallen leaves echoed behind him among the symphony of crickets and owls and other nocturnal creatures—the deadliest one being his partner cursing like a sailor as she made her way to him. He crouched before the weathered grave with Anna's name carved into it and picked up the only envelope remaining, hands shaking as he opened it.

"Take a carriage to the Arrowwood Grill and be careful of the sun, for your day has only just begun," Aiden read aloud, fighting back an eye roll at the rhyme.

Theo gave him a nod, and he returned it, a silent truce for now only because they needed to work together. "A carriage should be easy to find," she said, and then they were off.

11

THEO

FOR THE FIRST TIME IN THE GAME, THEO FELT EVEN MORE GUILT-ridden and angry than she usually did. Where the adrenaline rush and Aiden had dulled some of that persistent noise caused by feeling *everything*, it now came back in waves. The sensation was enough to nearly knock her off her feet as she led the way to an empty carriage trotting down the street toward them.

The look on Aiden's face upon finding out they were last...it bothered her more than it should, and a part of it was due to the fact it was her fault.

She'd been too cautious, played things too close to the vest, which she had never been one to do. Maybe she could blame the mate bond and its persistent throbbing throughout her mind and heart and, *damn*, her body. More than once, she'd checked out Aiden's forearms or the cut of his jaw when he swallowed or studied the scar through his brow.

They leaped into the carriage, Bridget and Dylan sitting up front with the driver as they filmed. Aiden's body brushed against hers. It wasn't so much that he was tall in stature—he was only slightly taller than her—it was that the space was so small.

No wonder most couples think the carriage rides are romantic.

The soft stroke of his hair on his arms tickled Theo's bare skin, and she was caught in that awkward in-between of not wanting to move because she enjoyed it, and also wanting to move because if she didn't, it might appear she was into him—into the very partner that she'd just severely pissed off. *Whatever.* She had a plan to fix things, to be proactive.

"We're going to win the chalice, Aiden. I can promise you that. I've waited entirely too long for this moment to let it slip through my fingers."

"Why do you want to be human so badly?" Aiden's voice came out as barely a croak.

She didn't want to give him everything. That equaled power. Besides, it had been hard enough to admit the truth to Andreas, but she knew she had to give Aiden *something.*

"Because I'm tired of being immortal and feeling so much, and I don't want to die quite yet, in case you're wondering why I just don't step into the sunlight." She fidgeted with her hands in her lap. "I'd like time to experience things...as they should be, perhaps? Things I didn't get a chance to enjoy because of my choices."

Aiden shifted slightly so he could look at her, *really* look at her, or at least that's what it felt like, as he watched her for a moment before dipping his chin and turning to face the front again. That signaled the end of their conversation.

For the rest of the ride, they listened to the symphony of horse hooves echoing through the night. When a strong breeze blew in, it brought with it the scent of rain. A storm was brewing—in more ways than one.

The carriage stopped outside Arrowwood Grill, a small restaurant downtown, past Rainbow Row. The entrance was tucked away, an awning with the name and logo heralding its presence.

Theo's stomach gurgled at the sight because she couldn't eat human food...and Max would know that. So if that were the case, then why were they here? Somehow, she managed to tamp down all her questions as Aiden reached up a hand, helping her out of the carriage.

For a split second, she felt like a fairy-tale character being helped down by her prince—the image as intense as it was frightening. She cleared her throat as they made their way inside the establishment, which had clearly opened just for the show.

A woman in her fifties, with red hair twisted into a neat chignon, dressed in a black dress with enormous pearl earrings, grinned at them. "Hi! You must be Theo and Aiden. I'm Marysa. Come on back with me." She waved for them to follow as she moved from behind a hostess stand.

The restaurant had a dimly lit romantic vibe. Edison bulbs crisscrossed the ceiling, and a bookshelf doubled as a bar against the back wall, the booze interspersed with the books. Pristine white linen covered the tables, little rustic lanterns with faux candles the centerpieces of each. But they didn't venture farther into the actual dining room. Instead, they turned down a white hallway laden with gorgeous artwork of scenes around the city.

Marysa led them through a wooden door that looked like a historical artifact itself and into a bright party room that appeared to be transformed into a cooking show set—several tables stocked with kitchen appliances and ingredients...and, of course, filled with the rest of the contestants. The noise stopped for a moment as they stared at the new arrivals, but then they quickly went back to work. "Work" being cooking.

Oh no.

Marysa stopped at an empty table at the back, thankfully away from everyone. Bridget and Dylan shifted around them.

"You two will be cooking together tonight, but as we all know, vampires can't eat human food, or they'll get deathly ill. So that's why tonight's task will be a little difficult and will challenge the relationship you've built as a team." Marysa clapped her hands together as Theo and Aiden stared at each other, both with a single brow raised and an *Oh, shit* look splashed across their faces.

Continuing, Marysa gestured to the table behind her. "So, Theo, you'll be the chef tonight. Aiden will guide you on how to make everything—but he can't taste it. He can only direct you. As you see, all vampires are the chefs, and humans are the guides. You have one hour to complete the task. Once finished with the dish, you'll present it to our judges, who will be arriving shortly and will be waiting for you in the dining room. Any questions?"

Theo stepped around the woman and up to the table, already strapping on an apron and pulling her hair away from her face before washing her hands in the sink.

"No. I think we've got it. Thank you, Marysa." It had been centuries since she'd had to cook anything. Saying she was rusty would be a horrendous understatement.

Aiden chimed in, "Thank you, Marysa," as he moved to stand across from Theo, reading over the recipe card.

"Shrimp and grits shouldn't be too difficult."

"Says the one not cooking," Theo muttered as Aiden began lining up ingredients. A smile played over his lips, letting her know he'd heard her smartassery. *Good.*

"The first thing you need to do is cook the grits. Boil the water and then pour them in. But..." He leaned in close and whispered the next part against her ear. She tingled down to her toes but listened carefully. "Replace half the water with milk and add in two tablespoons of butter."

Theo did precisely that, and after she took a step back, they set their timer. "Grits remind me of porridge, and I hated porridge." She leaned against the countertop, eyeing their competition.

"Did you eat a lot of that in your human life?"

She nodded. "I did. We ate a lot of seafood too, especially since we lived near the port." Pausing, she offered Aiden a grim smile. "But if it's all the same, I'd really rather not talk about that time in my life, at least not right now when we've got a challenge to win."

One team squealed with happiness as they finished first. Marysa led them out to the dining room with their dish. Brandt and

Paisley's gazes locked on the winning pair, all kinds of deadly things moving behind their calculated stares.

Theo nudged Aiden's shoulder, tilting her head toward the villains. "See? What did I tell you?"

His lips twisted, but he said nothing. Instead, he looked down at the recipe card, preparing the next set of ingredients.

Unable to help herself, Theo leaned against his shoulder, suppressing a smile when she felt a surprised jerk roll through his muscles.

"You're still mad at me."

It wasn't a question. She knew damn well it was true.

Shifting his head so it rested atop hers, he nodded slightly. "I am. Maybe a little?" She swore she felt him kiss her hair. "But it'll be okay. I'm just worried because we're going to be last." He paused. "We haven't even started on the shrimp yet."

"Maybe we'll get a pass if we cook really well?"

He hummed against her hair before gently moving away, his voice kind when he spoke. "Maybe so."

Turning his attention to the grits, he began to direct her again, instructing her to put in butter and salt and pepper, along with cheese.

One by one, the other teams filtered out, leaving Theo and Aiden alone with their camera crew. To Aiden's credit, he was an amazing teacher. He was patient and calm, directing Theo carefully with cooking and even asking for her input.

By the time she plated the meal, she found herself adding this dish to her bucket list for when she became a human again. It smelled delicious.

Marysa led them to the dining room, where three judges sat at a table. One a younger man, probably in his thirties, and the other a little older, perhaps early sixties, along with a woman possibly in her forties.

Off to the side stood the other teams. Some looked smug as if they'd already won, while others shuffled nervously. Theo hadn't realized they'd all still be here, but then again, of course they would. They had to be in order to see who the winner was. Her nerves were getting the better of her, throwing her off.

"Judges, here we have the final team's rendition of shrimp and grits."

She gave Theo and Aiden an encouraging smile as she motioned for them to set the plate down on the table.

The judges almost grimaced, turning green at the sight of yet another helping of the same dish. Fidgeting with the hem of her shirt, Theo watched as the judges reluctantly, scooped a small serving onto their plates. Theo could barely breathe. Her hands sought out Aiden's, his squeezing hers in return. If nothing else, they needed this win to prove they were a good team, and maybe, just maybe, Max would reconsider eliminating them. Hope fluttered through her veins as the older judge's eyes lit up.

"This is very good. Quite possibly the best of the bunch. What do you think, Pete?" He looked over at the other judge.

He covered his mouth, chewing, and then spoke. "It's superb. This one's the winner, in my opinion. Don't you agree, Staci?"

"Absolutely." Staci put her fork down with a grin. "It seems congratulations are in order, since you won the challenge!" She steepled her fingers. "Now, you'll need to go to the Foxglove Hotel to collect your prize. Best of luck, you two. You're quite a team."

If that were the case, why did Theo dread the moment they arrived at the hotel? Somehow the human had grown on her, and she knew she'd hate losing him due to the Solis Occasum, which more than worried her. She'd set out to win, not be tempted by a cute man. *Mate*, a voice reminded her in the back of her mind.

Way to make things difficult, Theodora.

12

AIDEN

Raindrops fell in large splats across Aiden's forehead as he and Theo rounded the palmetto-enshrouded corner. They'd worked hard to make sure they didn't come in last, but what if next time there wasn't a challenge to save them? On top of that, there was no guarantee winning the cook-off saved them in the first place —not after how everyone dashed out of the room before they had the chance to move.

What would his life even be if it weren't focused on Cassidy and revenge and protecting his remaining family members? Theo's lovely face flashed in his mind, and he couldn't help but think about her or her lips that were no doubt as soft as they looked, or the way she often trailed her fingertips along her neck when she spoke—she did it absentmindedly, but it entranced him all the same.

"Almost there!" Theo called out as they jumped over a fast-forming puddle on the sidewalk, the rain now falling in earnest and causing Aiden's shirt to stick to his skin, raindrops running down his back, his face, everywhere.

They found the hotel, painted a lovely shade of purple, with a large black awning protruding from its entrance and spanning out to the end of the sidewalk. Beneath it, Daniel waited, looking intense with his arms crossed over his body.

Before turning to face the host, they maneuvered under the covering, making sure the camera crew had room. Although he and Theo all but ran to the hotel, they were both barely out of breath. Thankfully Aiden had conditioned for times like these.

A frown tugged the corners of the host's lips down as he swung his gaze from Aiden to Theo. Dramatic music played in Aiden's head, filling the tense silence—aside from the pitter-patter of the rain—because he knew when the show got edited, that's how it would play out. He drew in a deep breath. Damn it. This was it. It was over. The reprieve he thought they'd surely get from winning the challenge was nothing but a pipe dream.

"Theodora, Aiden." Daniel bowed his head slightly, his voice somber.

Theo grabbed Aiden's hand tightly, weaving her fingers through his, as she shuffled closer to him, something she'd done during the challenge. Her floral scent mixed with the rain, and her shirt plastered to her chest; it was almost too much. Aiden cleared his throat as he drew his focus back on the host.

"You arrived last out of all the contestants."

Although this was something they'd already known, it still hurt to hear. Theo gasped as her nails dug into his waist. He held her tighter as he muttered, "No." He scrubbed one of his hands down his face, the ridge of his eyebrow scar raised slightly beneath his fingertips.

"Unfortunately, yes," Daniel continued.

The moment felt strung on a flimsy string with beads that were entirely too heavy for it, threatening to break at the slightest disturbance. Breath got bottled up in Aiden's throat as his mind whirred with the *what-ifs* and *what do I do nows*?

"But..." The host paused as he tugged down the cuffs of his shirt. "Since you had the best dish in the challenge, you will not be eliminated from this round. You are safe, as is the team that came in before you—as they had the second-best dish. Therefore, no teams will be eliminated tonight."

Theo's response was quiet, barely heard over the rain. "Wait, what?"

Aiden stepped away from her, his nervous hands rubbing the back of his neck, his heart beating a thousand miles a minute.

Daniel grinned. "Lucky for you, right? But you and the team before you have something to think about." He turned toward the door, and out came the other group.

The host pointed to the vampire in the pair, who looked to be in her forties, a little shorter than Theo, with long ash-colored hair. "This is Aria." And then he angled his head toward the human. "This is Elsie." Her teammate was tall, her black hair cut to her chin in a severe bob. They looked at Aiden and Theo warily, and he wanted to say the feeling was mutual but was still too stunned to speak.

Thank God he and Theo had made a good team in the kitchen. Of course, there was still a tiny part of him that wanted to snap at Theo for getting them into this predicament, but he also knew— probably better than anyone—that everyone made mistakes. He was definitely more than a little conflicted at the moment, and then add in the fact that he had started to enjoy her hard-earned smiles or small huffs of laughter, and that made things even more complicated.

Daniel clasped his hands together before speaking again. "And for our next great plot twist. You now have the option to switch partners! You'll take the rest of the night to decide if you want to and must let us know tomorrow. Get plenty of rest as your next destination is Salem, Massachusetts."

Theo swayed on her feet, bumping into Aiden's arm. He shot her a glance, his brows dipping down, and she just shook her head, straightening, crossing her arms over her body, a fierce look slowly etching itself onto her face.

"Both teams must agree, or the switch doesn't happen. We'll

meet tomorrow night to discuss. We'll let you know when." Daniel's gaze swung over to Dylan and Bridget. "If you two will follow Rita, over there"—he gestured to a crew member who materialized from thin air—"she'll take you to your rooms."

The crew waved to them, following Rita, leaving behind the other team. Aria and Elsie eyeballed Aiden and Theo, their gazes speculative, causing his heart to race. Just because he didn't agree with how Theo played the beginning of the last challenge didn't mean he wanted to lose her as a partner. Now he knew without a doubt that she would get them to the end...and then they'd handle things accordingly. That part made him shudder. Maybe that was the very reason he *should* consider a partner switch up? Could he really stake Theo as her stunning blue eyes stared back at him? A sour taste rose on his tongue, acid coating his mouth, his thoughts, this moment.

Daniel grew somber again as a roll of thunder startled nearly everyone else, a crack of lightning striking nearby, casting light upon the scene. Aiden turned to Theo, seeing doubt flicker across her expression for a split second. The same was probably mirrored on his face.

"You'll share rooms tonight. You are dismissed." The host gave them a nod before disappearing.

Rain began to pour sideways, the wind blowing it beneath the awning and onto them. Everyone scurried inside, the other team casting one last backward glance before heading to their room. Hell, Aiden and Theo didn't even *have* a room yet.

Thankfully the lobby was warmer, the smell of freshly baked chocolate chip cookies wafting in the air. It was a vampire hotel, so he had a feeling those were made especially for the human guests and crew members. His stomach growled at the scent. When was the last time he'd eaten more than a granola bar?

He noticed their backpacks sitting to the side of the reception desk. It was nice not having to worry about that during the challenges. Wordlessly, they marched toward the reception desk.

The place was incredibly swanky. A layered chandelier dripped from the ceiling, and tall cream-colored sofas sat beneath gilded wall sconces, the marble floors mirroring the intricate lighting of the space. Vampires loved their fancy stuff.

Lightning flickered across the hotel, the ground rumbling under Aiden's feet as he stopped at the desk. "Is there a hurricane coming this way?" he asked offhandedly.

Living in the coastal South, hurricane season was something he was used to, especially where his Georgia hometown of Harper's Grove was located—just one hour from the coastline and about thirty minutes from the Florida-Georgia line.

The receptionist pushed black hair from her eyes, smiling slightly. "No, but it is a strong line of storms that are due to cause a lot of damage." Her drawl matched Aiden's, all her words drawn out. He didn't miss the way she fluttered her lashes at him. "But maybe it won't be so bad. I always hate sleeping alone during storms like this."

Theo snorted beside him and moved up so that one whole side of her body pressed against his. When she spoke, she was polite.

"Hopefully, we can monitor it. I'd hate to think Max knew about this the entire time."

Which Aiden was almost certain Max *did*. He seemed like the type who wouldn't move his plans for anyone, not even nature.

Theo smiled and continued, ignoring Aiden's presence altogether. Like old times already.

"We are so exhausted and hungry, so if you could direct us to our room and deliver a room service menu, that would be the best thing in the world."

Nodding, the receptionist got their room settled. The walk was silent, like passing through a crypt, which in a way they were. They took the elevator down into the basement of the building to B4. The lights flickered as soon as they stepped out into the purple-carpeted hallway.

"That can't be good," Aiden said as he moved slowly down the pathway, looking for their room, 422.

"Definitely not," Theo murmured in agreement.

Still riding the rush from earlier, Aiden hadn't really thought about the implications or anything regarding sharing a room with Theo. It would be like the cabin all over again...except no Bridget and Dylan to run interference.

A purple-and-black damask placard on a wooden door noted room 422, and Aiden scanned the keycard, letting Theo in first. He caught a hint of her flowery perfume, nearly feeling sunlight on his skin from the scent alone. Ironic that a vampire's scent could make him think of sunshine.

She flipped on the lights, illuminating the surprisingly spacious room with what appeared to be an equally decent-sized bathroom with the most enormous shower he'd ever seen.

A bed sat off to one side, and on the other was a large, sleek black coffin raised off the floor and opened to reveal rich maroon lining matching the dark, macabre theme of the room.

"A deluxe coffin. It's one that's built for two and was specially manufactured with human paramours in mind, given the air vents and all," Theo piped up, noting where his attention had gone.

He walked over to where she stood next to it and messed with the air vents, opening and shutting them from the inside. "Human paramours, you say?"

Scoffing, she headed over to where she'd dropped her backpack. Even though she'd broken the silence, the tension between them still stretched taut.

Unable to help himself, Aiden spoke up as he went through his pack, looking for what he needed to take a shower. "This is probably one of those scenarios where we're destined to be together."

Theo straightened, holding a change of clothes to her chest, her nose scrunching in a way that shouldn't have been attractive but unfortunately was. "Really? A really bad storm, or well, set of storms is about to be raging, so I'd say that's a bad omen."

"Have you never watched a 90s or 2000s teen drama show? A storm, such as the one we're experiencing now"—and as if on cue, the lights flickered again, thunder rolling above them—"typically brings two unlikely souls together." He moved closer to where Theo stood frozen, her gaze following him warily. What was he doing? He didn't even know and was acting on pure adrenaline at this point. "We'll probably have to hold each other at some point because—"

"I'm not scared of storms, Aiden. I'm a vampire. I'm not scared of anything."

Aiden laughed and arched a brow, loving the vehement look on her face. "I'm not talking about you, Theodora. I'm talking about myself." He pressed a hand to his chest while managing to look offended. "I'm terrified of storms, especially if I'm stuck in one with a beautiful woman." She rolled her eyes, but he continued because he could see a crack of a smile begging to come through. She liked him at least a little bit despite the act she put on. "So you'll have to hold me when it gets really scary. What a nightmare." He punctuated it with a wink.

Theo snorted. "You're ridiculous. We almost get eliminated, and you're trying to put the moves on me. Just because we're sharing a room doesn't mean—"

"I never said anything about expectations, Theo. Shows where your mind's at."

She narrowed her stare. "I'm taking a shower before the storm gets worse. If the room service menu shows up while I'm in there, I'd love blood—straight from the vein. *Anyone* will do." Her smile was a little sadistic and showed fang, the impact hitting Aiden in the chest. No one had affected him like this since Cassidy, and here Theo pretty much did with zero effort.

Aiden reached out and lightly grabbed her wrist as she walked by.

She came to a stop, arching a brow at him. "Yes?"

Taking a step closer, Aiden finally told her the truth, his voice barely recognizable—gravelly and filled with wanting. "I don't want to switch partners, Theo."

Her breath hitched, his stare dropping to her chest with the movement, finding her nipples hard through her wet shirt. He swallowed and somehow managed to drag his gaze up to meet hers again. Something shifted in her eyes—*lust*.

In barely a whisper, she spoke. "I'll kill you on that final challenge, Aiden, if I have to. I don't want to, but I will."

His lips kicked up at the corner. "Okay. I can live with that as long as it means you want to be my partner and not switch."

Thunder rocked the basement.

Something softened in Theo's expression as she bit her lip. "I don't want to switch." There was a pause before she looked at him again, desire swimming in her blue flame eyes. "I want you."

13

THEO

Theo cleared her throat, hoping maybe it would dispel some of the intense sexual tension floating between her and her gorgeous partner.

"I meant as a teammate, of course," she added, even though she knew he knew she wanted him. Say that five times fast.

But sex and romance should be the last thing on both of their minds. They'd nearly gotten eliminated, had the offer to switch teams, *and* there was a series of rough storms moving through because of course there was.

"Of course," Aiden finally spoke, breaking through her thoughts, letting go of her wrist.

A spark flared in her belly as she realized she missed his touch more than she should. God, what was happening to her?

"So we're a team from this point forward, yeah?" Aiden dipped his chin. "We make decisions together, and we do what we do and don't stress the rest? If Brandt wants to come after us, I have no doubt we can be ready. Cool?"

Theo released a breath. "Yes, cool, definitely." Damn, she was anything but.

"So..." Uncertainty flashed across Aiden's expression. He

took a step back and shoved his hands in his pockets. The moment hung between them, brimming with possibilities, and then a loud crack of lightning shuddered, and the lights went out.

And this time, they didn't come on again.

Both of their phones beeped, illuminating the room and their faces. Theo put down all her toiletries and clothing in the open casket and then read the text aloud.

"We apologize, but the storms are much worse than expected. You are safe within the walls of the Foxglove Hotel since you're below ground. We'll be communicating with you via text until the next leg of the race for safety reasons. Your crew is now being moved to rooms next to yours and will reunite with you tomorrow night. Keep your phone with you at all times. Also, please be on the alert. We have lost contact with Aria and Elsie. Let us know if you see them."

Theo's head snapped up as her gaze collided with Aiden's. "Brandt," they both said at the same time.

She was never one to tattle or be a rat or whatever newfangled name it got called. Were the kids calling them snitches these days? But seriously, in this case, it needed to happen. One too many instances had been allowed to slide.

After punching in Max's cell number, she moved the call to speakerphone just as he picked up on the first ring.

"Hello?" His Australian accent filtered through the phone.

There was a lot to say, so she steeled herself and let it fly. "So I guess the rumors on *Forever After* were true, huh? That you don't care about your contestants, especially, oh, I don't know, if they start dropping off one by one?"

Being a vampire, her night vision was fantastic, and she caught Aiden giving her an impressed look, lips twisted, brow lifted. It shouldn't have made something expand in her chest or send goose bumps dancing along her arms, but it did.

Max chuckled, and it wasn't husky or sweet like Aiden's. It was...

devoid of emotion, actually. Disturbingly so. Sociopathically so, which actually would explain *a lot.*

"Theodora. I've been expecting your call for quite some time now. Shocked it took you as long as it did. I always heard you were a stickler for rules." He clucked his tongue to punctuate his statement, and it rankled Theo to no end.

A stickler for rules? *Her?* Um, she was set to be hanged in 1692 because she didn't fall in line and do what was expected of her. She had a feeling Max knew that, too. He seemed the type to do his homework.

"You know that those contestants aren't missing. We literally just saw them—"

"Hmmm...maybe that puts you on the suspect list? It's interesting that you saw them and—"

Theo gestured with her hand, every part of her body wanting to scream with irritation. "Well, then I guess you'll have to add Daniel and our crew to the list as well since they were there too." She gritted her teeth and gathered herself enough to speak again. "I see I shouldn't have called. You don't care about anyone but yourself. I should just quit."

Those four words came out unexpectedly, and once out there in the universe, she couldn't get them back. They were there permanently. Her eyes widened as Aiden sucked in a breath from where he now lay on his bed.

Max, ever the one for theatrics, allowed silence to fill the line for what felt like forever. Theo refused to speak, refused to show that she'd just messed up and knew it.

"Well..." he drawled. "You could do that, I suppose. But how would you get the Solis Occasum, Theodora?" She'd always loved her name, especially her nickname, one that her husband had always called her in such a melodic lilt, but now? She loathed it, hated the way that dick of a director said it. "And we all know you really want the chalice because more than anything, you want to be human again. And tell me this, how many enemies have you procured over your time as a vampire? One? One hundred? *More?* I'd be cautious what you say next because you don't want to make an enemy out of me...especially if that human you're paired with doesn't beat you in the final trial...remember how weak you'll be."

A growl built in her throat, begging to be released, but somehow, she managed to tamp it down. "Maybe you've got this all wrong. Maybe *you* should be the one to be scared of me—human or not."

And with that, she hung up.

Aiden sat up on the bed, eyes squinting into the darkness. Sure, they could use the flashlights on the cell phones, but they didn't dare risk killing the batteries—knowing Max, he'd withhold chargers next. Then there was the fact that she could see perfectly fine.

"Damn, Theo. That was..." He shook his head, a little crooked smile curling his lips. "That was incredible. Badass. Hot."

If she weren't a vampire, she would've blushed at his words. Knowing he couldn't see her in the darkness, she allowed herself to smile back before rummaging through one of the drawers in the nightstand, pulling out matches and a few candles, lighting them one by one.

Once finished, she sat next to him on the bed. God, he smelled so good, and she hated that she was aware of these little things.

Their hands were so close on the mattress, their pinkies almost touching as she turned to face him, finding his face gilded in the candlelight. "We're going to have to go rogue and not follow Max's rules, before we even find the chalice, Aiden."

"And I'm prepared."

"I know you are. We're alike, you and me. We're willing to do what it takes to get what we want."

His gaze drew further inward as his lips pressed together in a firm line. "Right. Which has me thinking, *wondering*...what's your story, Theo? What happened with your husband and... I'm not the brightest guy, but I'm no slouch. I think I put two and two together and was able to gather that you're from Salem. Am I right?"

She looked up at the ceiling, weighing each of her following words. This was something she guarded carefully, but apparently, most of the world knew anyway. Still, it was sacred to her, a sacred action to share this part of herself, and while she liked Aiden, she also knew the end game. A small voice in the back of her mind tempted her, asking her to maybe stop thinking so much, to just let go for once.

What would that even be like?

She would give anything to feel that fire she once knew. That's exactly why she wanted to become human again, and now...

Looking down at the black bedspread again, seeing Aiden's fingers spread out there, gave her a sort of thrill. If she were to inch hers over the slightest bit, they'd touch. And then what?

Stop thinking.

Stop thinking.

And just do.

So she did.

Her pinky touched his, and that electricity, the spark she'd come to recognize as something so very Aiden, shot through her body like lightning in her veins.

Her mate. Something she still couldn't get over.

Aiden turned, his pupils wide, his mouth slightly agape. He felt it too.

"Sometimes I want to turn it all off, Aiden," she whispered into the half darkness that shrouded them, the storm raging on outside and within these four walls.

He locked his fingers with hers. When he spoke, his voice was husky, a low timbre wrapped in honey and velvet. "Let me help you with that, Theodora. *Please.*" She swore his voice broke on that last word, that plea.

Her heart grew hummingbird wings and fluttered in her rib cage, tickling her chest. Pressing her other hand there, she couldn't believe how long she'd gone without feeling anything like this. Guilt and regret? Oh yeah, she had both of those in spades—she lived, ate, and breathed them on the daily, but happiness, albeit brief little flickers, found within these strangely intimate moments? They were more than she ever expected, ever even knew she wanted.

"Yes." That one word jumped from her lips without a parachute, free-falling into the world between them.

Aiden shifted slightly, both of his hands coming up to the sides of her face, cradling it as if she were something precious. If she had ovaries still, they would've flipped out at that move, at the surprising gentleness in his touch. And he was so *warm*—not only his skin but every single thing about him.

His forehead rested against hers, his breath tickling her mouth, her stomach tumbling with the knowledge that his lips, those lips that she'd admired for a few days now, were *so close*. Just like with his hands, all she had to do was move the slightest bit, and she'd know what they felt like.

"You're still thinking, Theo," Aiden whispered, a smile in his voice. His eyes were closed, and Theo decided maybe she should close hers too instead of being a creepy-crawly stalker and staring at him.

She brought her fingertips to her lips, unable to believe the happiness she found there. She was smiling and not one of her guarded ones either—the kind that hurt one's cheeks and that caused the eyes to crinkle. "I guess you'll have to fix that, won't you?"

"Gladly," was Aiden's final reply before the time for talking had gone. He moved slowly, brushing his mouth once, twice across hers, testing, teasing. And then finally—*FINALLY!*—he pressed his lips against hers in a measured, sweet kiss. It was the perfect dance as they took their time learning each other.

He tightened his hands in her hair, sweeping his thumb delicately against her face, and Theo was...*gone*, momentarily gone as she drank his kisses as if they were an elixir to all the world's problems, including her own, as if it was the last first kiss she'd ever experience.

So many feelings roared through her, things she hadn't felt in hundreds of years. Starbursts and spring days and the sun on her face, the ocean roaring at her back—all while sitting in a candlelit room, with Aiden leaning into her body, his hands on her skin, hers draping across his strong shoulders, clasping at his neck like her favorite shawl.

The pressure of his lips increased, his tongue slipping into her mouth, making heat pool in her stomach, *everywhere*. Lava ran through her veins, replacing the ice that usually dwelled there.

After what felt like too brief a time, Aiden pulled back, resting his forehead on hers again, his breathing heavy. The moment, while hot and everything in her buzzed with alarming clarity, it was also incredibly tender.

Tender. Sweet. Those were the things that described Aiden. She'd known that deep down from almost the moment they met. This was what he'd be like if they had sex. And that would most certainly undo Theodora Nash, something she couldn't allow.

Tears welled up in her eyes, clouding her vision a little and making her thankful the candles didn't shed light on her completely. Things between them would not end this way—a happily ever after. They wouldn't end in bloodshed either. She knew now that she couldn't kill him, and instead...she'd have to figure out a way to win on her own once they got closer. Yeah, it was against the rules but sometimes, and well, *a lot of times*, rules were made to be broken.

She understood that the reason she didn't want to make him— or anyone—into a vampire was selfish. It was too much for her to carry around, to add to her guilt because what if that person changed their mind? What if they hated being a vampire? She couldn't be responsible for such a life-altering choice in someone else's life.

"Aiden," she whispered, shattering the silence.

"I know," he inhaled sharply.

With one more kiss pressed to her lips in an almost dreamlike state, he slipped away, but not before dropping one to her forehead as well. The touch, the connection, centered Theo in a way she hadn't felt in years. *Centuries.* Jonathan used to kiss her on the forehead. The image of him, his kind eyes and lovely smile after he'd do that, was enough to break her, to make her scramble to her feet.

Clearing her throat, she ran a hand over her black-and-silver ombre hair. Her hands shook when they made their second pass, and she *knew*, she knew beyond a shadow of a doubt, that she'd regret pulling away from Aiden nearly more than she'd regret anything...aside from her final months as a human. She didn't want to like him—she'd fought the attraction, and then with the added knowledge that he was her mate, well, that made her thrash even harder.

But now? With the memory of his lips on hers, his ocean scent lingering on her skin, his fingers wrapped in her hair, in her mind, in her heart? In her veins?

The game had just changed.

The question was, what was she going to do about it?

14

AIDEN

Not long after their kiss, Theo complained of chest pain—something that happened to let her know it was time to get to her coffin regardless if she was in a safe place or not—and then crawled inside the maroon-lined space.

The storm raged on outside, Aiden unable to search for any sort of information on it since the phones only allowed texts and calls to and from approved numbers—i.e., Max or Daniel—during all hours and then web search during task hours. Seeing Theo snap at Max and put him in his place made him like Theo even more. Something about her fiery side called to him.

He rolled over on the bed, unable to sleep, his mind racing as fast as his heart. Kissing Theo had been a revelation, a moment filled with quiet desperation and...unfortunately for him, a most likely unrequited yearning for the woman in the casket. He wanted to get to know her more, to understand her past—he'd only been able to piece together so much. 1692, Salem. Salem Witch Trials? Maybe? Her husband was killed, and there was talk of a best friend. What happened back then?

His blood began to boil at the thought of anyone hurting her or someone she loved—she bore deep scars from whatever happened that day, and he had a strange desire to...fix it? To help her heal?

Scrubbing a hand down his face, he blew out a ragged breath. He liked Theo. He liked the woman he was supposed to kill, and he'd kissed her. Kissed her with all the tenderness he could muster because something spoke to him in his soul and told him that was the balm she needed at that moment. What about another time, or place? Would she want him to be rougher with her?

Ah, hell.

Somehow, he managed to drift to sleep with dreams of blood and stakes and empty coffins terrorizing every second.

The next night, Aiden woke a little earlier than Theo, turning on lights as a text from Daniel came through. Dread filled his mind, coating his thoughts, and the last thing he wanted to do was open it, especially since Theo hadn't awoken yet. They never did get a room service menu or eat, so he knew she had to be starving. He definitely was. Since the power had come back on, he figured the storm couldn't have been too bad.

Daniel: *Due to the storm, we must delay filming for another day. We're still searching for Aria and Elsie. If you see them, alert us immediately. Also, we urge you to stay inside as a safety precaution. Room service menus have been placed beneath each door.*

Being stranded in Charleston with Theo wasn't the worst thing, especially after last night...and finally getting food sounded like heaven right about now.

A squeaking drew his attention over to the casket. Theo stretched catlike before tilting her head to take him in.

"Morning, sunshine." He grinned, unable to help himself.

"Ack. We're stuck here another night. Did you read the text? It woke me up, and I was having a good dream too..." She stopped suddenly, her eyes going large, mouth forming a little O, which only intensified when she scanned him from head to toe.

He hadn't thought it'd be a big deal to sleep in only his

underwear, mainly because he figured he'd get dressed before Theo even woke up...but the text had thrown him. She looked so adorably sleepy that his mind stuttered and stammered.

But *her* being flustered? Now that was interesting. Aiden leisurely sat up on the edge of the bed, trying to flex everything as he did so, partially to keep that expression on her face and partially because he worked hard for his body. Although it had never been about appearances, but rather his revenge plan.

He ran a hand over his chest, slowly down his stomach, finding more courage with each passing moment that Theo looked her fill, her pupils blown wide with desire.

"It's okay to stare, Theo. As a matter of fact, I welcome, encourage, and wholeheartedly endorse it."

She snapped her gaze to his, closing her mouth with a click of teeth. After clearing her throat, she shrugged nonchalantly. "I can't help it if I like pretty things."

The words shouldn't have flown inside his chest and burrowed there, but they did because the enigmatic Theo said them.

"That sounded oddly like a compliment. You do realize that, right?"

"Don't get too used to those," she deadpanned.

Aiden stood, stretching his arms overhead, aware of how every plane of his body was highlighted. Theo swallowed audibly, the sound spurring him forward.

"Oh, is that so?" One corner of his mouth kicked up, and he scrubbed a hand through his hair as he took a step closer to where she sat in the coffin. "Well, if you're going to give me a rare compliment, then I'd like to do the same for you."

Blinking several times, Theo finally managed a barely there reply. "All right then. Be my guest."

Aiden stopped right in front of her, gripping the edge of the casket, his fingertips brushing her cool skin, her legs exposed from her sexy sleep shorts.

"I think you're stunning, Theo, but I'm pretty sure you already know that, don't you? You're aware of the way I look at you."

Her brows furrowed, not moving from where his fingers rested ever so lightly against her skin, his touch featherlight as he stroked back and forth. She leaned forward just enough so he could see the gray specks in her blue eyes. Her breathing came heavy, making him glad she couldn't see the hard-on he was starting to rock. The things this woman did to him, and none of it made sense. She should be his enemy because she stood in the way of everything he'd wanted, no, *needed* these past three years.

Her tinkling voice broke him from his thoughts. "And what way is that exactly?"

"The same way I've caught you looking at me. There's desire there." He paused, shifting. "When I first saw you, I thought to myself, she's too beautiful. I almost hoped we wouldn't get paired up because I knew you'd distract me and I...I haven't been distracted in quite some time."

"Me neither, if I'm being honest."

Her raw vulnerability shredded the last of his resolve. "Well... we have to stay inside tonight. And remember what I said about storms? We didn't really get close enough last night, and maybe..." He smirked. "I'm scared now."

A laugh burst from her pink lips, and then she shook her head, her hair messy and making him think of other ways to get it disheveled. Damn. He needed to get himself under control, and he couldn't tell where the adrenaline began and where reality ended because...because things were escalating. He had no interest in putting on any sort of brakes. Who knew what awaited them next? Maybe it was finally time to live life to its fullest.

"Oh my God, please. You are *not* scared, Aiden. You're..." Her gaze dipped to where he was hidden, where she would've gotten an eyeful had the coffin not blocked her view.

She shook her head again, biting back a smile. "You're

something else. So what's your plan here? Are you using me to pass your time?"

He scooped up one of her hands and brought it to his lips, kissing it softly. "Definitely not." He traced his fingertips gently over the area he'd just kissed, his heart rattling with each movement. "All I know is that I feel drawn to you. And that kiss last night...it was a pretty incredible first kiss, wouldn't you say? I thought maybe you might like a repeat or an encore performance? Something along those lines?"

"You are such a sweet talker. What did your fiancée think of that?"

Aiden flinched but quickly recovered. Theo brought her hands to her face, covering it while releasing a pretty epic groan along with a, "Shiiiiiiiiiit."

Prying her hands from her face, Aiden tried to smile at her. "It's okay."

"It's not. I didn't mean to be insensitive. I just...I guess I wanted to know more about you and about Cassidy. I would've reacted the same if you were to bring up..." She drew in a deep breath and exhaled. "Jonathan."

"I wonder if it's time we did? Maybe we could help each other in more ways than one."

"Does one of those ways include the heat you're packing in those boxers?" She wiggled her brows.

Aiden laughed, loving the sparkle in Theo's eyes and liking the fact she diffused the situation effortlessly. He looked down and then back up at her, smiling.

"How could you even see it since I'm standing behind the coffin?"

"X-ray vision is a vampire specialty."

"Is it really?"

"No, I'm messing with you, although it would be pretty handy, huh?" She lifted a shoulder. "I just wanted to make you smile because it got serious there, but...I think that's okay. I think it'd be good for us to talk about them. Breakfast date?"

Aiden tried to ignore the heady feeling enveloping him at those words, at just being in her presence, but it was impossible. "A breakfast date sounds perfect." He took a step back and placed his hands on his hips, giving her the opportunity to check him out. "Shall I remain in my boxers for your pleasure and perusal?"

She nibbled her lip, a move that sent a zing straight to his stomach and lower.

After stepping out of her coffin, it was her turn to smirk at him. "Why not?"

His breath hitched, his voice halting, practically disbelieving. "And you'll stay in that?" He pointed to her hot little shorts and T-shirt thing she had going on.

"Yeah. Yeah, I will because I think this is gonna be a good night for the both of us, don't you agree?"

Unable to help himself, he grinned at her. "I do."

They ordered room service, which arrived speedily. With barely a word, they devoured their breakfast. Although Theo wasn't too pleased with the literal blood bag. Aiden offered for her to drink from his neck again, and while her fangs protruded over her lips at the idea like her own hard-on, she refused.

To be honest with himself, Aiden kind of wanted her to bite him. Last time he'd been scared to death and his mind had been a little fuzzy, too, thanks to her putting him in a trance. Now he wanted to be fully awake and aware for all of it. The realization shocked him, but didn't lessen the desire.

Once their meal was finished, they both lay on the bed, side by side, arms over their stomachs as they stared at the ceiling. The flickering of the fake candlelight sconces cast light across them.

"All right, Theodora Nash, tell me why you froze when Daniel mentioned Salem." He shifted. "I already know a little about your life, but if you're comfortable, I'd like to know more."

Theo turned her head slightly on the pillow, granting him a small smile before she deflated back into the bed, her gaze on the ceiling again. She looked as though she'd been borne of flame and trials, the way her eyes resembled the bluest part of the hottest fire, the candlelight cutting shapes into her beautiful face. But it wasn't just her looks that had Aiden tripping over himself as of late. Actually, he'd gotten to know her slightly more, and that had him even more intrigued, had him feeling like teenage Aiden about to knock on the door of his crush to take her to the Homecoming dance, or when he knelt and proposed to Cassidy.

Cassidy.

Her brown eyes flashed in his mind, her bright smile, and then with a blink, the memories were gone, burrowed deep into a safe place in his soul where he could keep and cherish them. Not once in three years had he thought about moving on, even when his sister, Aurora, all but begged him to, or when his parents said they'd set him up with the daughter of one of their friends. He'd figured he'd had Cassidy, and she'd been the one great love of his life, and that...that would be enough.

And then Theo had come along and shot all that to pieces.

Cassidy would want him to move on, but he was in the strangest situation with this woman next to him. They'd already marked each other as good as dead at the end of this, and then there was a psychotic vampire plotting their demise, and another running the show they were on.

"1692...let's see." She blew out a breath. "I was thirty-two years old, and...I was Theodora Herrick." A smile lifted her words as she began to tap her fingers on her stomach in a slow drumbeat. "Married to Jonathan Herrick. Our marriage was arranged by our fathers because we were both from wealthy merchant families, and why not increase wealth through marriage, right?" She let loose a self-deprecating scoff at that.

"Jonathan and Theodora Herrick. It has a good ring to it. Did he call you Theo?"

She nodded, finally turning to make eye contact with him. Sadness painted broad strokes across her features, her eyes no longer flames but ice, her grin a watered-down version of what he'd come to know.

"He did. He started it to tease me because he liked how I blushed when he said it, but after a while, it just stuck because I loved it."

Aiden smiled. "It fits. *Theo.*" So many questions burned into his mind, and he fought against the tide of greed and instead decided to narrow it to one for now. "Did you have any children?"

"No. We didn't want children, which was...not viewed well during that time, as you could imagine. Back then, the Puritan way was rigid, and I was expected to basically have more than two babies and only be around my female friends when chaperoned by a male, and then the whole healer bit didn't help..."

"Healer?"

Theo shifted away, her gaze upward again. "I've said too much. It's just...everything that happened the night they were taken was a nightmare that I relive every single day of this long, monotonous, immortal life." She blew out a breath. "And I miss Jonathan so much and wish I could go back in time and do things differently. That he wouldn't have died because of me." A tear tracked down her face, and Aiden wiped it away with a fingertip. Theo leaned into his touch, that ever-present jolt rushing through him at the contact.

"I can't speak to the immortality aspect, but I understand the guilt that can weigh you down so heavily. Why do you think I want this?"

Her mouth pulled into a frown. "You don't want it, not truly. I'm not even saying that to get you to drop out of the race or to give me what I want." She flicked her gaze to his. "But I believe only certain people enjoy being vampires. And I'm just not one of those people, not with my history and how I became one, and what I did immediately afterward. Honestly? I think your guilt would only grow if you were to change."

Aiden stiffened at that. He'd had one goal for so long...and for someone to speak against it, well, it didn't sit right. Dropping his hand from her face, he rolled back to his side of the bed but didn't move his gaze from hers.

All sorts of arguments crowded along his tongue, but instead he decided to ask her something. Something he'd been wanting to know for a while now.

"What did you do immediately after you were turned?"

She winced. "I...I exacted the revenge you so badly want to."

"Did it help?"

Her chest rose with the breath she pulled in, one that seemed to give her strength. "It did."

"There you go. That's what I want, Theo. I'm not trying to be a dick here, but if I need that revenge to douse this pain, this hurt in my chest"—he thumped it slightly, his voice getting choked up with emotion—"then that's what has to happen. I need to become a vampire, and I *will* do it, and I won't allow anyone to stand in my way. Not even you. *Especially* not you."

Theo sat up, but he remained still, unmoving, irritation snaking through his veins, wrapping around his heart, further encasing it in the bitterness and anger he lived with from day to day. Muscles in his jaw feathered and ached from how hard he clenched it.

Slipping her hand into his, Theo cast him a meaningful look, one that swirled with so many emotions, but he refused to dissect which ones. Doing so could be his downfall. "This is not who you are, Aiden Archer. You and I are alike in a lot of ways, and sucking —sorry, no pun intended—as a vampire is one of those ways."

He left his hand in hers, hating how it weakened his frustration, how these little things about her rammed and battered the walls around his heart that he once thought were impenetrable. "Why do you care so much? Is it just because you want the Solis Occasum? Is it some kind of twisted mind trick?"

He moved to get up, uncertain as to where he could actually go, but instead, Theo straddled him, pushing him back into the mattress. His eyes went wide with surprise.

So that took a turn I did not see coming.

Not one bit.

And he found he could not move, even if he wanted to.

Theodora Nash had him fully entrapped in her web, and as much as he loathed to admit it, he liked it.

15

THEO

"You're so freaking stubborn, Aiden. You forget that I'm trying to help you and make sure you don't make the same mistakes I did because you can't change it; you can't fix it once it's done." She lifted a shoulder, arching a brow. "You want to be a vampire? Fine. But then what? You do everything you set out to do, and you're stuck as a creature of the night *forever*. There's no return. Trust me, I've looked and searched my entire life, and this is the first opportunity I've found."

Theo's chest heaved with emotion, everything hot all of a sudden, a feeling as foreign as sunlight on her skin, something only Aiden seemed to bring out in her. On top of that, she fought back anger at seeing the large scar on his shoulder—she wanted nothing more than to kill the vampire who put it there, the intensity enough to cause her breath to hitch.

Aiden studied her, shock still written in his expression. And well, she was shocked too as she sat straddled on him, her hands locked around his arms, leaning over him as he lay on the bed. Her shorts barely had enough material to actually be called shorts. Because of that, they'd slid up, allowing the soft, dark hair of his legs to brush her inner thighs.

His boxers had ridden up, exposing a tempting tan line, and she felt what waited just beneath her, his length that continued to grow even in their little squabble. The friction was almost too much to bear, and she knew if she moved just so, he'd hit exactly where she needed it, that he'd feel how affected she was by him and his little show tonight, walking around the room in just his gray boxers that clung to him like a second skin.

What on earth had she been thinking?

She *hadn't*. That was the problem when it came to this man. Her *mate*.

The air became thick, almost humid with tension as they engaged in a battle of wills, a stare down, neither budging from their positions. Theo strengthened her grip around Aiden's arm as she fought to catch her breath and not pant.

Finally, Aiden dragged in an inhale, the movement causing Theo's gaze to drop—his shirtless chest on display with a smattering of dark chest hair leading down to where she sat. She met his eyes once more, not really sure what to say or do but knowing she had too much pride to back down. Andreas had always told her this, and she never listened. Maybe he was right after all.

"Damn you, Theo," Aiden finally spoke, his voice thick and gruff. Hunger painted his eyes in a deep black. Every single part of him pulled taut with a lust that burned in Theo too. A lust that had been pent up for entirely too long.

And then he pulled her down so that their mouths were nearly pressed together. She trailed her fingertip down the strong column of his neck, his pulse thundering beneath her touch. If only he knew that she was already slick with need and desperate for him to take care of it, to take care of her.

"Damn you for making me want you, for making me question everything," he spoke against her lips, their noses brushing.

This must be what drowning felt like. With a stuttered breath, she reached her arms around to cradle the back of his head. His silky hair tickled her fingertips. She held him in place with her grip, giving him consent to do whatever he wanted.

"Damn you," he whispered once more before kissing her.

This kiss was not like the one from last night. This was a claiming, a devouring, and she loved it. She wanted to bury herself in it forever. Wild and feral, it was everything she never knew she needed.

Aiden's hands dug into her hips, having slipped beneath her cropped shirt, the warmth enough to burn her cold skin, causing her to gasp into his mouth, which he greedily gathered up. Then he had her flipped over onto her back as he continued to work her mouth like he would no doubt work another part of her body. The thought had her moaning and grinding against his impressive erection, completely lost to the moment.

To her relief, Aiden thrust his hips against her, allowing her to wrap her legs around his waist. His muscles flexed as he moved and drifted to her neck, kissing and licking, before playfully biting.

When he pulled back, his eyes were glazed over. "You tell me how far you want to go. It's always, *always* your call."

She shook her head, shooting him a smile, with her fangs poking over her lips. Sometimes they did that when she got exceptionally turned on. No one but her own hand and her handy-dandy vibrator had done that in entirely too long.

To her surprise, Aiden didn't shy away from her fangs. Instead, he leaned down and kissed her mouth fervently, his tongue dancing with hers before pulling away, tugging at her lower lip.

"I want," she panted as he fingered the neckline of her shirt. "I want you," she admitted finally, shifting so he could raise her shirt up and over her head.

"Of course every inch of you is beautiful," he all but growled as he took her in, and then he palmed her breasts, bringing one to his mouth so he could flick and tease her hardened nipple.

"I like it a little rougher than that," Theo said as she arched into his body, enjoying the feel of him, his mouth on her skin.

"I'll do my best," Aiden said with a smirk before he moved to the other nipple. He bit it slightly harder than the other, eliciting a cry from her. He soothed the tiny hurt with his tongue and she was utterly in heaven. He could read her like a book, knew exactly how to follow her demands.

He gathered her hands above her head before licking down her chest, between the valley of her breasts, a fire scorching in the wake of his tongue. He only let go when he reached the hem of her sleep shorts. He nipped at them before snapping them down her body, leaving her only in her underwear...which weren't sexy at all. It was the pair she wore on laundry day, but with the way he bit his lip, Theo would have thought she was wearing something else, like a sexy little black thong.

With a groan, he slipped his fingers beneath the top of her underwear before taking his time sliding the fabric down her body, one slow torturous inch at a time—which was more erotic than she'd ever anticipated.

Once he finished, his hands were on her thighs, a wicked smile on his lips. "I think it's time you were treated like the queen you are."

Anticipation lit her from the inside out, her hands on the bulge in his boxers. Her grin was positively feline. She'd never felt so powerful, so sexy.

"Is that so?"

He nodded once, not taking his gaze from hers before thrusting into her palm, once, twice, his jaw working in the sexiest movement she'd ever witnessed. What would he look like when he came? More than anything, she wanted to find out.

When she was about to demand he strip so she could feel *all* of him, he lay down next to her, tugging her body so she was hovering over his head. He further parted her knees with his elbows so they bracketed either side of his face, and holy shit, she was so ridiculously turned on that her eyelids fluttered as she bit her lip. Her nerve endings caught fire. This...this was new territory for her, and she was prepared to chart it out with Aiden more than she wanted her next breath.

"I want you to do what you need to, okay? Just hold on." He paused, gesturing for her to grip the wooden slats of the headboard. "Grind into me, whatever it takes to get you off, okay?"

Her one-word response was shaky, lust making her ache as she felt Aiden's breath on the most sensitive part of her body. "O-o-okay."

Jonathan hadn't even done that, and they had been...extremely compatible in bed. One of Aiden's hands bit into her thigh, while the other hand slid between them. He slipped one finger inside her, making her moan as she held tighter to the bed.

"Fuck, Theo. You're so wet for me," Aiden rasped.

She panted as he began thrusting into her before adding another finger, curling them so they hit her inner walls. His thumb pressed against her clit and her eyes nearly rolled to the back of her head. Feeling sexier than ever, she started riding Aiden's fingers, her body pulsing with need.

Just when she got into a rhythm, his mouth was on her clit, his tongue flat against her. A groan rumbled from his chest. The vibrations sent shockwaves through her body as pleasure coiled tight within her belly.

She didn't think; her body knew exactly what to do. Moans, whimpers fell from her lips as he licked her incessantly while she ground against him, his fingers working her into a frenzy. The headboard of the bed cracked beneath her grip, but she didn't care.

Nothing else mattered but Aiden and getting off.

For a minute, she wanted to take a vacation from being Theodora Nash, controlled and thinking everything through.

Instead, she focused on the way Aiden's mouth felt against her, the heat of his breath as he alternated between long, torturous licks and sucking her clit, the strength of his fingers as he crooked them again, hitting her even deeper, the way she felt like a goddess with her breasts swaying with each frantic grind. She'd never been wetter in her life.

Finally, she threw her head back, everything within her tightening as she found her release, Aiden working her harder, not letting up. She trembled and shook. Her vision went hazy, her head dizzy, and all she could say was Aiden's name, those two syllables tumbling off her lips with so much want because while that was incredible, she wanted *all* he had to give.

He smiled against her still sensitive bundle of nerves before giving her one more flat lick, and then he flipped her onto her stomach. He kicked off his underwear, revealing his hard, beautiful cock, more than ready for her. She had to wipe a little drool from the corner of her mouth at the sight. Even hotter was what he said next.

"Get on your hands and knees for me, gorgeous."

Um, yes, please. Nine of the hottest words a man could utter.

Before moving, she purred, "But don't you want me to return the favor?" Her stare dropped to his length, and she arched a brow.

He licked his lips, sweat dotting his forehead, causing her to squeeze her legs together. "Another time. If you're sure you want to do this, I'd rather come inside you."

"Yes," she hissed. "Do it then. *Please.*"

"Do you want a condom? I don't have any. I haven't really needed them..."

Theo shook her head. Vampires couldn't get pregnant or get diseases. "I'm good, and you're good."

And then she got on her hands and knees, arching her back, shooting him what she hoped was a seductive look over her shoulder. Her pulse still raced erratically from her orgasm. Aiden gripped her waist just as he ran the tip of his cock over her wet heat, teasing her, back and forth until she was a shaky mess.

"Aiden, please," she whimpered, fists tightening into the sheets.

"That's a good girl," he grunted as he positioned himself at her entrance. Her body instinctively moved against him to feel more, still not getting enough.

Suddenly, their phones went off. *Phones plural*, meaning it had to do with the game.

Aiden cursed, his forehead falling against her back.

"Shit," Theo cried, still wet and more turned on than she'd ever been in her life.

They broke apart, each reaching for their devices.

It appears that we can move ahead with filming, so please read this text carefully. Today is a test of will on several accounts. First, we have yet to discover Elsie and Aria and have alerted the authorities so that they may step in. If you suspect foul play, please alert the director. Theo all but rolled her eyes at that, but kept reading.

*Secondly, now that the airport has opened back up, we've decided to leave and make this next part interesting. You will actually need to travel to Salem **tonight**. No private jet this time. You have to book it on your own. Once you arrive there, meet Daniel as quickly as possible for the next clue. Don't forget to take your crew. Mics will need to be turned on once in the hotel lobby.*

"Freaking cockblockers," Theo snapped as she started gathering her stuff in a furious flurry, changing into clothes and shoving her discarded ones into her backpack.

"Worst possible timing." Aiden's voice was so sex soaked, it nearly made Theo say screw everything else. She just wanted to screw him. Especially when she got another glimpse of his impressive cock, as he searched for his underwear.

But then reality set in as a knock came at the door, no doubt Bridget and Dylan.

Within minutes, she and Aiden were ready and out of the room in a flash, their camera crew leaning against the wall, waiting for them.

"Y'all ready?" Bridget asked as she hefted her camera, and Dylan followed suit.

Theo shrugged before sliding a fiery glance to Aiden, who was already watching her with a new spark in his eyes, one that should've incinerated her clothes right there on the spot. And oh, how she wanted them to. She wanted to finish what they'd just started.

Somehow, she managed to speak without her voice sounding horny or sexually frustrated, her first-release buzz long gone since she was already riled up for round two.

"Ready as we'll ever be, I guess. We need a taxi."

Everyone shoved into the elevator as Brandt's team emerged from their room.

Theo growled and pressed the close button on the elevator a million times, cursing it with everything she had. "C'mon, just shut, you stupid doors!"

Aiden positioned himself in the center of the entrance as if to... what? He was human, and this guy was slaughtering vampires on the reg, so what did he think Brandt would do to him?

He cracked his knuckles as if he could hear her thoughts. "Like hell he's stepping foot on this elevator."

A snarl curled Brandt's lip. A heartbeat later, he transformed into a bat, Paisley on his heels.

Bridget dug in her bag, pulling out a stake, sharpened to a very pointy end. She held it by her side, careful that no one outside the elevator could see it. "Let him try."

Theo arched a brow, surprised at the other vampire since Max had outlawed stakes from the show and even searched for them before filming began. And it wasn't like vampires just carried them around either. She'd have to ask Bridget about that later.

The doors closed, Brandt's bat form slamming into them with a squeak.

A relieved cheer went up inside the tiny space before Dylan gave Bridget an inquisitive look. "You know we're not supposed to have stakes, right? Max said anyone—staff or contestants—found with one is done for."

Bridget lifted one shoulder as she shoved it back into her bag.

"And? I'm not scared of Max. You really think I'm not going to have some sort of protection after what happened on the last show? What if the other vampires aren't as chill as me? Like that guy." She hooked a thumb toward the closed elevator doors. "He'll kill you without hesitating."

"She's not wrong," Theo added. "Aiden, do you want to book our flights since you've done that the majority of the trip?"

Aiden dipped his head once and pulled out his phone, his thumbs going to town on the screen. Within seconds, the amount of time it took for the elevator to take them to the lobby, he had their flights booked and ready. Everyone clicked their mics on.

"Got 'em. Last four tickets," Aiden announced.

They just had to get there before Brandt and Paisley did. Hopefully they weren't on the same flight.

She didn't think he would strike in front of a crowd, but who knew? He was clearly unhinged, and the thing was, she still didn't know his damage. Why did he need the chalice so badly if he was already so powerful? He had to be at least a thousand years old, practically indestructible, so he was definitely not turning into a human. And if he wanted a bunch of vampire baby sires running around, all he had to do was perform the process. And bam! Offspring all over the place.

Theo made a mental note to call and ask Andreas what he might know about the situation since he was the oldest vampire she knew personally. If only she could find a pay phone or something to use since hers would only call out to Max-approved numbers.

She desperately needed to talk to Andreas. He seemed to have an answer for everything.

The only thing was...they were headed to Salem.

A place she'd promised to never set foot in again after losing her husband and best friend.

She sighed, her shoulders lifting almost to her ears with the movement.

Looked like it was time to confront the ghosts that had trailed her for the past three hundred and thirty years.

16

AIDEN

THE RACE TO THE AIRPORT PROVIDED A MUCH-NEEDED DISTRACTION from everything Aiden and Theo just did and everything they hadn't had a chance to finish. He swallowed hard when he thought about Theo's ass in the air, the breathy moans she made, the way her fingers tightened and clawed at his skin, in his hair, on the back of his neck. He loved it way more than he should.

And to say that complicated things, was an understatement. But he struggled to think about anything else at the moment, especially the fact that he wanted all Theo had to give. The thing was, her mind was a vault. It was impossible to know what she was thinking.

Last he checked, even though he'd given her what sounded and felt like one hell of an orgasm, that didn't mean she'd changed her mind on making him bleed on the final leg of this race. And she didn't know he'd decided he could never hurt her.

But he hadn't changed his mind on the part where he'd let her win.

There was no way he could do that, no matter how much he liked her personality, or her taste, or touch, or any of those things.

Thankfully, they were able to get on their VampJet flight without any issues from Brandt and his team—seeing as how they were on two totally different flights. The problem would be beating sunrise once they arrived in Boston and grabbed a rental car.

And then there was the fact that Theo had shared more than she had previously, but there were still so many skeletons in her closet, so to speak.

Once the plane landed, a vampire bat appeared in the aisle, next to Aiden, a small envelope in its grip. Reaching for it, he furrowed his brows, seeing that the word "Urgent" was scrawled on the outside.

Shooting Theo a confused look—glad to see that she at least had stopped shaking as she had the entire flight to Boston—he opened the envelope. Inside was a small card that Aiden read aloud.

"The first team to get the clue will automatically go first in the challenge and earn more time to rest, relax, and prepare beforehand. Better hurry and better plan."

Theo's posture went rigid as she folded her hands into fists once before loosening them. Aiden waited for her to speak, to say something, *anything* but only got a terse nod as she stood from her seat.

"I guess we need to pick up our rental car and get to the hotel," she finally managed, without meeting his stare, as she hefted her bag on her shoulder.

He figured they wouldn't go after the first clue with sunrise coming within the next two hours. Salem was a thirty-minute drive from the airport, and that didn't factor in possibilities for things to go wrong. With Theo, he'd rather not risk it.

Gesturing to the gangplank in front of them, he attempted a smile. "Let's do it."

She still refused to look at him as she shouldered past to head down the gangplank and into the airport proper. He followed her without a word. Her dismissal stung way more than it should.

As she walked, her shoulders drooped, her entire body curling into itself. That caused Aiden to switch gears on how to handle her

sudden change in mood. He gently brushed her wrist, drawing her
to a slow stop. Bridget and Dylan were in filming mode, but it didn't
matter, not with that broken look on Theo's face.

"Hey," he spoke softly, his brow furrowing slightly.

Theo tightened her fingers on the strap of her backpack, her
black nails shining in the fluorescent light, her pallor more
pronounced, along with purplish crescents beneath the icy eyes
that usually held some sort of spark. Right then, they were flat,
dead.

Her lips twisted to the side as her gaze shifted over his shoulder,
moving to the check-in desk, and finally to Bridget and Dylan. She
motioned for everyone to turn off their mics, which they did. He
was surprised Bridget and Dylan didn't argue, but then again this
was Theo. Most people didn't argue with her...most people except
him. Arguing with her had become a sort of foreplay that he'd
better not think about right now.

"We don't have time to talk right now." She glanced at the show-
issued cell phone in her hand. "We need to rest because there's no
telling what Max will pull this round, since I pissed him off by
threatening to expose him"

He weighed his response carefully though there was so much
he wanted to say. Yet, Theo had already began shutting down right
there in front of him. Finally, he nodded. "Right. Well, if you need
me, you'll let me know?"

With a pinched look that included a cute scrunched-up nose
and narrowed eyes, she shrugged. "What would I need you for?"

Ouch. They really were going to just brush off everything that
had happened between them only hours ago. Picking his pride, and
maybe even a tiny shard of his heart, up off the floor, he held up his
hands in surrender.

"Nothing, apparently."

Her jet-black and moonlit-silver hair kissed her cheek as she
tilted her head, but she said nothing before turning on a booted
heel, leading them to the rental car service area. He checked his

phone, thankful they would at least make it to Salem before sunrise. It sucked that they were both needed to show up at the Witch House there to gather their clue. He would've gone while she slept in safety to save time, but it wasn't allowed. Both or none, those were the rules. Now they'd lose hours, and Team Nosferatu Wannabe, and whoever else, would show up.

At least the ride to Salem would be short. Short and filled with all kinds of awkward tension. Aiden jumped at the chance to drive because at least then he'd have something to focus on instead of whatever was going on between him and Theo.

About five minutes into the silence that seemed to stretch a million miles, Dylan leaned forward and asked, "Did something happen between you two? Because I'm sensing a little extra edge to the tension today."

Bridget smacked his shoulder lightly. "Leave them be. They like each other and don't want to admit it. They probably already banged it out and hate that they enjoyed it and want more."

"I don't like him," and "I don't like her," were both said at the exact same time. Aiden looked over at Theo, and he tried so hard not to smile, but then she laughed, and he couldn't help but join in.

"See? What did I tell you?" Bridget piped up from the back seat. Aiden rolled his eyes at her in the rearview mirror.

He looked at the clock on the car dashboard and gritted his teeth, hands tightening on the steering wheel. "Theo, how's your chest?"

Dylan snickered in the back seat, and Theo arched a brow at Aiden, causing him to shake his head and smirk. "Sunrise. Does it burn?"

"Oh. No. I think we're going to be okay."

"Good." He turned his attention to the other vampire on their team. "Bridget? What about you?"

Thankfully, she gave a thumbs-up in response.

The rest of the trip passed by quickly, and as soon as Aiden pulled the car into Salem, he let out the biggest sigh of relief, knowing they'd beat the sunrise for at least an hour. He just didn't expect Theo to throw a wrench in everything.

The illumination from her phone lit her face in blues and whites as she spoke up. "Turn right up here."

Aiden twisted to look at her for a moment before swinging his attention back to the road. "I thought the hotel was farther in."

Steel lined her words. "It is, but we're going to the Witch House to get the clue."

"What? Theo, are you serious? Sunrise is in—"

"I know when the sun rises. So does Bridget. Now, are you going to turn, or are you going to throw away a chance to fully regain first place after that debacle in Charleston?"

He tried not to flinch at her words and bit back any response because Theo was a strong woman and knew what she was doing. If she said she had this, then she did. He trusted her, even if it terrified him. Besides, if Bridget was willing to do this, then surely it had to be safe.

As he made the turn, he caught Theo's leg bouncing out of the corner of his eye. "Are you okay?"

"I will be once we get this clue and can move on." She fidgeted with the hem of her shirt. "I just hope we don't have to go anywhere else that brings back memories."

He wanted to ask if Jonathan was buried here, why and how he died, and what she did that she regretted so deeply. Whatever it was, it painted her expression in fire and embers, erasing the usual guilt and regret she wore. All she'd told him was that those actions were coated in revenge.

Before he had the chance, Theo jerked forward in her seat, pointing ahead to a historic dark-colored home illuminated by streetlights. "There! There it is!"

There wasn't exactly anywhere to park, so Aiden spun the car to the side of the road, and everyone filed out, rushing inside where Daniel waited.

As usual, he was dressed in a suit, not a wrinkle or sign of travel or wear on him. When Aiden first met him, he thought maybe he was a vampire simply because of his impeccable style and demeanor, only to be shocked to learn he was a human.

"Welcome to Salem. You're the first team to arrive."

Theo drew Aiden into an embrace with a squeal. She took him by surprise but he quickly recovered. He tightened his hold on her waist and lifted her off her feet, murmuring into her hair.

"We did it because of you. You're amazing, Theo."

She laughed as he put her down, straightening her shirt all while still smiling at him. Damn, this woman was magnetic.

"First, as you know, your prize is that you get extra time to rest —meaning you don't have to rush to get to where the next challenge takes place. On top of that, I'll give you extra material to help you prepare for that challenge." He smiled as he handed a packet of papers over to Aiden, which appeared to be ghost stories about Salem. Aiden shoved them in his backpack to look at later. "Now, here is your clue for the next challenge." Daniel gestured to a vampire bat arriving on the scene.

Theo grinned as it came to a halt in front of her. "It's got good taste," she joked, taking the envelope from its tiny claw before it disappeared into the bowels of the house.

Of course Aiden wanted to agree that the bat had good taste— anyone who chose Theo did—but instead he bit the inside of his cheek.

His heart raced loud enough that it roared in his ears. He couldn't believe it. They were the first team to arrive. And all thanks to Theo braving the sun.

He wrapped an arm around her as she opened the clue, her hands shaking again, her breathing grew loud and ragged, so much so that he felt her trembling against his body. Knowing she'd hate attention drawn to it, he said nothing and instead held her a little tighter, letting her know he was there.

She leaned into him as she read the card aloud. "We have to give a ghost tour tomorrow night, and the team that does the best—

gets the most votes from the patrons—gets the next clue first for a head start."

Daniel cleared his throat, interrupting them. "Per the show rules, Bridget, you'll come with me."

Bridget's gaze volleyed between them, a crease forming between her brows. "What?"

"Vampire crew are not subject to the same rules as contestants regarding sunrise. Please remain behind. You'll rejoin your team tomorrow." Concern marred the host's expression. "The rest of you, be safe."

And then he walked away with a visibly and audibly irritated Bridget, who appeared to be fighting them tooth and nail about staying behind. Of course Max would protect his crew this time.

When Aiden turned to complain about it to Theo, she looked like she might throw up, Dylan cursing under his breath.

Theo's hand flew to her chest, her eyes wide with a sort of stoic panic—she didn't make a fuss, only seemed resigned.

"I knew what I was risking," she whispered, reading every single emotion that Aiden knew he had flitting across his face.

No, no, no.

Only moments ago, he'd been excited and glad she'd been motivated to do this despite the impending sunrise, and now...

"It's fine. We can get you back to the hotel in time. I'll break every traffic law I have to, okay? We just need to go *now*." He wanted to cause a scene, to demand Daniel take Theo too, but then they'd lose precious minutes to get to safety—besides, he already knew the answer would be no, each contestant had signed the waiver, understood the risk.

Theo nodded, still unable to speak. Without thinking, Aiden threaded his fingers through hers and led her outside to where he parked the car...or where he swore he'd parked the car.

It was gone.

"Is it just me, or did the car disappear?" Dylan turned in circles even as he filmed.

Aiden pressed the key fob frantically while tightening his hold on Theo with his other hand. No sound of a running motor, no alarm, no nothing from the car.

Desperation threatened to sink into the pit of his stomach, but he refused to let it land. This was not how they were going down. They would fight, and he would get Theo to safety if it was the last thing he did.

"Okay, at least we have our bags with us, so that's a start. Now to find somewhere that might have a coffin..." He paused, feeling slightly stupid for having to ask this question, but wanting to be absolutely sure. "And you have to have a coffin for sure, right? I can't find a brick building to hide you?"

"I need a coffin." Her thumb swiped across his wrist. "And we're a team, Aiden. I'm not just going to sit by and burn up to a crisp. The first thing we can try is a funeral parlor, maybe?"

Aiden dipped his chin. "Okay. We can do that and then if that doesn't work, we go to a cemetery."

She cocked a brow at him as if he'd said something outrageous.

"I will dig up a grave and get you in a coffin that way, if I have to. I don't care what it takes."

"Damn, you're sweet." Awe laced her voice as she brought his hand to her mouth, pressing a kiss to the back of it.

Though he was still dizzy from the kiss, he whipped out his phone and searched for the closest funeral parlor. Following the blinking blue dot on his map app, they took off at a full-out run, with Dylan at their side. But when they got there, they discovered the funeral home was locked down like Fort Knox. Aiden had no qualms about breaking and entering if it meant life or death, but there were bars on every window, exit, and entrance.

"There's another one down the street. Let's try it," he said in a huff. "Maybe it doesn't have bars on everything."

She gave a weak thumbs-up, and then they ran faster than he thought possible, and with each heavy footstep thudding on the pavement, the anger in his veins grew until eventually, it was a raging inferno. He knew exactly who to blame for the car—Brandt. Their flight must've left right on their heels, and this was his way of marking them, or at least trying to knock off Theo. But that wouldn't happen, not on Aiden's watch, not when he wanted more moments with that woman.

The next funeral parlor had to be it because the sun would be up any moment. Theo no longer spoke but instead gripped her chest, her face twisted in silent agony, which made Aiden's own chest clench with pain.

Even Dylan stopped filming so he could move faster—no doubt Max would be pissed about that.

Sweetwater Funeral Home stood out like an oasis in the desert, its door old-school and wooden. Aiden didn't hesitate to kick the shit out of it, feeling the first bit of relief flood his body when it partially gave way. But it didn't open enough to let them slide through.

Theo began to groan and cough, and he noticed the sky lightening. "Fuck!" he snarled. He kicked the door again.

Theo started to grow red as if burning, and Aiden ripped through their packs to cover her with a jacket before turning to Dylan. "We kick the door in on the count of three," he directed.

Dylan nodded, camera equipment tossed to the side.

Fear coated his tongue, his thoughts, as Cassidy's face danced across his mind, as a little voice taunted him, wondering if he would let another person die on his watch.

"One, two, three!"

He and Dylan kicked the door at the same time. It didn't give in completely, but it splintered enough he could reach in and unlock it. Shards of wood cut into his arm, but he didn't care.

Just as smoke started to rise from Theo's body, her groans growing louder, he got the door open. Knowing full well she was capable of saving herself by walking in, but wanting desperately to do this for her, he scooped her into his arms. He hated the way she whimpered and shook. His jacket smoked as he ran through the parlor, frantically seeking a casket.

In the back of the building, he found one and gently placed Theo inside. Second-degree burns marred one side of her face. He cursed. "I swear I'll stake Brandt before this over, Theo. I *swear* it."

She shot him a shaky smile before reaching up and only managing to touch his chin. "Thank you," she croaked.

Hand waving weakly, she motioned to the lid. He kissed her cheek next to her burns, knowing they would need tending to when she arose tomorrow night, and then he shut the coffin lid. He collapsed on top of it, angry tears leaking onto its shiny surface.

"She's safe now," Dylan whispered.

Aiden nodded, not ready to move away from the vampire that had inched her way into his heart. All he could think about was what he would do to Brandt the next time he saw him. He would not stand by and let him try to kill Theodora. Over his dead body.

And knowing that asshole was roughly five hundred years old, that would be a very likely possibility. But it was one Aiden was willing to take.

17

THEO

THE NEXT NIGHT, THEO AWOKE TO EXCRUCIATING PAIN. IN THE darkness of the coffin, she stroked the side of her face that had been burned. She knew blood would heal the injury, would give her much-needed energy, but the truth was she dreaded opening the lid of her sleeping quarters because there was going to be hell to pay.

First, she would heal, then they had to go through with the ridiculous ghost tour, and then she would stake Brandt through his heart. If he could get away with taking out the competition, then so would she. Max evidently had given him free rein—and *why* and for *what*?

Her mind flashed to Aiden—sweet Aiden, whose face had contorted in fear and rage when the sun came up. She knew she'd have to contend with him to get first dibs on Brandt. His vow to stake the older vampire the next time he saw him still echoed in her mind.

Her heart, that traitorous little organ, fluttered about in her chest. Then, of course, her thoughts strayed to hotter, sexier things, like Aiden's mouth on her body, his rough grip on her thighs, the way he'd ordered her to get on her hands and knees.

Oh, how she wanted to be alone again...but also not. She had tried to go with the whole "let's forget that happened without having the talk" aspect. But she'd seen the way it hurt Aiden, how he'd winced.

She hated herself for it, which confused her more than it should have.

Then throw in the fact that they were in Salem, and she would have to give a ghost tour of the very streets she and Jonathan had walked down, past the spot where they were married, where he was executed, where she'd... She squeezed her eyes shut.

It was time to do this. Her future depended on it.

Slowly, she lifted the lid to the casket, her gaze landing on a nervous Aiden—he was pacing the floor, hands rubbing through dark stubble on his chin. He froze, his stare searing her to the core, and then he was in front of her in a flash, one of his hands entwined with hers, the other cradling her unharmed cheek.

He all but deflated over the lip of the coffin, his touch causing butterflies to emerge from long-born cocoons. His voice was hoarse when he spoke.

"Thank God. I was getting nervous, but Dylan and Bridget—"

She perked at hearing the other vampire's name, and Aiden nodded. "Yeah, she just got dropped off. They're outside." Aiden hooked a thumb toward the closed door. "They told me to give it time, that you were okay." His expression turned sheepish. "And then we scared the owners to death, who actually turned out to be pretty cool. They've agreed to let us stay here as long as we need."

Bringing her hands to rest on top of his, she leaned into his touch as if that alone would heal her. Terrifyingly enough, it felt like it very well could.

"Thank you for everything last night." She offered him a soft smile as she looked down at their joined hands. "I guess I owe you an apology for scaring you."

A smirk twisted those gorgeous lips of his before he pressed a kiss to her forehead—their unspoken agreement from the night before shot to pieces thanks to a near-death experience. She was okay with it...for now.

"Is Theo Nash apologizing to me? Hell has surely frozen over."

Unable to help herself, she let out a little laugh, surprised at how coarse it sounded, like nails in a blender. She shook her head, still smiling.

"You are such a smartass."

He lifted her hand and pinned it against his chest, a crooked grin tilting his mouth up on one side. "You like it, though."

"I do."

She was too exhausted to lie.

His eyes widened slightly. "I think this is more disturbing than your normal persona, Theodora. You need blood, and you need it quick."

Without hesitation, he pulled his shirt over his head, throwing it on a nearby chair.

"I can't drink from you again," she fought, albeit not as strongly as she probably should.

The fact was her mouth watered with the idea of drinking from her mate again. She'd always heard how different their blood would taste, how it would awaken so many things inside her. And it was all true, no matter how she tried to ignore it or tamp it down.

Aiden brought his hand to the back of her neck, dipping his head down so he could meet her eyes. "Please? And then afterward we can prepare for the challenge. I didn't get the chance to tell you—Daniel gave us ghost stories to better prepare for tonight."

She released a heavy sigh, the pain in her face throbbing along with it. "I do want to win this challenge." Biting her lip, she lifted her stare to his. "Do you want me to...?" She allowed the words to trail off. She couldn't bring herself to say the rest out loud, couldn't outright ask him if he wanted to be put in a trance again due to his history with vampires. The last thing she wanted to do was make this situation traumatic for him.

To her surprise, he shook his head and brought his thumb to her lips, tugging slightly at the bottom one. "Drink, Theo."

Swallowing back any other arguments or misgivings, she nodded, threading her fingers into the hair at the nape of his neck, recalling how lovely it felt, how good *he* felt.

She was determined to make sure this experience was decent for him, because after all, he'd saved her life when he could've just as easily let her die—especially when she was his opponent down the road when they won the chalice, not *if* they won, but *when*.

Her nose brushed against the side of his face, and then she moved to his lips, kissing him ardently, throwing her entire body into it as much as she could. All she wanted to do was pull him over and into the coffin, shut the lid, and have her wicked way with him.

Aiden groaned, the sound sending a bolt of lust straight to her core. An answering whimper escaped her mouth. She was so turned on and tired and hungry and scared that she didn't give a damn.

She playfully bit his lip, which earned a rumbly response that came from the depths of his chest. Then she moved to his ear, biting slightly on the lobe and then alternating before nibbling. She was really reining those fangs in hard as she kissed, licked, and laved. She gently scratched one hand down his chest, sliding down to his scrape along his belt buckle.

Theo was glad the camera crew wasn't in the room with them— this was something she didn't want to share with anyone else. This moment felt more precious, more fragile than expected. She wanted to cradle it in her hands and protect it to the best of her ability.

Pausing the kiss, she drew her fingers beneath his chin. His eyes snapped open, hazed and filled with lust. Wordlessly, she stepped out of the coffin and stood in front of him.

"Theo—" he began, but she pressed a finger to his lips, effectively silencing him.

She kissed him again, pouring all she could into him, allowing her body to grind into his, to feel his length grow between them, letting her take what she needed.

She moved her mouth to his neck once more, and then she bit him. A sigh of ecstasy released from him as his grip grew more possessive. She moaned against his skin, reveling in the taste of salt and Aiden on her tongue, on her lips, in her veins. It was as if a film had been pulled away from her eyes, making everything brighter, sharper, the clarity almost startling.

A familiar refrain throbbed and thumped in her chest, in her bloodstream. *Mate, mate, mate,* and she smiled this time, allowing it free rein—at least for now. She was hedonistic in that way and was past tired of denying herself pleasures as penance for so long. Fuck that. Speaking of which, she'd like to fuck Aiden.

She would. She was sure of it.

Not today, but *soon.*

Finally, once she felt her skin heal, her cheek mending itself back to brand-new, she licked the wound and then her lips, pulling back to meet Aiden's eyes.

He brought his fingertips to her healed cheek. "I hated that you were hurt," he admitted, his voice soft as if he were worried about shattering the moment like Theo was.

"I hated that you were worried." She maintained his stare, undoing his belt buckle and then his pants.

He covered her hands in protest. "Theo, you need to save your energy—"

Since they were first in getting the clue, they had plenty of time before the ghost tours started. Theo didn't know when they'd have another chance to be alone like this, so now would do. Shaking her head, she allowed a feline smile to curl her lips.

"Aiden, you should know by now that I get what I want, and I *want* to do this—unless you don't want me to. If that's the case, tell me, and I'll step away from you."

She stilled her fingertips at the waist of his jeans, having yet pushed them down.

He swallowed, and she loved the way his Adam's apple bobbed and worked. Seeing him so flustered and turned on got her even hotter.

He finally answered. "I want this, damn, I want it, but I worry—"

"Let me do that. You worry enough for the both of us. Let me take care of you for once, okay?"

Giving her a heartbreakingly tender smile, Aiden nodded. Without wasting time, Theo unzipped his pants, tugging them down before getting on her knees, pulling his underwear down, and freeing his length.

"*Hello,*" she whispered, not meaning to speak out loud.

Aiden laughed softly. While she'd already seen his cock before, it was a sight she wouldn't grow tired of. But right now, she wanted to make him come undone. Her thighs squirmed as an ache built in her core. She wrapped her fingers around his length, giving him a pump.

One of his hands went to her hair, his hold firm enough to give her delicious goose bumps—as always, he knew what she wanted, when she wanted it. He slammed his other hand against the side of the coffin, gripping it tightly, which made Theo feel like a goddess.

After a few strokes, she swirled her tongue around his tip, then along the underside of his shaft. A guttural moan filled the air as Aiden's grip on her hair tightened. She took him in her mouth, sliding him as deeply as she could. When she began to suck, Aiden's knees all but buckled.

He thrusted his hips forward, the movement jerky, as if he were holding himself back. It made her smile. She scooted back slightly, lifting her eyes to him.

"Don't be shy. I won't break." She batted her lashes a few times before taking him in her mouth again, working him from tip to base, slowly.

"I want to fuck that mouth, Theo," he all but growled.

She drew her hands to his ass, digging her nails into his skin and driving him forward, showing him he had her consent. He hissed, and got the message pretty quickly once she picked up her pace.

Watching him thrust in and out of her mouth was almost enough to get her off, especially with the way his eyes seared into her, burning their wicked, delicious path across her skin. Every muscle in his corded body bunched as he worked to hold off and enjoy the pleasure for as long as he could.

She moved her index and middle fingers to the perineum, first applying pressure gently as she stroked the sensitive area and then intensifying it. Aiden grated out, "Fuck, I'm going to come."

She let go of him with a slippery pop, pumping him in her tight fist once, twice, and then he released into her hand, his chest rising and falling so fast she thought he might pass out on the spot.

He stumbled slightly, bringing one hand through his hair, moving a dark tendril off his brow. Then he grinned at her, so beautifully, a smile she realized he'd had on reserve, one that was ridiculously addictive that she feared she'd spend the rest of her vampire days trying to earn another of the very same from him, despite their differences.

Reaching over for a box of tissues, he wiped her hands, cleaned up the mess and got his pants and underwear situated again.

"Let me take care of you," he rasped.

Her smile was wicked. "Later. We've got a challenge to study up on."

He looked like he wanted to argue, but she pressed the button on her cell phone, revealing that their time was dwindling. They still had prep work to do for tonight's tour.

Arching a dark brow, he shot her a grin. "Later then."

Then his hands were on either side of her face. He kissed her thoroughly, pulling her up on her tiptoes. The force of it made her sigh and he swallowed it up. His fingertips fisted in her hair as she held onto his muscular shoulders. It was just a kiss, but it was everything. She felt like she'd been reborn.

What a funny thought for a person like her, especially one born of revenge and guilt and bitterness.

How had she gotten here, to a place where she found a semblance of happiness, a spot of sunlight that didn't burn her skin but instead her heart?

Aiden broke her from her reverie by lifting the packet of papers Daniel had given him as their prize for getting the clue first. "I guess we should get started then?"

She nodded, the movement robotic and stiff. "Sure. Let's give it a look." Even if it felt like knives sticking into her heart. The rehashing of all the history that was her life.

Thankfully, Aiden made it a little easier.

"So at the start of the tour, do you want to introduce me as your boy toy?" He paused, cracking a wolfish grin. "But they didn't have boy toys back then, did they? What would I be called?"

Theo snorted. "Paramour, perhaps?" She lifted a shoulder, not even bothering to suppress a smile. "I'm not as versed in all that as you seem to be."

Aiden shook his head. "Paramour sounds too fancy for me. I'm sticking with boy toy, I think."

"Boy toy it is." She smirked. "And what would I be introduced as?"

She was almost a little afraid to see what he came up with.

He leaned forward, kissing her on the nose. "The most beautiful woman in the world."

The happiness she felt, that foreign emotion, continued to yawn and unfurl in her chest as the night went on. Aiden always seemed to know exactly what she needed.

That wasn't scary at all.

18

THEO

THEODORA HADN'T VOMITED SINCE 1692. YET HERE SHE WAS, A THREE hundred-and-thirty-year-old vampire who swore she was about to upchuck the blood she'd drunk from Aiden as they walked up to Daniel standing on the outskirts of Proctor's Ledge, where so many of those accused during the witch trials had been executed. A chill skittered up her spine, one having nothing to do with the cold Massachusetts air.

She knew this would come, knew she'd have to face it. More than likely, she'd be giving a ghost tour around each place she and Jonathan frequented, probably the jail he and her best friend and fellow healer, Elizabeth Croft, were held alongside her. They had not gotten the chance that she did. No, they were executed before her, before Andreas entered her life. She drew in a deep breath to calm herself, but it was nearly impossible when memories filtered through like a faded film roll.

Recalling that day always hurt. Even now she felt Jonathan's phantom touch, how his brown eyes memorized her face and the way he held her as best he could through the prison bars, in a poor excuse for a hug, a last kiss. Uneasiness threatened to pull her under, but Aiden's hand at the small of her back—reassuring, present, warm—definitely helped keep her afloat.

Brandt and Paisley were currently MIA, but two of the other teams were spaced around the memorial to the victims of the witch trials. Theo wanted to cry as she walked past each ledge, looking at the names. She knew most of them. And then she saw her husband's name and Elizabeth's etched into the stone, right toward the end. A buzz filled her ears, drowning out the sounds of everything else around her as she gently traced her fingertips over the inscribed names of the last people she ever loved.

Jonathan Herrick.

Elizabeth Croft.

Aiden stiffened beside her. When she met his stare, it was evident he wanted to do something to help, but what could one do in this case? The people Theo loved were dead and gone, and she was here. She was grateful. She'd lived what felt like a thousand lifetimes, had done more than most. And now, more than anything, she wanted to feel the sunshine on her skin; she wanted to eat a piece of pizza because it looked and smelled delicious. The food she ate while human had been far more limited than the plethora of options now.

But her truest, deepest desire had begun to float slowly from the murky depths she had buried it in. Maybe she no longer wanted to be alone anymore. She knew she had Andreas and Davina, but it wasn't the same.

Daniel clasped his hands together, snagging everyone's attention as they stood impervious to tourists milling around them and their camera crews. The host dipped his head and then began speaking.

"We're waiting for one last team to join us, and then we'll get started. Make sure you've turned your mics on, please."

Everyone flipped theirs on in a flurry of motion.

"What kind of stunt are they pulling?" Theo whispered while eyeing the crowd.

Aiden tightened his hands into fists. "I don't know, but when I see Brandt, I'm going to beat his ass."

Theo gripped his bicep, wanting to revel in the hardness of the corded muscle beneath her touch, but not when they were standing in the place where she found both life and death.

"Aiden. I know we said we would, but now we've slept on it, and I'm okay. I'm fine." She stood on her tiptoes, shooting him an overly bright smile, one she was pretty sure she'd never sported once in her life, and pointed to her healed cheek. "See? All thanks to you. So do me a favor and maybe don't get kicked out of the competition because we are"—she pushed her pointer finger and thumb a scant bit apart—"so close to winning this thing."

Aiden shook his head, his jaw clenching. His nostrils flared as he slanted a look at her.

"You nearly died, Theo. And my concern for you, at that moment, and even right now, has *nothing* to do with a damn chalice."

He turned away from her, his words providing a warmth that she shouldn't allow. But she did. She wanted to. She opened her mouth, dying to give him the same gift, to explain that she didn't want him kicked off the show because she wasn't ready to say goodbye to him, whatever that meant.

A rumble through the crowd drew their attention, and there was Brandt, walking tall and smug, Paisley next to him looking equally proud. Their gazes slid over to Theo and Aiden, slight surprise registering at seeing them there.

"Thought you'd killed her off, didn't you?" Aiden snarled, taking a step toward them.

The host's brows furrowed as he moved to get in between Aiden and Team Asshole. "What's this about?" he asked, head swinging back and forth like a tennis match spectator.

Anger vibrated from Aiden. Theo tried to calm him by wrapping her arm across his shoulders, even though it was lopsided since he was a little taller.

"Aiden..." she warned, feeling a growl of her own building inside her chest.

Brandt's gaze collided with hers, and in that instant, she changed her mind about being calm, cool, and collected regarding the whole situation.

"What are you looking at with your crusty ass?" she taunted, tilting her head to the side with a sweet smile. "You thought for sure I was toast, quite literally, last night, huh? Well, guess what? I don't die that easily."

"You better be glad this woman is one hell of a fighter. If it wasn't for her, I'd already have staked you," Aiden snapped. And then, under his breath, so Theo was the only one who could hear, he muttered sideways, "Or at least tried, shit."

She fought a laugh.

Daniel, having had enough of playing referee, straightened. "You're not insinuating that Brandt and Paisley tried to kill you?"

Theo rolled her eyes as Aiden scoffed while answering the host. "That's exactly what we're saying. And there's no *insinuation*; it's one hundred percent fact."

Brandt pressed both of his hands to his chest, fluttering his lashes. "Me? I didn't do anything. It's not my fault if you can't recall where you leave your car." And then he smirked. Aiden started to lunge for him, but Theo held him back.

"Enough of that!" Daniel exclaimed.

An audience had started gathering on the street.

But Theo had one more thing to add, wanting to make sure it was caught on all the cameras. "Just like with *Forever After*, the vampire dating show that Max ruined, he's at it again, not caring who gets taken down in the show's wake. The question is why, though? Why does he want Brandt to win the Solis Occasum? What's in it for him?"

"There will be none of that. We won't besmirch Max's name. Don't forget—you signed a waiver," Daniel said as he rubbed his forehead.

This was most likely way above his pay grade, and she was sure he was getting paid pretty handsomely.

"We're moving on and will handle all your grievances later." He shot Brandt, Paisley, Aiden, and lastly, Theo a hard look before continuing, almost daring them to speak up again. "Tonight, each of the four remaining teams will take turns giving a ghost tour to our volunteer tour group. You will be given costumes to change into, along with a script to study. You'll all take the same route, and it's up to you to make this information yours, to engage the audience." He paused, allowing his stare to rake dramatically over each team.

No doubt the editing team would cue the melodramatic music at this point. "One team will be eliminated tonight, and the final three will head to Ireland for the next to the last task."

Theo had never been to Ireland. No doubt Max would pick the creepiest place in the country to film—maybe a haunted castle or abbey. Anything would be a lovely distraction from the ghosts of her past, especially when they came rushing back once Daniel ushered them over to where the wardrobe department passed out costumes for the night. He then directed them to put all their belongings in portable lockers. If she weren't so keyed up, she would have laughed at the idea of wearing clothes from her human days.

"Looks familiar, huh?" Aiden asked as he bumped her shoulder, his earlier anger having faded.

She nodded, fingering the black dress and white apron, a white coif cap on top of the stack of clothes in her arms. "It does. It's something I hoped to never see again." With a sigh, she looked off to where makeshift changing areas had been erected on the side of the street. "I guess I'll be back."

And after a few minutes, she looked exactly as she had in 1692, except paler, and her lips turned down almost naturally now.

When she met Aiden at their starting point, she fought back a gasp at him in black breeches, a white linen shirt topped by a black doublet. Her mind instantly went to Jonathan, but she shook those thoughts away, instead choosing to focus on Aiden and how he actually made the stuffy clothing work for him. He cut a fine figure, as if he could have been a nobleman in the old days, one with very nice...*assets*. The thought almost made her smile.

His eyes lit up when she approached, scanning her from head to toe, leaving a scorching fire in its wake. "Damn, girl, who knew Puritans could be hot?"

If she could blush, she would've, but instead, she pretended to be preoccupied with their script, although she could barely comprehend what was typed on the page. All she could think of was Salem, 1692, Jonathan, Elizabeth, Aiden, and then rinse and repeat.

"Apparently, we get to go first since we pissed off the powers that be," Aiden added after a beat.

She swallowed hard. "I'm not surprised. The sooner we can get it over with, the better. Nothing against the town, it's lovely, but my memories are too big if that makes sense?"

Aiden nodded, fiddling with what was known today as a Pilgrim hat. "I get it. That's why I sold the house that Cassidy and I bought. I didn't want it because the grief was already suffocating. Living there and running into her ghost would break me completely." His smile was sad as he looked down at his own script.

Two damaged, wounded souls that had somehow managed to find each other amid the storm. *Mates*. Something that Theo wanted to take to her grave if she could. Aiden didn't choose it, and she wasn't sure he'd be ready for something so permanent. There was no need for him to know, especially if she was going to change back into a human—and she *was* going to change back into a human.

"Someday, maybe you'll tell me the whole story?" His voice broke through her thoughts. "Why you were in jail, how you turned...*all of it*."

Theo still wouldn't meet his gaze as she nibbled at her lip. "You don't want to know that stuff. It's boring."

His hand came to rest on hers, the one holding the script, his warmth seeping into her ice, threatening to thaw her if she let him. "It's anything but boring, Theodora. It's you, and I already said I want to get to know you."

Sweet words, sweet man, wrong time, wrong century. Determined to mollify him until she could find the courage to tell him her story—*if* she could ever find that inner courage—she gestured to her dress.

"You're getting a pretty good look at me circa 1692. I literally wore clothes like this, so the costume department is spot-on with their research and accuracy."

Aiden wiggled his brows playfully. "And it's sexy as hell."

Unable to help herself, Theo snorted, covering her mouth with her hand. "You're ridiculous."

"But you like it." He shot her a wink.

True, she did like it.

Before she could respond, Rita, one of the crew members, approached, interrupting their discussion—or flirting, rather.

"Excuse me, we're ready for you. We're going to try to get ahead of the storm that's coming in." Rita pointed to a group of about five tourists ranging in age from twelve to maybe seventy.

Wordlessly, they followed. Aiden pulled Theo against him and placed a kiss on top of her hair, a move so inherently tender it should've broken her on the spot, but instead, it wove its way into her veins, attempting to mend her deepest, darkest hurts...if only she'd let it. As it was, she was stubborn as all get out.

"Welcome to our tour. I am Theodora, and this is Aiden," she spoke, affecting an accent more like that which she'd been born with, one of old. "Join us as we tour through Salem..."

As long as they didn't go by Federal Street, which was where the Old Witch Gaol once stood, where she, Jonathan, and Elizabeth were held, she might be able to make it. She *had* to make it.

For her and Aiden.
For a chance at life.

19

AIDEN

THEO WAS FALLING APART BEFORE AIDEN'S EYES. EACH SMILE GREW shakier even as she lifted her head higher. When they passed a bronze plaque on Federal Street, something crumpled in her stare, her shoulders hunched. With a quick clip, she moved past it.

"Wait a minute, I'd like to know what happened here," one of the tourists called out, stopping right in front of the plaque.

Aiden fell back and squinted into the darkness, seeing the words 'Old Witch Gaol' on the sign.

She froze, turning on them, her eyes wet, a cool breeze blowing ebony and silver wisps of hair across her lips.

"You want to know what happened? I'll tell you." She took one step closer toward the group. "Innocent people lost their lives because humans can suck. I lost my husband and best friend. I had to sit in the jail that once stood there and watch them get taken, had to wait, helpless and heartbroken, knowing that they were being hanged for nothing! For simply being different. And then, when I was offered a way of revenge, I took it. I *fucking* took it and welcomed the blood lust that came with turning into a vampire, and do you know what I did?"

Her chest rose and fell frantically, but the group was transfixed, hanging onto Theo's every word while Aiden had to fight down the urge to hold her. Here he was, finally getting some of the answers he so desperately wanted. But he hadn't wanted them like this.

"I went to the home of the people who accused me, my husband, and my best friend of being witches—me and Elizabeth because we were healers and without children, my husband simply because he was rich and married to me. Those assholes who accused us of witchcraft knew with the ridiculous law that our riches would go to them since we didn't have any brothers or heirs."

Her eyes flashed in the glow of the street lights, drawing the tour group in.

"So that night, I, a newborn vampire, tore through their house and killed them all, drained them dry, and that's the only thing I haven't regretted these past three hundred and thirty years. So now, if you'll excuse me, I'd like to go nurse my heartbreak somewhere else, somewhere in private." After a sniffle and straightening of her apron, she told the audience, "Thank you for going on this tour with us. I hope maybe you'll vote ours as the best so we can win, and I can become a human again and stop reliving my guilt every day for eternity." Her hands were trembling as she clicked her microphone off.

The smile she gave them was brittle, and when Aiden went to follow her, she lifted a hand gently. "Give me five minutes, please." Her voice cracked on her plea, and Aiden was slowly beginning to realize he'd pretty much give her anything she wanted. Just not the chalice. Although he understood a little better now why she wanted it. He still wanted to know more about Andreas, about *everything*, but that would come another day, another time.

He turned to face Dylan and Bridget, and everything he felt must've been written all over his face. Bridget shifted her feet. "We'll give you both a few minutes, okay?"

Dylan paused, looking at her as if he might argue. And he eventually did. "Max said—"

Bridget shrugged, her voice a hushed whisper. "I don't care what Max said. Let's go."

She didn't give Aiden a chance to thank them. She and Dylan's heated argument echoed through the streets as she marched off with him in tow. The crowd of tourists dispersed in a rush of whispers. Aiden tried to smile at them and thank them, but it felt off, fake.

Aiden turned around, seeing Theo's silhouette still in the distance. With a sigh, he turned off his microphone.

Although watching her walk away, in pain and knowing he couldn't do anything about it, made Aiden anxious, he headed back to their tour starting point. She needed time, and he would give it to her.

The evening had grown colder, and not as many people wandered about, or at least not in the area where he was. A faint cry drew his attention down one of the alleys that had welcoming white bulbs strung across the top of it.

Narrowing his eyes, he saw a heap splayed out in the center. Another cry came from it, and Aiden picked up the pace, jogging over to the body. It was a human woman, one of the remaining team members, with a stake poking out from her chest. Aiden turned her head. Blood dribbled from her mouth, one final breath rattled from her, and then the night fell silent again.

His hands shook as he realized what he'd just witnessed. In the shadows near the wall of the building on his right lay another bundle, a vampire with a stake sticking out from his chest. Aiden gasped and stumbled back a step before gathering his courage and moving over to them. The male vampire's skin was a sickly shade of gray and blue.

He scrambled back, away from both bodies. "Shit," he bit out as he ran a hand through his hair, standing up to his full height.

Someone had taken them out, and he knew without a doubt it was Brandt and Paisley. Their illustrious host Daniel had to know

Max knew this was going on, but they didn't care. It was *Forever After* all over again.

Another sound came from the back of the alley. The crunch of something beneath the bootheels of a murderous Brandt, maybe? On instinct, Aiden pulled the stake out of the vampire's chest, hating the sounds it made as he did so. But he wouldn't stand defenseless against a murderer. Not again.

An irritated meow came from the shadows seconds before a cat scampered away. *Only a cat.* He turned the stake in his hand and then dug his phone out with the other to dial. Who? The police? They might be able to help—at least they'd do more than *Night Race* would.

Just as he was about to call 911, a shrill shriek came from the mouth of the alleyway. Fucking Paisley. She held her hands to the sides of her face like Van Gogh's *The Scream*, a siren, a beacon for the rest of the contestants and crew to come running.

"Holy shit, he killed them!" Brandt exclaimed, false terror in his voice.

Max and Daniel fought through the remaining two teams and their camera crews to where Aiden stood with the bloody stake in his hand. This did not look good. He released the piece of wood, watching it hit the asphalt and roll at his feet.

"What's this?" Max bit out.

Aiden shrugged, anger simmering beneath his skin. "I don't know. You tell me."

"Aiden!" Theo called, her shadow moving toward him.

She threw her arms around his neck, either not noticing or not caring about the scene around them. It was as if she had a singular focus when it came to him, or at least maybe in his dreams she did. Yet when he released her from his grip, she took in the dead bodies not far from where they stood, the stake at his feet. Her brows scrunched in wordless question.

He gestured to the corpses. "I found them like this. I heard her dying, and I came to investigate. They were like this when I got here." He turned his gaze on Theo, beseeching. "You've got to believe me."

"Right, this coming from the guy who's been heard on more than one occasion talking about staking other vampires. Stakes are forbidden, and hell, killing contestants is too," Max snarled.

"Oh, it is, huh? Sure could've fooled me and most of the world with everything that went down on *Forever After*." He ran a shaky hand through his hair. "You know I didn't do this. This is a fucking setup."

Theo's eyes were wide, her lip pulled between her teeth as she took in the scene once more. Was that a flash of suspicion in her gaze? There was definitely a certain hesitancy in her movements as she took a small step back. The action was something no one else would think much of. But Aiden had grown to read her so well he knew the gesture was monumental.

"Theo," he barely whispered, turning to her, his hands at his sides even though they wanted to reach forward and brush her hair from her face, to hold her. The ghost tour already had her in a vulnerable place, and then she had to find out her so-called teammate was being accused of murder.

She took another step back, this time noticeable, her expression heartbroken, as she fisted the coarse fabric of her dress. Could she really think he'd do this? She knew him better than this. Or at least he thought she did.

Max shook his head, looking around the crowded alley, and then after releasing a loud breath, he spoke. "Brandt and Paisley, your team will go to Ireland. Sheila and Laurel, your team will go to Ireland. Daniel will get with you soon regarding that."

Aiden rubbed the stubble on his chin in disbelief. "Two people are dead, and you're worried about continuing on with the challenge? Are you serious right now?"

"What's that cliché? The show must go on?" Max arched both brows. "I've invested too much time, energy, and money in this show to let it fall apart just because you hate vampires," he seethed.

"I don't—" Aiden began.

Max held up a hand. "Save it. We all heard you threaten to stake Brandt. Where's your backpack?"

With furrowed brows, Aiden gestured toward the street, to their makeshift camp in the center of the city. "In my locker."

Max gave him a nod and motioned to someone Aiden couldn't see in the crowd. What was even happening right now? Aiden studied the spectacle, attempting to calm his breathing. He needed to think his way out of this.

Theo had backed against the brick wall, her arms held over her body in a hunched pose that caused bile to burn Aiden's throat.

"Here!" a voice called from the back, working its way up to the front, the small crowd parting for the crew member who hefted Aiden's familiar pack in the air.

Max snatched it, opening it with zero gentleness. Four sharp wooden stakes clattered to the ground. Everyone gasped, chattering at the sight. Aiden whipped his head to Theo, who held a hand over her mouth, absolutely appalled, yet...when she met his stare, hers was surprisingly blank, like a slate wiped completely clean. Something about that niggled at his mind, but he obviously had bigger problems right now.

"Those aren't mine," he gritted, holding back all he could to keep from snapping completely.

Max scooped the stakes up, lifting them in one hand like one would a hand of poker. "Then how do you explain them being in your pack, Archer? Security!"

Heart pumping, Aiden looked around. The alley was a dead end, and the other way was everyone else, who would no doubt love to be a hero and capture him. He was trapped.

He was stuck.

And alone.

Theo wouldn't even look at him, her hands tapping an impatient rhythm over her crossed arms.

"Those were planted on me, and you know it, Max. You and Brandt, and I swear—"

Max's deranged chuckle cut him off. "Swear what? You'll stake us? Again, further proving my point." He shook his head. "We won't be calling the authorities because we want to handle it in-house first. Good television and all that. Once we've dealt with the situation, we'll alert them to the dead bodies, which we'll move for now." He signaled toward someone in the horde.

A tall, beefy, bald guy with bluish, pale skin and arms bigger than Aiden's entire body sliced through the crowd, his black shirt stretching across his chest. Aiden might be fit, but he had nothing on this wall of muscle.

The guy shoved his arms behind his back before using zip ties to tie them together. Baring fangs at him, he hissed a warning. Great, a vampire. Now he really didn't stand a chance.

"What's going to happen to him?" Theo finally spoke, her voice the softest thing about that moment.

"He's going to the old jail," Max answered without hesitation.

"It's abandoned, though. I wouldn't say it's safe," Bridget spoke up from somewhere in the crowd.

Max shrugged, an evil grin curling his lips as he ignored the camerawoman and faced Theo. "As for you, you may not have had anything to do with the murders of these innocents, but because your teammate is disqualified, we cannot let you move forward with the challenge. All mics need to be stripped from you both."

To punctuate his answer, he shoved the stakes back into Aiden's pack and handed it off to another crew member. More members of the crew moved forward. One took Theo's microphone pack and another tore Aiden's from his body.

Aiden looked at Theo again, his heart cracking in his chest at the utter devastation splayed across her face. He knew it wasn't his fault, but he still hated seeing that look there, and he resolved to get out of this mess, not just for himself but for her too. They would find the Solis Occasum, and he knew all hell would break loose between them once they did, but it was something they had to do, something they *would* do. No way would he ever let Max's scheming get in the way of their goal.

Anguish carved deeply into her features, Theo took another step, a wince following close behind. This had to be a horrible sense of déjà vu for her—Jonathan locked up, now him. He could only pray he didn't end up dead as well.

"Can I...can I speak with him once you've locked him away?" she asked in a quiet voice.

Briefly, Max looked to Daniel and then to the security guard, who jerked Aiden to prove a point. "I know this is hard for you given your past, so I'll let you know when you can speak to him, although I can't understand why you'd want to. *Unless...you were in on the plot?*" Suspicion sparked his eyes.

Theo shook her head vehemently. "No. I wasn't involved in any plot." She paused for a moment, rage transforming her face into a scary visage, her eyes fiery blue pools of hatred, her fangs exposed over her lips, begging for blood, her fists clenched in fury. "I only want to make him pay for what he's cost me."

20

THEO

THEO HATED SEEING UNCERTAINTY AND THEN HURT IN AIDEN'S STARE, but she had a plan—one that would inevitably fall apart if she showed any tenderness toward that man. But below the surface? Deadly anger threatened to boil over, slithering through her veins like a cobra, ready to strike.

She waited outside the abandoned jail, one that had nothing to do with the witch trials, thankfully, her jaw sore from keeping her irritated mask intact. Thunder rolled in the distance. Lightning flickered through the sky like a spider web. It wouldn't be long now before she got soaked.

In the scheme of things, that didn't really matter. Not with Aiden behind bars. She knew without a doubt that Aiden didn't have anything to do with the murders. The stakes had clearly been planted on him.

Theo cursed under her breath at the situation they'd found themselves in, and when thinking about everything leading to this moment, she got even more pissed off. If Aiden had held it together a little more... *No.* She couldn't blame him for provoking Brandt, not when she wanted and *had* done the same. She'd even enraged Max. Was this all her fault? Was she reliving her past all over again? Just a different day and age, different man, same old Theo?

Angry tears, the kind she hated, stung her eyes as she forced everything down deep for later perusal. Right now she needed to focus on Aiden. She couldn't let him down.

"He really did a number on you, didn't he?" Max all but crooned.

Theo turned around to find him leaning against the chain-link fence surrounding the jail, his legs crossed, the very picture of innocence and calm, but she knew better. This vampire was a lion ready to pounce. Little did he know she was too. And her bite was bigger. Or at least she hoped.

Pushing her bottom lip out into a pout, she batted her lashes ever so slowly as she made her way over to him. "He really did. I feel so stupid."

Max snickered, shoving off the fence and sauntering toward her. "Don't. We all make mistakes, which speaking of..." He rubbed his smooth chin. "If I let you do this, if I let you in to see the human... that means you're putting this little beef"—he gestured between them—"behind us, yes? After all, I'll let you get first drink."

It took everything in Theo not to flinch at that, especially knowing and understanding Aiden's past. "Deal," she croaked and cleared her throat. "That certainly would persuade me to bury the hatchet, so to speak." The smile that curled her lips felt nothing less than feline.

And Max would be the canary.

The bastard had no idea.

"So? May I?" She gestured toward the jail. Another rumble of thunder rent the air. The storm was getting closer now.

"Of course. Where are my manners? Follow me," Max said over his shoulder as he led her through the gate and toward the boarded-up yet impressive building. "This place is rather spectacular. I wish I'd thought to use it for a challenge." He huffed a laugh while Theo remained silent.

Just as they entered the gray stone part of the building, the rain began to fall in earnest. Lights flickered overhead as a shock of lightning lit up the old building. When the power returned to normal, Theo spotted another door at the end of a short hallway, most likely separating them from the cells. *Perfect.* That's what she'd hoped for.

"Don't mind the power outages. The storm should pass soon." Max shrugged before striding over to a rotting desk in the middle of the floor. He swiped a large, rusty key ring from it and handed it over to her. "Here's the key. And be sure to lock up when you're done. I'll be at our base camp, getting things ready for the next leg of the race."

Her face fell at the mention, which wasn't part of the act. This couldn't be the end of the road for her. Not after she'd wanted it for so long. She refused to accept that and lifted her chin with a new determination.

She let out a growl, partly for show, and partly because she couldn't hold it back. The lights flickered above her once more.

"He'll pay for costing me the chalice." She held up the key ring, the jingling the only other sound in the creepy building. "Thank you for this."

Max nodded and then shoved his hands into the pockets of his tight jeans and slid from the building into the storm.

Theo released a loud breath but still held herself in check because who knew if he had cameras wired here and there, all for the sake of entertainment or money.

Keeping her head held high, she walked down the dimly lit hall that looked like something straight out of a horror film. The power surges added to the eerie vibes, but there had to be a way to use them to her advantage.

Unlocking the large door, she stood in the heart of the small jail. There were five dilapidated cells with stripped-down bunks and rust and rot. Her heart twisted as she thought about Jonathan's strong hands gripping hers between the bars. She blinked those memories back along with a few unshed tears. She knew this was a different place, but it didn't seem to matter.

At the end, Aiden sat on the pillowless cot, head in his hands, only raising it to meet her gaze upon hearing the door open. Like her, he'd been allowed to change back into his modern-day clothing, but he also now sported a black eye and a split across his cheek—on the same side as his eyebrow scar that she'd found so incredibly sexy. Anger burned through her. His knuckles weren't any better—busted and bloody. Whoever had done this to him hadn't gotten a free pass. Aiden had attempted to fight back.

Her stomach lurched at the idea of him going through that, but it was better than the alternative that awaited him if she didn't get him out of here. He'd be a walking blood bag and would be Max's next "missing contestant."

Uncertainty laced his deep velvet voice as it slid over her, reminding her of her task. "Theo?"

She said nothing as she made her way down to the cell. Her hands were clenched in fists as she tried to steady herself and keep the flashbacks at bay.

"Aiden." She dropped her voice even lower. "I need you to listen to me very carefully and don't, for God's sake, *don't* ask fifty million questions, okay?"

He attempted to furrow his brow but winced from the pain. "Right. Okay."

Shooting a glance above them, she noticed a camera. If she angled herself just so, they wouldn't be able to see her lips move inside or outside the cell. This plan wouldn't work if they could make out everything she said.

She lifted up the key ring. The words that followed came out in a rush. "I'm going to unlock the door and come in. Don't look when I say this, but there's a camera in there. I need to be angry with you, and you're going to react as if I am. Then I'm going to pretend that I'm drinking from you, but here's the thing. We need to pretend as if I've killed you from overdrinking."

Leaning back, she met his openly curious gaze. "I thought…"

"*Questions*, Aiden. Answers later, remember? We don't have a lot of time, and I don't know what sort of traps Max has laid out in case he's on to me, so we need to make it look real. Blink a few times if you're good with this plan."

Standing, albeit a little wobbly, Aiden blinked. It was too risky for him to speak. Not when she couldn't be sure that he wasn't in a blind spot of the camera feed.

Theo wasted no time unlocking the cell, stepping inside, and angling so she blocked Aiden from the view of the doorway, just in case. She tilted her head so that the camera wouldn't be able to make out her words, her body language mimicking anger and irritation.

"I'm pretending now that I'm telling you how upset I am," she whispered, moving closer, her fingers at her side, itching to touch him, to soothe his hurts. The lights went out momentarily, but she could still see Aiden clearly in the darkness.

He scrubbed a hand down his face, talking as his mouth was covered. "And I'm apologizing. Genuinely, because I feel like I'm the reason we're in this mess, and I thought you were really angry with me, that you'd…" He stopped and shook his head, looking away. He tucked his hands into his pockets.

If she knew if they were one hundred percent alone, she'd touch his cheek, bring his gaze back to her. Instead, she kept talking, desperate to get this over with, desperate for her heart to stop thundering so quickly in her chest—yes, she knew it was partially from the mate bond, but it was also majorly from the fact that said mate was in trouble.

"Thank you for that. I had to act, you know? If I stayed by your side right off the bat, they'd never have allowed this. As soon as I saw you over the bodies, I knew it was a matter of minutes before you were pinned with it. Now…I'm going to put my mouth on your neck, okay? I need…" She swallowed and then bit out a curse. "I don't know, just…act like I'm drinking from you."

She didn't want to see Aiden's face, knowing she'd probably find a mirror image of what she felt—whenever she thought of blood now, she got all hot and bothered thinking of Aiden. It really did change the game, as other vampires with mates had warned her. The lights flickered back to life. But for how long?

Her hands went into his hair, one along his neck, as he wrapped his arms around her instinctively, his touch burning into her skin like a brand.

All that could be heard was their ragged breathing. Aiden's chest brushed hers, his fingertips smoothing back and forth at her waist. Her lips pressed against his skin, her fangs begging to come out and play, especially once she tasted the salt there, reminding her of last time. It was almost Pavlovian.

As if sensing her thoughts, Aiden tightened his grip. "You could do it if you wanted to, Theo."

"There are a lot of things I want to do with you, but right now...I can't. We need to focus on getting you out of here."

He moved so he was able to nuzzle into her hair. "And looking like I'm dead will do it?"

"Yes. In case more shit hits the fan. Now the next part...you're going to have to trust me."

"I trust you. Tell me what I need to do."

"We need to make this believable. They can think I'm lulling you into my clutches, and now...now we're going to rough it up. You're going to struggle, and eventually you'll go limp—"

"I'd never go limp around you, gorgeous."

Theo smiled against his neck. Damn him. "Aiden," she said coyly.

He grinned at her, looking like a boxer who'd gotten his ass kicked in the ring.

"Ready?" she whispered, pressing her lips into his neck a little harder. On instinct, her tongue darted out, tickling his skin.

His sharp intake of breath told her all she needed to know. This had turned out to be slightly more sexual than she intended, and it would've been okay if they weren't in a jail cell and likely on camera.

"Sorry, now are you ready?" she rasped.

"Always," came his reply.

"Run as fast as you can once I get out of here, okay?"

"Wait. You're not coming with me?"

"I am, but I'll meet you. If we both run now, it's over. I'm telling you; I feel it in my veins Max has cameras in here. This was all too easy. So if I can make it believable, it'll buy time."

"What are you going to do?"

"I'll walk out the front door and distract him. You'll grab the car I have parked at Salem Common; keys are inside under the seat. I'll meet you there in forty-five minutes. If I don't show up, leave without me."

Aiden shook his head against hers. "No."

"You have to. I can hold my own. I'll be okay." She pulled back a little. "I need to get you out of here, and then we regroup. Our second meeting spot, if we don't connect at the first one, will be the Old Burial Hill Cemetery in Marblehead. It's about thirteen or fourteen minutes away, and the location is just random enough maybe Max won't catch on."

"I don't like this..."

"Never asked if you did. Sometimes we have to do things we don't like. Now fight me."

Then it was like a switch was flipped. Aiden began to struggle and pull against Theo. She was careful to keep her hair shielding his neck, holding him tightly against her.

Their bodies tangled and danced, a violent choreography to anyone watching the cameras. What shocked Theo the most was how much Aiden trusted her, given his past with vampires. If only things could be simple between them.

Theo turned so they were out of view of the camera. She made sure to meet Aiden's stare before she explained the next part of the plan.

"So now I'm going to lay you down. Keep your eyes shut until you hear the door close."

Aiden pursed his lips, already forming an argument, but they were running out of time. Theo pulled away. Thankfully, he played along and became dead weight in her arms. She laid him down on the floor in what she hoped was a blind spot. To be safe, she positioned him so that he was slumped, his neck angled toward the wall so that no matter where a camera was, it wouldn't be evident he didn't have a single mark on his neck.

Thunder shook the old jail, and after a loud crack of lightning, the power went off—this time with a loud pop that indicated it would likely be for good.

With her heart thudding violently in her chest, Theo turned on her heel, leaving his cell wide open, the keys sitting next to him should he need them.

But as she did, an epiphany crashed into her, one that sent her stumbling a step or two, emotion clogging her throat.

Why did it feel like she was leaving her heart behind?

21

AIDEN

As soon as the door shut behind Theo, Aiden sat up, reaching for the jail keys she left. His eyes slowly adjusted to the darkness as the storm raged on outside.

Everything in his soul wanted to run after Theo, but she was right. She was tough as nails and could handle herself. This was a brilliant plan, and if he allowed his feet to do what they wanted, then he'd only ruin everything, and they couldn't afford that now.

So he managed to skulk through the creepy-as-hell abandoned jail, thankful now for the horror vibes as they provided cover for him, as he found a back exit. He released a breath, allowing the small victory to urge him forward to Salem Common in the pouring rain, where he would meet up with Theo.

A moment that couldn't come soon enough.

The streets had emptied out even more since everything went down. His hands itched to check his cell phone for the time, but he'd left it behind out of fear Max had a tracker on it. He was almost sure that was the case, especially with how conveniently Aiden had stumbled upon the two dead bodies of those contestants, and with how close by they were to hear Paisley's scream.

The thought had him curling his fists, his nails biting into his palms, but he kept moving. He added a few more names to his Revenge Tour. Now he needed that chalice more than ever, something that he knew would be a point of contention with Theo. He blew out a ragged breath.

One crisis at a time.

Eventually the rain came to an end. The power remained out, so that provided another layer of cover with the blown streetlamps. Aiden slipped through the streets, constantly looking over his shoulder. Vampires still had night vision and could pop up at any moment. Every shadow turned into a foe, had Aiden ready to fight if needed, but thankfully Theo had delivered on her promise. Had he really doubted she would? The woman was incredible.

There, parked along the edge of the park, was a sedan. Aiden wanted to fist pump or cheer, but he kept his lips in a flat line as he all but tiptoed around to it. Sliding inside, he located the keys, cranked up the engine, and locked the doors, breathing in a jagged inhale.

He wouldn't be able to breathe fully again until he was with Theo.

Gaze flickering to the illuminated green clock, he knew he had about fifteen minutes before she showed, or he'd have to head to their next rendezvous point. Who was this guy? This buttoned-up veterinarian from small-town USA now thinking about rendezvous points and getting the shit kicked out of him by vampires. Only to turn around and realize he was…he was slowly falling for another.

One he was almost certain he could never have.

He thumped his hands nervously on the steering wheel as he stared at the clock, counting down the minutes. The old adage "a watched pot never boils" came to mind, one his fiancée used to say all the time when he'd stand in front of the microwave, waiting for his bacon to cook.

But seriously, the waiting was torture. His stomach pitched, his mind wandering through all the possibilities of things that could go wrong.

When their appointed meeting time had come and gone with no sign of Theo, Aiden knew he was right to worry. His chest rose and fell in frantic pants. He swiveled in the car's seat, looking this way and that, on constant alert. Ten minutes turned into fifteen, and he kept seeing her face—the intensity when she told him to leave if she didn't show up.

"No," he croaked into the empty space.

It couldn't, it *wouldn't* end like this. He refused to let it.

So he'd play it Theo's way first. He'd go to Marblehead, and he'd wait like she asked. If she didn't show tonight, he'd do everything he could to find her. He needed to be sure she was okay.

With Theo, he would always need to be sure.

About everything.

22

THEO

Theo hadn't expected to run into Max so soon. He wasn't waiting at the center like she anticipated. Instead, he leaned against an SUV parked down the street from the jail. She really hoped Aiden had gotten to the getaway car and that he listened to her when she said to leave if she didn't show up on time because this could take a while.

They'd meet up at the cemetery in Marblehead, but first, she had to take care of this narcissistic baby vampire. She wasn't going to let Max stand in the way of what she wanted, let alone hurt someone she...someone she cared about despite desperately trying not to.

Wiping the corner of her mouth with her thumb, she shot Max a smirk. "Thanks for the snack. I hope you don't mind that I killed him."

Max's eyes widened at that. "*What*? Are you kidding me, Theo?"

She shrugged. "I figured I earned it since I was his partner. Now, tell me about the next clue for this race, Max."

The director looked at her anew. Her fingers itched for the stake she'd tucked in the waistband of her pants, ignoring the way the point stabbed at her flesh with each step—tiny pinpricks that were worth it for the end goal.

Regaining his composure, Max straightened the cuffs of his jacket. "I can't tell you that. You're no longer a contestant on the show."

Before she could respond, a recognizable presence caused the hairs on the back of her neck to rise—that familiar scent of leather and spice, wrapping her up in memories of the day her life changed and every moment since then.

Andreas.

"Andreas Donovan," Max all but spit onto the sidewalk between them. "What are you doing here?"

Andreas shrugged, looking as cool, calm, and collected as ever. He even went so far as to dust the invisible dirt off the shoulder of his perfectly fitted black peacoat. Theo bit her lip to keep from smiling.

"I'm here because I don't answer to *anyfuckingbody*, Maxwell."

Theo's head jerked to the side. "Maxwell? I did *not* see that one coming."

Not that there was anything wrong with the name, but Max was such a douche, and she had to needle him somehow.

Andreas chuckled, the sound dark and menacing. His expression turned murderous as he addressed Max again. "As I said, I don't have to explain my whereabouts to you, leech. Come on, Theodora." He tilted his head toward the misty street. "We have places to be."

Max sputtered. Theo didn't even deign to give him a second look, although she wanted information on the location of the Solis Occasum since they'd gotten kicked out of the race. As if reading her mind, Andreas shook his head. Damn it. He was too good at always knowing what she was up to.

As they walked away, literally into the night, Theo waited until they were far enough away to whirl on her sire.

"What are you doing here? I was about to do a little stabby stab, and you know I *never* have murderous tendencies aside from that one time when I first turned..."

Andreas snapped his fingers, and a sleek car as dark as the sky above appeared before them. She'd never understood how he did things like that, and he wouldn't tell her either. All she knew was she'd never quite met a vampire with powers like Andreas, and she still didn't know how old he was. A million? That's what it felt like sometimes when she watched him do these sorts of things.

"You can't kill that leech. You know if you kill another vampire, the council will come for your head."

"Okay, point taken there. I'd like to keep my head firmly where it is, on my body. But what's with the nickname, *leech*?" Theo asked as she slid into the car, across the leather interior.

Andreas revved the engine and took off.

"Vampires are what they are, but there are some that are vile and wretched that suck the life out of everything, blood or no, and that's Max."

Theo's brows furrowed. "So how did you know exactly the right time to show up? Notice I didn't say 'save the day' because, as I said, I had that under control."

Andreas chuckled again. "I know you did, Theo, but this show isn't what it seems. It's all a great big ruse for Max to get what he wants—through Brandt. He's using him, but the ancient vampire is planning on stabbing him in the back the first chance he gets." He let out a sigh. "I placed a spy in her your midst—"

"Who?" Theo's eyes went wide. Her mind ran through all the possibilities of who Andreas could've sent.

He smirked. "You'll find that out in due time, Theodora. But my intel said things were getting too dangerous for you and the human. So I came to make sure you were okay since I couldn't get in contact with you."

Theo held up her hands. "Yeah, they made us give up our devices and replaced them with their own phones."

"Of course they did."

Drumming her fingers along the center console, Theo gestured to the GPS screen in the car. "We have a lot to talk about, but first we need to go to Old Burial Hill in Marblehead and meet Aiden first."

Surprise flitted over the older vampire's face. "You made a friend, Theo? I'm so proud." Sarcasm dripped from his words as one hand clutched his chest like a proud parent.

Theo couldn't help but grin and flip him off. "Whatever. Aiden's my..." *No.* She wouldn't tell him about the mate thing yet. "My partner in the race. He just got beat up by one of Max's goons, and I need to find him, and then we need to find the Solis Occasum." She released a heavy sigh, leaning back into the seat, her eyes on the dark street ahead of them. "Although you just ruined any chance I have at getting a clue as to where it is."

Andreas took his eyes off the road for a moment and cast her a sneaky smile. "Or did I? Maybe I know more than you think."

After a minute of silence, she shrugged and crossed her arms over her chest. "Fine. Be secretive then. I don't know how Davina stands you half the time." The man was a little too much like a father at times, which made her react like a daughter.

"Ah, it's not a hardship, let's say that."

Theo groaned.

They pulled up to one of the oldest cemeteries in New England. Aiden sat on the steps that led to the hill with the gravestones, his leg bouncing.

"There he is!" Theo pointed to him, barely able to contain her elation.

She felt Andreas studying her out of the corner of her eye. "Something's different about you, Theo, and I think I know what it is."

"We're not talking about that right now." She swung the door wide open before Andreas even put the car in park.

Aiden leaped up from his spot on the stairs, relief splashed across his handsome face. Not wasting any time, Theo ran to him, jumping into his arms. She wrapped her legs around his waist and her arms around his neck. It was as if she couldn't get close enough to him.

He was so warm, so alive. She squeezed her eyes shut in thanks, happy to be enveloped in him again.

"Thank God, Theo. I was worried sick," Aiden spoke into her hair as he kissed the side of her temple, smoothing his hand over her head, her tresses, to her back, squeezing her tightly against him.

"Me too. Me too," she murmured.

His muscles tensed around her. "Who's that?"

Slowly she disentangled herself from Aiden, turning toward Andreas, who'd gotten out of the car, watching them with such a smug expression. "That's Andreas."

"*The* Andreas?"

"In the flesh." Andreas reached forward and shook his hand. "I'm here to help as much as I can, and we can start by getting the hell out of here. Come on." He walked around to the driver's side of the car. "I'll explain on the way."

Aiden looked to Theo, and she nodded. "We can trust him."

And then they slid into the back seat like a bunch of teenagers.

"Oh, I see how it is. No one's going to sit up front with me? You're going to make me feel like I'm the dad dropping off my kid at a middle school dance, huh?"

"Sorry, Andreas." Theo shrugged while beaming. She felt lighter than she had in days. Twisting toward Aiden, she dropped her voice. "Are you okay?"

"I'm okay," he answered softly with a smile, taking her hand in his. His gaze flicked to Andreas. "I didn't expect an ancient vampire to have jokes to be honest."

"I like to stay current with the times. No one likes a crusty vampire," Andreas joked.

Everyone laughed. It felt good to be together, for everyone to be okay.

Theo knew she shouldn't tighten her grip considering Aiden's wounds, but she did, careful to avoid the raw edges of his knuckles. Leaning her head against his shoulder, she fought back a smile. Andreas caught her gaze in the rearview, arching a brow in question, but neither said anything.

The interrogation was coming, though. Andreas loved sticking his nose all up in everyone's business, especially hers and his other vampire children.

"So about the Solis Occasum," Theo began.

It could've been a trick of the light, but she swore she saw his fingertips tense around the steering wheel. "Right. Well, the thing is you're going to hate me, and I've tried to put it off for as long as I could. But now...now I have quite the story to tell."

Theo sat up. "Then you better start telling it, Andreas."

"Well, I'm what is known as a Guardian."

She tilted her head to the side, feeling her face scrunch in confusion. "Like of the galaxy with that tree guy and raccoon? I'm not following..."

The man who sired her, who gave her a chance at revenge, at some sort of life after death, released a heavy sigh that encapsulated them in the car.

"No, although I do feel cheated to not have my own tree or raccoon sidekick. No. Guardians are...how do I put this? We are highly guarded, no pun intended, secrets. We are vampires who were created by the Old One, the first original vampire."

Theo's jaw dropped. Andreas was...he was definitely old. "So... I..." She struggled to find words. "Okay. So you know the first vampire?"

He nodded. "I do. Orion is thousands of years old and is actually not as stuffy as one would think. The story around his creation, though, is shrouded in mystery—no one really knows how he came to be. All we know is that after he was created, the Old One saw a need for checks and balances and more. So as a part of that plan, I was created as the Guardian of Revenge."

Goose bumps dotted Theo's arms as she recalled the night Andreas came to her. "I always knew you turned me because you understood my need for retribution, but I don't..." She shook her head. "I still don't understand."

"It's been my job for centuries. To ensure innocents get their revenge. Sometimes it requires turning them into vampires—that's a last resort. But other times, I'm simply a guide." Andreas paused a beat before speaking again, looking at Aiden in the rearview mirror. "So, Aiden, your last name is Archer, correct?"

He stiffened next to Theo. "Yeah. Why do you ask?"

"Because Orion also chose certain human lineages to become Guardians, one being the Archer family, the Guardians of Balance, the Guardians of the Solis Occasum. The very chalice you seek now."

23

AIDEN

"Come again with that?" Aiden leaned forward so he could better see Andreas's face.

The older vampire, Guardian, whatever the hell his title was, pulled off onto a dirt path, clicking buttons on the dashboard of the car. The ground opened up right before their eyes, revealing a large, descending vehicle ramp.

As Andreas guided the car into the darkness, lights flicked to life along the drive. The earth closed back up behind them, and then they were in some sort of underearth garage.

"It's true. The Old One felt things had gotten out of hand, so he decided there needed to be balance, thus the cure for vampirism was created. At first, this was well-known and common knowledge, but a large fraction of vampires hated that, hated being weakened in any sort of way; as you see, humans also used this knowledge."

A very loud, very stunned gasp came from Theo. Clearly, she'd been in the dark about all the information as well.

Andreas went on. "So a large group of vampires hunted down the Archers, the Guardians chosen century after century, and slaughtered them, eventually erasing the knowledge of the cure, leaving only the chalice, which your family has guarded...some unknowingly."

Aiden clenched his jaw, struggling to make sense of everything. This felt like something out of a movie, not a moment in his actual life. The soft touch of Theo's hand in his kept him grounded at least.

Once the car parked, they all emptied out into the underground garage, a white door before them.

Andreas faced him. "*You* actually guarded the Solis Occasum at one point in time, Aiden. I looked into you, and I know what happened to you and your fiancée. I'm truly sorry for your loss. The vampire that took the chalice from you was hired by Max to do so. He was a Tracker, one who was killed by Max as soon as he handed over the chalice."

Dizziness struck Aiden in a wave. He rubbed his temples and began pacing in front of the car in the dimly lit garage. How could any of this be possible? Then again, vampires and witches were real.

He turned to the Guardian. "I didn't have the Solis Occasum at any point in time. I...I don't understand."

Andreas was quick to answer. "Magic cloaks it and makes it appear normal—it could've appeared to you as an old goblet tucked away in a box somewhere. You couldn't see it before because your magic wasn't activated."

That made sense, but then another thought struck him. "So are you saying Cassidy was killed because of me? I already carry so much guilt because I couldn't save her, and now I learn it was also because I had a stupid chalice that I didn't even know about?"

Andreas moved in front of him, a strangely calming presence. "Your predecessor died without teaching you the ways of guardianship, and thus it fell to you without knowing. The Solis Occasum knows and will transport to the next Archer worthy of the cause, but once lost from their clutches, you must fight to get it back or lose it forever."

"Where was it then? So the vampire knew to find me because he was a Tracker? I guess they have special abilities, too, then?"

"Yes, and Max had been waiting for this for years. As you know, he has endless resources and time. The Tracker located the Solis Occasum in the house you'd bought with Cassidy and wanted to ensure you didn't return—that's why he attacked you on the street."

A hand held up to halt his words, Theo interrupted. "Wait a minute... So how did he not know he had the chalice then?" Her brows furrowed in confusion.

"The chalice makes itself known to its owner on the first full moon of ownership, if the Guardian hasn't already discovered it. A Messenger was dispatched—"

Aiden shook his head. "A Messenger? We have Guardians and Trackers and now *Messengers*?"

Andreas chuckled. "The vampire world is very intricate, but yes. A Messenger is similar to a Guardian, but they are to help communicate destinies. Unfortunately, the Messenger sent to you was murdered shortly before you were attacked. That night was to be the night everything was to be revealed to you, which is why Max chose then to strike." The Guardian blew out an unsteady breath. "And of course, once Max got the chalice, a lot of things happened, which we'll get to eventually. But the moment you applied for the show, he knew he had to have you. Had to erase another Archer from the earth." Andreas paused, his expression turning hard. "We need to get the Solis Occasum from Max as soon as possible. He's already abused its power."

Aiden's mouth went dry, his body tensing. "It's been used?"

"Yes. Max had the most powerful witch, Alecto Bloodthorn, enchant it so that it could be used as many times as he wanted... and has since killed her and her entire lineage, so the spell can never be replicated. He's mixed different blood types in it in order to gain different abilities. I don't know if you all watched *Forever After*, but if so, you'll recall Ruelle, the werewolf that was found dead."

Aiden and Theo nodded slowly.

"That was all Max. He needed her blood. Now he's able to shape-shift. I believe his ultimate plan is to become indestructible, which you already know is dangerous given how evil he is. Brandt is helping him, hoping for the same prize, so they both are problems right now. That's why Brandt kept trying to take you both out. That was his job."

A thunderous look crossed over Theo's face. "I have so many questions, but Andreas, why didn't you tell me about the chalice? Especially after knowing how badly I wanted to be human again."

"I couldn't tell you then, but I've since gotten special clearance for you and, apparently by proxy, your mate." Andreas's eyes went wide, quickly realizing his error. "I apologize—"

Aiden's heart raced. Sure, he'd been falling for Theo, but not once had she mentioned anything about mates. He whirled toward Andreas. "*Mate*? What do you mean by that?"

Theo let out an awkward chuckle. "It's a funny story, really."

"Let's tell it inside instead of this dusty garage," Andreas said on a cringe as he ushered them to the door, mouthing a "Sorry" to Theo, thinking Aiden wouldn't see, but he totally did. Theo looked chagrined, and Aiden just wanted to know what was going on.

They stepped inside a bright, crisp, and clean white entryway and followed Andreas to a sitting room decorated as if it belonged in a magazine spread—white walls, rugs, brick fireplace, couch, chairs, the only pops of color being red pieces like pillows or candles. Andreas folded himself into a chair that was fit for royalty, which now made total sense considering his age and station. Aiden remained standing. He was too amped to sit, to be still.

Theo moved in front of the fireplace; her mouth twisted like she'd tasted something sour. She met his stare. "Okay, so...I suppose I should just come right on out and say it. You're my mate."

Aiden tilted his head. "What do you mean by that, though?"

There were so many possibilities. He'd watched a lot of vampire movies, but none of them really covered the realities he currently faced.

Theo found something random on the wall to look at as she answered. "Vampires have soul mates, and when they meet them... at some point, their hearts start to beat faster than usual, and then when you drink from a mate, their blood is unrivaled."

Although he was aggravated, Aiden couldn't help but ask, "Was mine?"

"You drank from him?!" Andreas rumbled.

Theo bit her lip. "It was unlike anything I've ever tasted..." And then she looked at Andreas and rolled her eyes. "And yes, *Dad*. I drank from him. I had to, or I would've died." She swung her gaze back to Aiden. "But I'm sorry for not telling you. I didn't know if I should because, well, we both want the Solis Occasum, and I won't even be a vampire for long enough for it to matter, you know?"

Ouch. Hearing Theo minimize their connection like that stung. Surely she couldn't be so clueless about the depths of his feelings for her? He let loose a staggered breath. "It matters to me, Theo. That's the part that stings."

She took a step toward him, and he held a hand up. "Let's...let's just focus on the chalice and forget about everything else, yeah?" Of course. Mates or not—whatever that meant—here they were, each vying for the chalice.

Andreas shifted, clearly uncomfortable. He spread his hands along the arms of the chair. "Good idea. Although, you really should talk about the mate thing afterward because"—he skewered Theo with a look—"it's kind of a big deal."

"It is. I just didn't want it to be at this point in my life," Theo conceded with a sigh, meeting Aiden's stare.

It was as if she held his heart in her fist and crushed it to dust. No, he wasn't in love with her, but he was well on the way, falling for her more each and every moment. The danger they'd just experienced had shown that to him quite clearly. This was a woman he could easily love, someone he *wanted* to love, and he hadn't thought that was possible again after Cassidy.

A new wave of guilt crashed into him, causing him to stumble back into the sofa and sit. He wanted to put his head in his hands, to be an ostrich, ducking into the dirt, but wants and needs were two entirely different things, and what he needed to do right now was act.

His voice held a deadened air, like a stale room that'd been closed up for some time. "So the vampire who killed Cassidy was hired and then killed by Max."

"Yes."

"Then I need to go after Max."

"*We* need to go after Max," Theo added.

He couldn't do this alone, even though he didn't want to be around someone who made him feel the way she did—the good and the bad. Bad, like her not telling him they were mates. He didn't know if he believed in all of that, but he would've at least liked an opportunity to try. But she'd shut it down, which was fine. It was her prerogative, and he'd respect it. And he'd learn from it too.

Aiden nodded at Theo, giving in. Relief caused her to hunch slightly, reminding him of a deflated balloon. "I still don't understand how my predecessor just...sent me a magic chalice, though."

Andreas leaned forward, putting his elbows on his bespoke pant-covered knees. "You already know it has been guarded by your family for centuries, whether vampire or human. Your predecessor may not have taught you what you needed to know, but they were able to send it to you before their final breath, thus keeping it intact. You see, you have magic in your blood, dear boy."

After Aiden straightened, something buzzed in his veins—was it the magic Andreas spoke of? If vampires hadn't stepped out into society, he wouldn't believe this moment, but as it was, he would pretty much believe anything supernatural.

"*Magic?*"

Andreas nodded slowly. "I can teach you how to awaken it if you so wish, to truly embody what it means to be a Guardian."

Theo sat down on the couch, far enough away from Aiden so that they didn't touch, wringing her hands. "So if we don't stop Max, he'll basically have free rein. He'll become too powerful to kill."

"Yes, exactly. And the same goes for Brandt, if, somehow, he manages to best Max. Which, although he's older, I highly doubt will happen. Now we need to beat them at their own game. The Solis Occasum is actually in Transylvania—"

Aiden and Theo both scoffed at the same time, sheepish expressions on their faces at the jinx.

"Let me guess, it's at Dracula's castle?" Aiden grinned.

"Yep," Andreas said with a shrug as he stood.

Aiden had only been joking, so the Guardian's answer rendered him momentarily speechless.

"Okay, so what, we just go to Transylvania and storm the castle while the show's filming in Ireland?" Theo asked, wiping her hands on her thighs. Nervousness radiated from her in waves.

"Not exactly. Tomorrow we have some work to do first, work that must be done quickly while they're in Ireland. Then, we'll go to Transylvania." Andreas rose from his seat. "Sunrise will be here sooner than you think. We retire for the night, and tomorrow we move." He strode toward a well-lit hallway. "Allow me to show you to your rooms."

The rest of the house appeared to match the living room, Theo studying it openmouthed. "How come I didn't know about this place?" she asked, her voice filled with awe.

"Only Davina..." He turned to Aiden and added, "My mate knows of this place. It's my safe house should I need it, which I haven't in a long time. She's actually the one who decorated it." He stopped outside a door. "Aiden, this is your room, and Theo, yours is right..." He spun to point to a door across the hall. "Here. I'll rise at sunset tomorrow, and we will begin. Good night."

And then he transformed into a bat, squeaking and wings flapping, as he disappeared down the hallway.

Aiden shifted to face Theo, pausing at the door. An awkward tension hung between them like rotten fruit. What was he supposed to say? Words eluded him, but as he gripped the handle, he winced, the pain from his knuckles still all too fresh. He didn't even want to know what his face looked like. That security guard had been a brute.

Theo rushed forward, her hands enveloping his as if it were a baby bird. "We need to get you patched up, Aiden."

Tenderness burned in Aiden's chest, in the hand that Theo held. As much as he wanted to push her away for hurting him, not really understanding anything between them with all the mixed signals and stolen moments and occasional resentment thrown in, he found he couldn't deny her.

He relented, allowing his fingers to wrap around hers. "Lead the way."

A smile curved her delicate lips, and she turned toward her bedroom door, guiding them inside. The room was like the rest of the house, although a large coffin—probably the largest Aiden had ever laid eyes on—sat centered in the middle of the room, raised up to about hip level. A rich onyx, it provided a startlingly beautiful contrast to the room. Propped open, it revealed a lavish burgundy interior with two plush pillows. In the corner, tucked against the wall, sat a sofa laden with more pillows in a rainbow of colors, almost clashing with the coffin. A short hallway led to what appeared to be the bathroom.

Theo didn't let go of his hand as she ushered them that way, flipping on lights as she went. Mirrors surrounded them in the bathroom, a large sunken tub in one corner, a shower behind the door, and a pristine gray marble-topped vanity with two sinks spaced far apart in the other, another door leading to the toilet.

"Take a seat right here, and I'll get you hooked up." Theo pointed to the lip of the tub, letting go of him to walk over to the medicine cabinet. After rummaging in there for a minute, she returned with bandages, antibacterial salve, and a wet washcloth.

Sitting next to him, she brought her fingers to his face, turning it so she could see it better, and began wiping gently at the cuts across his cheek and forehead. Her touch was so gentle it was as if he'd imagined it. But no, Theodora was right in front of him, her gaze locked onto his wounds, her hands cleaning them, her mouth pursed in concentration.

And he'd never wanted anything, *anyone* more in his life.

His breathing turned ragged as she moved closer, trying to better angle herself, but instead, her chest brushed against his arm, her softness making him want to bite his fist.

"Be still, Aiden. You're squirming," she whispered, as if she knew how delicate the moment was and wanted to be careful not to shatter it.

"I can't help it with you brushing against me," he all but growled with desire, although he was trying his hardest to be a gentleman. The fact he knew what her breasts felt like, how perfect they were in his hands, how she liked her nipple tweaked, the way it made her back arch... It made things hard in more ways than one.

Theo froze her ministrations, lowering the washcloth as she cleared her throat. "Oh," she breathed. "Aiden..." The way she said his name was more like an invocation, a plea, and it nearly took his breath away. "I'm so sorry about everything. For not telling you about the mate thing. I was scared. I still am." She chuckled softly. "I'm terrified, actually."

His heart swelled, filling to the brim with hope. Could it be that she felt the same? "Of what?"

"Of this. Of us. Of *possibilities*."

24

THEO

THEO TOOK IN AIDEN'S VULNERABLE EXPRESSION, HIS GUARD HAVING finally lifted from earlier, and placed the washcloth to the side, her hands trembling in her lap. She wanted nothing more than to grab his face and kiss him or...well, run. That was another feeling snaking through her veins—but that had more to do with the fear she'd just spoken out loud. She still couldn't believe she'd actually admitted it, but it needed to be said. She felt horrible and really liked Aiden.

More than liked Aiden.

She could close her eyes and see him as her future. It frightened her since, as of a few days, even hours ago, her future only consisted of finding a cure for vampirism. Which apparently his family guarded. And her sire was a freaking Guardian of Revenge, and there was an Old One. Her mind spun with the knowledge of *all* of that.

Aiden placed a hand over hers, stilling them. "Theo, I really fucking like you."

Her gaze snapped up to his. "You do?"

He nodded, a slow, sexy smile tipping up those lips of his, highlighting the dark scruff that now dotted his gorgeous, chiseled face. "Hell, yeah, I do. We don't have to talk about it now, but I wanted you to know why I was upset earlier, that's all."

Their fingers threaded together. Theo scooted closer, pressing her forehead against his. "I like you too, Aiden."

"Imagine that." He smirked.

She couldn't help but laugh, but it was quickly silenced when Aiden's lips touched hers. It was teasing and tentative, and she quickly to deepened the kiss, slipping her tongue into his mouth.

A groan rumbled in his throat, and then it was on; his hands caged the sides of her face in a move she'd grown to adore.

They devoured each other, a hungry desperation rooted beneath each touch, each sigh, each flick of the tongue.

Theo moaned, and then Aiden drew her onto his lap, her legs hanging over one side. "I want all of you, Theodora. At least for tonight. Can I have that?" he whispered against her skin.

Tugging at the strands of his hair at his nape, she kissed him *hard*. "Yes. You can take whatever you want."

With those words, Aiden stood and carried her to the vanity, giving her bottom a squeeze before placing her on it. Due to how the bathroom was set up, she could see them from every angle, thanks to the surround-a-wall of mirrors. All these years of living, and she never knew that could be a kink for her.

She studied Aiden as he lifted his shirt, her hands instantly going to his chest, loving the feel of him, warm and taut beneath her fingertips. God, it wasn't fair how good this man looked.

"I don't think I could ever get enough of this," she murmured, pressing her lips to the expanse of skin as he stood between her legs.

Aiden gave her a wolfish grin in response. "I feel the same way," he said before capturing her mouth again. It felt like he poured everything he had into that kiss, as though he was wrenching something from her and weaving it with his own essence.

Wrapping her legs around his waist, she yanked him against her body, loving the way he fit her perfectly. He rocked against her core, causing her grip on him to tighten as she nuzzled into his neck, kissing and licking him there. Proving she was pretty fantastic at multitasking, she began to unbutton his pants and then shoved them down.

He smiled against her lips and returned the favor but only pulled her jeans off. He kept her underwear on. For the first time ever, she was about to get it on while wearing something other than her stretched-out granny panties. Instead, she sported a sexy little red lace G-string. It had given her an extra kick of confidence for her task today. And now, it had been even more worth it for that look on Aiden's face.

His eyes darkened into two pools of lust, pupils eating up the forest-green irises as he tucked his bottom lip between his teeth. The move made him look entirely too sexy, especially when he scrubbed his chin with his thumb.

"Damn, Theo. I like you in anything or nothing, but that's—" He shook his head, his jaw working as his eyes tracked over her body hungrily. "I don't know what to do first."

"Do me and watch." She gestured to the mirrors surrounding them. "From all the angles."

She lifted her brows and wagged them a little, riding an incredible high, sitting there in her T-shirt and G-string and watching a man like Aiden get so worked up for her, and they'd barely touched.

Intoxicating was what it was.

"Fuck," he grated out. "You're killing me, gorgeous."

And then he kissed her once again, hard and full, before lifting her shirt over her head, a growl erupting from his throat at the sight of her in her matching red bra. She smirked at him but he didn't play fair. He dipped his mouth to the swell of her breasts, running his tongue along the edge of the fabric—so close but not where she needed him the most. She tugged his hair as she arched her back to give him better access, all but begging him for more. Instead of undoing her bra, he shoved the cups down.

"I like seeing you undone for me," he rasped as he palmed her breasts, thumbing the nipples. He lowered his mouth to each bud to bite and lave. The slight sting shot straight to her core.

"You have no idea how sexy you are," Aiden panted against her skin as he kissed her neck, his hand sneaking its way down her stomach, burning a searing path the entire way. She squirmed with anticipation and awe at finally having this man. They'd done other things, and while those had been amazing, she *needed* this.

She gasped as he gripped the inside of her legs, spreading her wider. His thumbs were on the top part of her thighs as he toyed with the edge of her soaked underwear. Heat coiled in her core as one side of his mouth kicked up. If he didn't move that hand or his cock between her legs she was sure she would die.

With a quick flick of his fingers, he unfastened the snaps of her bra, allowing the straps to fall down her shoulders like wilted petals. She wasted no time in getting the bra off and throwing it to some distant part of the bathroom.

A pleased hum sounded in Aiden's throat before he leaned her against the mirror at her back, in a reclining position where she was on better display. Nearly *all* on display save for the tiny scrap of fabric that made up her G-string. His ravenous mouth began to kiss her from the middle of her chest to where he held her firmly at her thighs, his fingers a welcome and delicious pressure there.

When he knelt slightly so he could kiss at the top of her underwear, she sucked in a deep breath as she tried to move, to get some sort of relief for the ache building within her. He nipped at the string on one side before snapping it completely, a sexy rumble erupting from him as he did so. Her hands flew to the vanity top, clutching it as she bucked with the movement, his finger thrusting into her.

"Aiden," she breathed.

He looked up at her, sin and temptation dancing in his heated stare. "I want to hear more of those filthy little noises you make, gorgeous."

Not giving her a chance to reply and with her underwear half on, he moved his mouth to her clit. Her pulse skittered as he pressed open mouth kisses there over the flimsy fabric before ripping it off completely. He licked her bundle of nerves, causing her chest to heave with feverish pants before he sucked on the nub. Theo held him there between her legs, her hands moving frantically in his hair as needy moans fell from her lips. She bucked against his mouth as he filled her with another thick finger. Low, rough grunts vibrated against her skin as Aiden devoured her and she could barely keep her heart contained in her chest.

When she happened a glance at the mirror on the other side of Aiden's head, she felt herself grow even wetter at the sight of his muscles bunching and flexing as he brought her to the brink. Pleasure spiked through her body as colors started to swirl behind her eyelids. Then it stopped, and Aiden backed away giving her a wicked smile.

"When you come, I want it to be around my dick," he said as he shoved off his underwear, his cock springing to attention.

Oh yes.

Theo licked her lips at the sight of his length, scooting closer to the edge of the countertop. Aiden stroked himself once—one long, hard stroke—and it made Theo whimper.

"You want this?" Aiden's voice was guttural as he fisted himself again.

"Yes. Yes, I want it. So bad," she whined.

He brought the tip of his cock to her entrance, sliding it through the slickness there. Theo gripped his shoulders, her nails biting into his skin. With his free hand, Aiden tweaked her nipple, a sweet sting shooting all the way to her core. She arched her body, nearly lifting off the countertop.

He brought that hand around her waist, yanking her to him before he slid inside her, filling her to the hilt. A gasp tumbled from her lips as her head fell to his shoulder, so wonderfully helpless against his perfect thrusts that made her entire body shake.

She breathed in the scents of ocean and sunshine from him and they made her even more desperate for him. For this man who'd crept beneath her skin, her barriers, her *everything*.

It excited her that he remembered she liked it rough, as he slammed into her, a choked groan wrenched from him with each movement. The erotic image surrounded them in the mirrors. She trailed her nails down his back, scratching his skin, before she dug them into his backside, pulling him even deeper. She'd never been a loud lover, but Aiden brought it out of her, making her moan, and whimper, and scream, as he led her to the edge again. Her head grew dizzy, her body coiling ever tighter as she tumbled over into the oblivion.

Her fangs extended. She wanted to bite him at that moment and licked her lips, dying for the taste of him. Aiden thrust into her so hard her breasts bounced, the feeling wild and untamed, exactly what she loved, and then he kissed her, *hard*.

"Bite me, Theo. Fucking do it," he growled against her sweat-slicked skin, playfully biting her neck, sending another shock to her throbbing core.

That was all she needed. She yanked his neck to her mouth, her teeth piercing the curve of his unravaged shoulder, that vivid burst of flavor and emotion riding on the blood that she drank deeply. Blood that she now knew was bursting with magic.

It was a heady thing, knowing the very essence of Aiden filled her, gave her life. Aiden tensed beneath her and he thrusted harder with a husky groan before finding his release.

She opened her eyes. The tableau meeting her on every side had her getting turned on all over again, ready and desperate for another round. Her memory went back to the night he had her on her hands and knees, and she wanted that too. She wanted it all with Aiden, and that was the problem.

25

AIDEN

THE NEXT NIGHT, AIDEN MET ANDREAS IN THE LIVING ROOM AFTER receiving a summons from the Guardian. He'd left Theo's room when her chest began to burn, alerting her it was time to get into the coffin. Of course, he wanted nothing more than to slip inside it with her, to hold her and nuzzle her.

But he was a human, and she was a vampire, and they were both seeking to become someone else. None of that mattered to his heart.

His emotions were still raw, as if everything he felt was on display as he approached Andreas.

"She cares for you, Archer," the Guardian said by way of greeting, standing from his seat near the fireplace that was filled with white Christmas lights instead of a fire.

Aiden had forgotten vampires were a little skittish around open flames.

As he shook Andreas's hand, he murmured a noncommittal "hmmm," not really sure what to say to the person who was basically like Theo's vampire dad.

"It's true—she does. I've known her for quite some time, and she's never been this way about...anything really. The mate bond never lies, Archer."

Aiden gave him a half smile. "Once we get the Solis Occasum, the bond won't matter."

Andreas got this dark, deep look in his copper eyes. "So you've given up on your own quest for revenge?"

He blew out a breath, scrubbing a hand over his head. "Not exactly. It's just...whatever happens when we find the chalice, I want Theo to be happy. I'm starting to realize that's one of my top priorities."

"The Solis Occasum belongs to you by right. What happens to it is ultimately up to you, which is why I've called you down here." He shifted his feet. "I've asked that Theo give us time to work, as I think we'd have better luck succeeding on our quest if we work on awakening your magic. That is, if that's something you want?"

Is it? Aiden had focused so solely on becoming a vampire these past three years that any other option hadn't really crossed his mind.

"I'd do anything to defeat Max. He's the reason Cassidy's dead."

Andreas gave him a quick nod. "I believe the lair will be a better place then. Davina would kill me if I scorched the pillows she picked out, although I'd love nothing more."

Aiden snorted, trying to imagine this ancient vampire arguing with his mate. It shocked him a little that the phrase came to mind when thinking of Theo. But it felt natural, right, to think of her as that. What it meant for the future, he wasn't sure. But now wasn't the time to overanalyze things.

The Guardian led him into another wing of the underground base, into a gray room with plenty of space in the center. Along one wall were various weapons, ranging from primitive to technological, and against the opposite side were weights, punching bags, everything needed for a small but decent home gym.

Andreas stopped in the middle of the room, motioning for Aiden to stand in front of him. "All right. First, you'll need to touch me."

Aiden's brows dipped. "Where?"

Shifting into a wider stance, Andreas crossed his arms over his broad chest. "Anywhere."

Aiden's lips twisted to the side in thought before he reached out and grasped Andreas's wrists.

"Now, from here, you're going to manipulate my mind to put me in a trance. This is very important—when you use this magic, those you use it on are under its power for approximately an hour. To break the trance before that, you need to touch them again and simply ask them to wake. The person who put them in a trance must be the person waking them if it's within the hour time frame. Remember this so that you can wake me up afterward."

That sort of knowledge made Aiden's stomach turn. A trance? Shit. That was a lot of power. "Okay. So how do I make you, you know, go into said trance?"

Andreas chuckled. "Patience. You'll simply say 'duratus,' which means freeze. Then you can manipulate their emotions. Whatever emotion you want to take over, you speak it while touching that person. It's as simple as that, really. The power is in the tongue. Without voicing your intentions, nothing happens." He paused a moment, eyeing Aiden seriously. "Got it?"

Aiden lifted his hands. "Wait a minute. How is this any different from the way vampires put people in a trance?"

The Guardian's brows jumped all the way to his hairline. "How do you know about that?"

His eyes widened. He hadn't meant to rat Theo out. Andreas studied him carefully, his head tilting a little to the side before he rubbed his chin. Meanwhile, Aiden said nothing. He'd already said too much as it was.

Suddenly Andreas snapped his fingers. "Theo. That's how you

know. Obviously. Then you know that's a secret you take to your grave unless you want to meet it earlier, yes?"

Aiden nodded, raising his chin. "Yes."

"Fine. I'm glad that's settled." He blew out a breath, although his shoulders still seemed to bunch up to his ears with tension. "Your power is different. It allows more manipulation, yet there's a time limit if that makes sense. With ours, there are no limits, aside from the fact that it can't be used on other vampires."

"That makes sense."

The Guardian rolled his shoulders a few times and then stood before him. "Now, are you ready?"

"I am." He tightened his grip around Andreas's wrist, narrowing his eyes. "Duratus."

A rush of electricity, power, *something* surged through his veins, but then it sputtered out before reaching his fingertips. Andreas still watched him intently.

"Clearly it didn't work," Aiden attempted to joke. He pulled his hand away and flexed his fist a few times, the phantom warmth and power still buzzing as if begging to be set free.

Andreas lifted a shoulder, unperturbed. "That's to be expected. I suspect your power was awakened when Theo drank from you— something about the mate bond, possibly. It's understandable you wouldn't grasp this right away." He extended his wrist once more. "Try again."

Not one to give up easily, Aiden tried again, attempting to focus as he gripped the vampire's wrist. "Duratus."

The same rush raced through him, but to no avail. He dropped the Guardian's arm and took a step back.

"What now?"

Silence stretched between them as Andreas circled him, tapping his chin as if in deep thought. He even let out a little "Hmm," as he sized Aiden up.

"I think I know exactly what we need." After digging his cell phone from his pocket, he fired off a quick text. He lifted a finger into the air as he directed his attention to the door. "It'll be just a moment, and we'll try again."

Aiden shifted back and forth. He shoved his hands in his pockets as he watched the door, wondering what Andreas's solution would be. He was the oldest vampire Aiden had ever encountered, so he sure hoped the man knew what to do. If anyone did, it would be him.

After a minute or two, the door opened and in walked Theo. It appeared she'd been up awhile and showered, since her hair still hung about her shoulders in damp tendrils. A smile curved Aiden's lips as he met her eye. She returned his grin with a brilliant, beaming one of her own. She shot him a wink before turning to the Guardian.

"You rang?"

The older vampire nodded. "I think there's a connection between Aiden's magic and you two being mates. There has to be since it was awakened when you drank from him." His eyes widened slightly. "So what Aiden needs is focus, and I believe you're the key."

Theo stepped to Aiden's side, playfully bumping his shoulder. "Focus, huh? I think I can help with that."

It actually made sense. Aiden's mind raced when he tried to bring forth his magic before, and Theo always brought such clarity.

"Let's get at it, then," he said as he took the Guardian's wrist in his.

Theo moved in closer, her floral scent enveloping him, putting his mind at ease. He closed his eyes, focusing on the woman he'd fallen in love with. His mate. The realization of what he felt for Theo, something that had been seeping into his bloodstream since that night she hissed at him when they met, nearly knocked him off his feet. He drew in a deep breath in an attempt to steady himself, to allow his epiphany to fuel him. Again, magic shot through his bloodstream, this time more powerful than before, and instead of sputtering out, he felt it all the way to his fingertips.

But it didn't quite work.

His gaze flicked to Andreas's, hoping he'd have an answer. A smile balanced on the man's lips. "That's more like it. Keep focusing on her. You'll get it."

Theo placed a hand on his shoulder, belief etched into the planes of her face. That alone made him feel like the most powerful man in the world. Wasn't that how love worked? That it made people feel as though they could do anything? Sure, they hadn't exchanged the words yet, but he knew she loved him just as he knew he needed his next breath.

He dipped his chin. "I can do it this time. I *will* do it this time." He pulled in a deep inhale through his nose and released it before taking Andreas's wrist once more.

Thoughts of Theo swarmed his mind, taking root. Her hard-fought smiles, her twinkling blue eyes, her snarky attitude. The magic raced forward, and a feeling akin to being lit up from the inside warmed his entire body. His pulse quickened as he finally spoke the word—"Duratus."

Just as the Guardian explained earlier, his eyes remained open, and he continued to stand, his movements completely frozen in place. A glazed-over look rolled over his face. Aiden released his hand and circled him, studying the effects of this magic.

It was strange to see the vampire so still, so he quickly touched Andreas's forearm and said, "Wake."

The Guardian blinked a few times and then met Aiden's wide-eyed stare.

"You did it!" Theo shouted as she wrapped her arms around him. She nuzzled into his neck as she gripped him closer. "I'm so proud of you."

Happiness spread through his chest, the feeling nearly enough to make him dizzy.

"Well done, Aiden. Very well done," Andreas added, breaking through the haze.

Theo disentangled herself from him before he faced the Guardian.

"Pretty easy once you know what to do, yes?" Andreas asked. He moved so that he could lean against the wall.

"Surprisingly, yes." Aiden looked down at his hands. "So that's it?"

Andreas shrugged. "That's it."

"But..." He twisted his hands this way and that. "Nothing shot out from my hands, no sparks or anything."

Andreas shook his head. "How do you think magic works?"

He shrugged. "I don't know. I figured it would be like the movies, maybe? But this is still pretty amazing."

"Now time for you to learn to manipulate emotions, which is actually incredibly simple, especially now that you just did that." He tapped his wrist.

"Do I need to stay?" Theo looked between them. "I can if you want." She directed that last bit at Aiden.

A mischievous glint sparkled in the older vampire's eye as his gaze bounced between them. "I think it's best that you go now. I may need you to contact my spy."

Theo crossed her arms over her chest, canting her head. "*Spy*? And who would that be?"

There was only one way to describe the expression on Andreas's face—smug. Aiden tried to riffle through their days on the show, wondering who it could've been.

"Bridget," the Guardian answered without hesitation.

"Of course, that makes total sense." It was obvious now that he knew. Bridget was one of the only people in connection with the show who genuinely seemed to care what happened to him and Theo.

Theo didn't appear the least bit surprised, although he knew this was news to her as well. "I like her," was all she said.

Andreas pushed off the wall. "Bridget has worked for me for quite some time and is a very skilled spy. She's been checking in with me along the way on her secret cell phone." He swung his gaze to the other vampire in the room. "Theo, I need you to verify with her that our plan to storm the castle is still a go. She was to procure an ancient map showing a classified underground tunnel we can use to sneak inside the castle once we get there."

Straightening, Theo gave him a nod. "I'm on it." She took a few steps toward the door before turning around and shooting Aiden another grin. "You got this."

Then she slipped from the room.

"You sent Bridget to keep an eye on Theo?" Aiden met Andreas's stare.

A small smile curled his lips. "She's family. Davina and I will do anything we can to keep her safe."

Aiden's brow furrowed. "So did you know that there would be trouble on this show?"

Andreas shrugged, moving over to a table and fidgeting with the vials—bottles of poison—sitting there. "I had a feeling, especially after all that business that went on with *Forever After*." He looked up. "Enough about that. Do you have any other questions for me regarding your magic before we practice manipulating emotions?"

A thousand questions ran through Aiden's mind, but he managed to settle on one. "How do I send the Solis Occasum to my next relative?"

"Ah. That is an excellent question. Let's work on that, and work on emotion manipulation. Then, I'll teach you how to properly stake a vampire, since I have a feeling you may need that knowledge as a last resort."

After what felt like an eternity but was only roughly two hours, Aiden knew how to manipulate emotions, as well as how to send the chalice onward should anything happen to him. The magic pulsing in his body was an exhilarating feeling, but he was antsy, ready to get the chalice and avenge Cassidy.

Andreas straightened one of his cuffed sleeves. "You've done well today, Aiden. And now the time has come for us to round up Theo and make our way to the chalice."

"Andreas?"

The Guardian paused.

"Thank you. For this. For everything." Aiden meant it. Who knew where he'd be if it weren't for the older vampire?

"Of course." Andreas smiled, and they continued moving.

They met Theo in the living room. She stood up straighter when she locked eyes with Aiden and beamed at him. It was pretty much the best thing he'd ever seen, the way it illuminated her face so completely, brightening everything around her.

"Hey." He grinned.

"Hey, yourself." She moved toward him. "Everything go okay? I see you're still in one piece, so that's good."

Aiden opened his mouth to respond but was interrupted by Andreas.

"Let's go, lovebirds. We need to get to the jet if we want to get ahead of the show. They're filming in Ireland as we speak, but you know how Max is—things could easily change. We also need to talk about Brandt and put together a game plan for him because he's going to be a problem."

"Yeah, no kidding. He's allegedly five hundred years old." Theo looked at Andreas with a wince, holding up a hand. "No offense."

Andreas shrugged it off as he began to lead them to the jet, calling over his shoulder, "None taken."

Then they were off—headed to Dracula's castle to get a magical chalice that Aiden's family supposedly guarded. As if that wasn't strange enough, magic ran through his veins and he was in love with a certain sexy vampire who wanted to be a human.

And he still wanted to become a vampire. Sure, the magic helped things, but if he wanted ultimate revenge, he'd need to be at the top of his game. The only way to do that was to continue ahead as planned, although his feelings for Theo complicated matters *a lot*. Talk about understatement of the year.

A year ago, if someone had told him this would be his life, he would've laughed in their face.

Yet this was reality. Time to kill some evil vampires and retrieve the Solis Occasum.

26

THEO

"Ardeliu Castle isn't Dracula's castle," Theo announced, her face scrunched as she took in the castle's sign at the mouth of the forest.

"This is the *real* Dracula's castle," Andreas cut in, strapping two swords across his back and passing Theo and Aiden their own back scabbards for their weapons—Aiden received two machetes, his preference when Andreas had asked him during their brief training. "It's kept a secret from the human world as it's sort of a cult favorite among vampires. With that said, it's not going to be easy to get there. You have to go through the Forest of Nightmares —there's no way around it."

Aiden tightened his scabbard over his shoulders, his muscles popping with the movement, and Theo fought not to react to the glorious sight. "And let me guess. This forest is going to be filled with all kinds of nightmares?"

Theo pulled one sword from her holster, feeling better with at least one in her hand instead of both on her back.

Andreas grinned. "You got it. That's where you come in, Magic Boy. You're gonna do your thing, and I'll help where I can, of course."

Theo walked to the old, faded sign marking the beginning of the path. As she wiped her hands over it, it started to glimmer in the darkness—clearly spelled. She jerked her hand back as dread settled heavy in her chest. This was way out of their league. With a sigh, she looked at Andreas.

"Are you sure you shouldn't be the one leading the charge? You're a Guardian, so aren't you basically undefeatable?"

Leaves crunched underfoot as Andreas and Aiden joined her at the mouth of the forest.

The Guardian shook his head. "I'm not. I can be killed by someone who's done their homework, which I have no doubt our boy Max has. He'll know the task is a gruesome, difficult one."

Nerves fluttered through her stomach at the thought of anything happening to Andreas or Aiden. They still hadn't really talked about what happened the night before. Up until then, she knew she was falling for the man, but she hadn't expected to jump over the ledge cannonball-style, and be all in and utterly one hundred percent in love with Aiden. How could she not be? True, they shared a mate bond, but it felt even more profound than that, like their souls knew each other from the moment they were crafted.

Yet the love aspect complicated things in a big way, and if she were to become a human...would he still want her? Would he hate her for taking away his chance at revenge? If he were to become a vampire, she knew she'd still feel the same way about him. After all, she'd walked this earth for centuries, and now it was as if her eyes were opened for the first time in so very long. After her husband, she didn't think she'd ever find anyone who could make her feel so full of love and life ever again.

Closing her eyes, she thought of Jonathan and pressed a fist over her chest. She would love him for as long as she lived—vampire or not. But it was time, wasn't it? It was time to let him go, to allow his memory to bring her happiness, to recall his laughter instead of the dark moments leading up to when they'd been separated. Her revenge had been exacted, and now she needed to stop letting the guilt to rule her.

When she opened her eyes, Aiden watched her in the dimness, a small, tender smile on his face as if he knew. He shot her a wink, and she returned it before straightening, pushing her hair from her face.

"Well. Are we ready to kick Max's ass or what?" Theo asked.

"Let's do the damn thing." Aiden grinned.

Andreas turned serious as he took the first step into the forest. "Now, Aiden, you'll need to use your magic where you can. To do so will require you to get close enough to touch, therefore don't be afraid to utilize the weaponry you've been given. And Theo, you're a vampire. You know what to do."

She nodded in understanding.

The Guardian skewered them with a serious stare, everything about him taut lines and worry. "Before we go, I need to warn you about this place. The Forest of Nightmares supposedly will show you your greatest fear. Also, the forest can alter time—one minute may be an hour. Whatever happens at that point, don't stop. The path is dangerous. There are things that could lure us away, but no matter what, keep moving forward. There are cliffs throughout that are cloaked, and one wrong step could lead us right off the edge. Tiny glow beetles will light our way, leading us in the right direction. Once they can no longer be seen, then we are headed in the wrong direction." He paused. "Got it?"

Everyone nodded. Satisfied, Andreas swept forward.

Darkness enveloped them, the tall trees blocking the sky, the stars, *everything*, like a suffocating brown mass overtaking the land. The path could barely be called that, as it was a little dirt thing tread into the ground and only had enough room to pass one at a time in single file. Andreas led, Theo in the middle, and Aiden at the back. She knew why they'd put her in the middle, and she'd fight them on it eventually, but she needed to get her bearings first.

A fog rolled in, creeping about their legs like slithering snakes, blanketing their world in gray so they couldn't see more than a few yards in front of them. A very faint glow illuminated the path—Theo had to squint to make it out.

"I don't think magic will help this," Aiden said.

"Brilliant observation there," Theo snarked as she smiled.

At least it gave her a momentary reprieve to think about something, anything else. She wasn't exactly scared—she hadn't been frightened of much since losing everyone she loved—but now she stressed about her guys, and she worried she wouldn't be able to protect them. That last bit petrified her.

"At least there's noise in the forest," Theo began, as she zeroed in on several small, nonthreatening sounds like wolves, owls, the usual thing. "It's when the forest goes silent that we need to worry."

Andreas remained quiet as he led them slowly with a staff in his hand that materialized out of nowhere, using it to test the ground in front of him.

Suddenly, an eerie, high-pitched screech of doom shattered through the air. Chills broke out along her arms. The forest went dead silent.

Here we go.

"Well, get ready, kids. Shit's about to hit the fan," Andreas called to them.

The sound of Aiden unsheathing both machetes echoed around them, and Theo pulled her second sword from its scabbard.

"What was that creature, Andreas?" she hissed.

"I don't know. I've done a lot of strange stuff, but traipsing through a spelled forest is a first for me. But I would've had to do it whether or not you fell in love with the human, since he's the last of his line."

Shifting footfalls thudded behind her, and then Aiden touched her forearm softly—he'd moved his sword to his other hand.

"You love me?"

She opened her mouth to speak when the ground literally shook beneath them.

A chorus of "oh, shits" and "damns," and other curses that would make their mothers blush, erupted from the group as they struggled to remain steady-footed. The fog thickened, curling into tendrils like beckoning fingers.

Trees falling and hitting the earth had Theo shuddering again. An enormous figure appeared on the path before them, moonlight silhouetting him. Theo squinted and made out that it was some sort of giant troll creature. Tufts of unruly white hair protruded from skin as gray as concrete. He was shirtless and barefoot but wore torn, ratty brown pants. In his hands, he held something that looked like a meat tenderizer...except it was massive and would no doubt kill them easily in one fell swoop.

No problem. She could do this. She could handle this.

"Aiden, I'll distract while you do your thing," she whispered from the corner of her mouth.

"Theodora—" Andreas began. This, she was used to—his reticence for her to be put in danger of any kind.

She raised her hand, effectively cutting him off. "Andreas, let me do this. Have my back, okay?"

The creature began moving toward them, releasing primitive grunts, which made Theo a little nervous. Why? Because it wasn't the same noise they'd heard moments ago, that piercing, nightmarish shriek. No, that freakish question mark was still waiting for them somewhere in the depths of this hellscape.

Andreas released a beleaguered sigh but maneuvered so she and Aiden could pass. She liked that Aiden didn't fight her on this —that he took care of her, but gave her the space and support to be a badass when needed. Tossing her hair over her shoulder, she sashayed her way to the front. The giant troll creature looked at her with filmy eyes reminiscent of the old man in Poe's "The Tell-Tale Heart." Its lips split into a sadistic grin, revealing a gaping maw with two rows of jagged teeth, and a roar echoed into the night.

The scent of rot and wet earth writhing with maggots filled the air. Okay, so the monster wanted to play it that way. Theo didn't care. She'd already faced things more terrible than this—what could be worse than having her heart ripped from her chest? Yet she'd crawled from the carnage and found a way to live. She'd come out of this too.

"Smells like you need a breath mint or a *thousand*," Theo called, lifting her chin high, swords held at the ready at her sides, warmth at the knowledge that Aiden had her back.

The troll took a step closer, shaking the earth. The trees quivered, leaves swooshing in tandem. She heard Aiden's sharp inhale and Andreas curse. Apparently, the creature didn't like her remark on his stank-ass breath, and Aiden and Andreas didn't appreciate her humor. It was certainly an acquired taste.

The monster continued toward them. The ground trembled beneath her feet with each step it took, but she remained steadfast. This was bigger than her now. This was about Max being an asshole, a murderer, and she'd do whatever she could to get the Solis Occasum back in its rightful hands, which were Aiden's, and then she'd help him exact his revenge.

Tired of waiting, she ran forward, shrieking into the night sky, the sound wild and unfurling something even more feral inside her. Sword raised, she danced around his large feet, which looked as though they were made of rock. The thought made her stomach drop because what if that were the case? How would they manage to subdue him if they couldn't *wound* him?

She knew of the Romanian folklore of the *Uriaș*, giants who were supposedly friendly. But this creature definitely wasn't. On top of that, it looked like it'd been crafted straight out of the side of a mountain. There was only one way to find out.

Lifting her sword even farther over her head so she could gain some momentum, she swung it as hard as she could. But the sword didn't penetrate. Nope. Instead, it clanged off the troll's rock-solid ankle, sending Theo stumbling backward. The creature released another roar, the nauseating stench of its breath nearly making her gag.

"Theo!" Aiden's frantic voice echoed around her.

She looked up just in time to tuck and roll out of the way of the creature's foot. She would've been smashed for sure, and she had no interest in becoming the latest sneaker trend for the giant troll.

"I'll keep him busy. You find some way to touch him!" Theo yelled.

"Aiden, grab his ankle and hold on for your life!" Andreas directed.

Not taking her eyes off the creature, she called out to her sire, "Are you sure you can't do this, Andreas?"

"I don't have the same magic as Aiden. He has to be the one."

She grunted in aggravation but glanced over to Aiden and gave him a nod.

He looked intense and a little bit scary, which turned her on *a lot*. She'd question herself about that later, but for now, she had a troll's ass to kick. After she moved farther down the path, she let out a whistle, loud and ear-splitting, which caused the monster to throw its hands over its ears.

"Hey, this way, asshole!" she shouted.

He turned around and then immediately began his earth-shaking charge toward her, giving Aiden perfect access to the troll's ankle.

Bile rose in Theo's throat as she tried to split her focus—distracting the creature and watching Aiden, a mortal human, run and link his arms around a supernatural being's leg.

"Duratus!" Aiden yelled, the sound nearly a roar itself.

And nothing happened.

Well, something happened, but it wasn't what Theo expected. The troll swiped at his leg, narrowly missing Aiden. Her heart leaped into her chest as she fought for what to do. All she could come up with was to poke the bear, so to speak.

Aiden scrambled around the troll's foot, and she knew his focus had to be shot.

"Focus on me!" she called out as she rushed closer, waving her sword to grab the creature's attention. Her plan of attack wasn't the best, but it would have to work.

There was no answer, but she could make out Aiden shuffling and moving. Then she went for it. She jabbed at it, her sword clanging off his hardened skin. Like rock. This wasn't good at all.

Of course, that only angered the creature more, but at least he started swiping at her. Hopefully it gave Aiden the reprieve needed to focus and zero in on his new magic.

She danced around, poking the troll, both hands tight on her sword to keep the vibrations from clanging all the way to her teeth. Finally Aiden's voice broke through the melee.

"Duratus!" he shouted, his voice strong.

The troll froze, one foot stilled in the air midstride, hovering in midair. Seeing that it worked, Theo released a huge breath. Relief flooded her as Aiden leaped from the ankle, wiping his hands over his hair. Excitement danced across the planes of his face.

Theo sheathed her swords, adrenaline vibrating through her body. She ran to the man she loved, jumping into his arms.

"Holy crap, you did it, Aiden! You did it!" she said as she kissed his temples, his cheeks, and then his lips.

He pulled back, face flushed from exertion. His lips curved upward as he reached a hand to cradle her face. "We did it, Theo. We're a team, remember?"

Andreas broke through the haze, clapping Aiden on the back. "Excellent job, Archer. Now you know what else to do."

Aiden nodded and stepped back up to the troll. He placed a hand on the creature's foot, closing his eyes. Guttural, husky words fell from his lips. The air shimmered with magic, much like the sign had earlier. Theo felt its pull fall over her skin like an evening shawl.

"What's he doing?" she whispered, although she had a pretty good idea.

"Manipulating the troll's emotions. He'll make it so that if we're to come in contact with it again or any more of its kind, that we will not be seen as threats."

"And what, the two of you covered this in Magic 101 the other day?"

His lips quirked up into a smirk. "Something like that."

A moment passed before Aiden joined them again. His eyes glinted in the moonlight, sweat dotting his brow. He looked absolutely exhilarated.

"How did you do any of this, with your magic so new?" She couldn't help but ask.

Aiden lifted a shoulder. "You were in danger, and that's all I could focus on. I wanted to help you more than anything."

Not holding back, she pressed a kiss to his cheek. "Thank you," she whispered.

Andreas cleared his throat. "While I am incredibly grateful that you were able to use your magic, we still have miles to go. So we should probably get moving."

Talk about a mood killer.

"What else awaits us?" Aiden asked.

"Things much worse than that," Andreas said over his shoulder.

Oh, great.

27

AIDEN

AIDEN FLEXED HIS HAND, MAGIC STILL COURSING THROUGH HIS VEINS. He hadn't felt as powerful when he used it on Andreas. With the way it pulsed and thrummed, he expected to see some kind of spark flickering through his skin, but there was nothing in the darkness.

Another terrifying shriek straight out of his nightmares alerted them that something waited in the gloom.

Urgency drove his feet forward. They couldn't get to the castle soon enough. He was ready for all of this to be over. With each step he took, he worried it was one step closer to something happening to Theo, to a repeat of everything that happened with Cassidy.

That was normal behavior—to worry about the person you loved.

Because without a doubt love encapsulated everything he felt for the badass woman who taunted trolls and told them they needed breath mints. He cracked a smile at that, shaking his head.

The forest was still eerily silent around them. Fog shimmered red and thick as it rolled in so abruptly he suddenly could barely see the lights on the path to guide him, let alone see his hand in front of his face. It seemed to have swallowed Theo and Andreas. His heart raced at a staccato rhythm.

"Theo?" he shouted.

Nothing came back to him but that scary movie-level silence that could suffocate. He imagined all sorts of evils lurked in it. Where was Theo?

He kept moving, picking up his pace, narrowing his eyes so he could keep his gaze on the faint light. The faster he walked, the sooner he could find Theodora. She had to be ahead of him. He'd not heard her step off the path, nor Andreas. They all knew how dangerous it was to waver from the trail.

Aiden opened his mouth, about to call out for Theo again when the air shimmered before him. A sudden breeze swirled the golden glow into a blood red. He froze midstride, unsure of what was forming before him.

It was the chalice.

The cup took shape, and Aiden swore that if he reached forward, he would actually be able to touch it. Something had him keeping his hands by his side, though.

Then Theo appeared. She scooped up the chalice and then moved toward him, a feline smile curling her lips.

"Follow me, and we can put this all behind us, Aiden. We can both get what we want." Her voice was a little higher than usual.

Emotions warred within him—was this really Theo? This was an enchanted forest, after all. Where was Andreas? He knew she wouldn't leave him behind.

Theo stepped off the path, away from the dim glow of the beetles, and pitched the cup into the air. "We can have it all. We can be together, Aiden. Don't you want that?"

That sounded more like her tone of voice, which caused Aiden to straighten.

"Theo," he finally spoke.

She grinned—one of the ones that he loved so much—and canted her head. "Come to me, Aiden."

His feet moved of their own accord, right to the edge of the path.

Then Theo shimmered. Just like the dust that caused the chalice to form. Aiden blinked and shook his head, as if shaking away the spell of whatever pulsed through the woods here. It wasn't Theo before him. Instead it was what he could only describe as a bog creature, a thing of myths. She had dissolved into the bog where she stood, mud matting her hair, covering her face, but her sharp teeth—those were most noticeable as they were bloodstained.

With whose blood?

A shiver racked his body as he took a step back. The bog lining the one side of the path would've easily trapped him, making him this creature's dinner.

When he moved firmly back on the trail, the bog monster let out a piercing wail, her mouth opening so wide it was like an endless void. Goose bumps danced along his arms, and more than anything he wanted out. He needed to find Theo to make sure she was safe.

Fear threaded its way into his mind, tightening its hold until he could barely think. He started moving again, determined not to look to either side of the path that had now lightened a little.

Then the sound of Theo's screams shook him to his very marrow. The end of it was cut off with a gargled noise. Horrible images of blood spurting from her mouth filled his mind. Had she been lured off the path?

Acid coated his tongue as he ran toward the sound. Nausea churned in his stomach as his heart sank—he hadn't even had a chance to tell her he loved her.

"Theo!" he roared. The force with which he called her name hurt his throat, scratched it completely raw, but he didn't care. He needed to find her, to hold her.

"Aiden!" she yelled, her voice sounding broken, but...also not hers?

Pinpricks dotted the back of his neck, a strange awareness crawling over his body. He slid to a stop, squinting into the sea of red.

Andreas's voice broke through. "Keep moving!" he yelled. "It's what I told you—it's not real. *Fuck!*" That last word sounded wrenched with anguish. Aiden couldn't even begin to guess what the Guardian saw.

Genuine relief flooded through him as he walked faster. Theo was okay then. Something happening to her was his new greatest fear. He pulled in a deep breath, although it did nothing to settle his mind, his chest, his heart.

Although it went against everything inside him not to stop and investigate, he made himself race forward. He had to trust Andreas and keep moving for Theo. So when another broken cry of hers echoed through the red fog, he ignored it, clenching his hands into tight fists that drew blood from his palms. *It isn't real. It isn't her.*

And he continued that way, one foot in front of another. Desperate to remain on the path, he conjured forth other things to occupy his mind. He thought of Theo's laughter and the way her body felt against his, how they were a perfect fit. How when this was over, he'd do whatever he could to be with her. The idea strengthened him, allowing him to keep going.

Finally, the red fog dissipated in a fast rewind sort of motion, revealing a worn-looking Andreas and a tear-streaked Theo, pacing back and forth on the path—it was wider now, the trees not as ominous or foreboding. Behind them stretched a clearing, and then the castle.

But right now, he wanted to focus on the woman he loved, thankful she was okay.

"Theo!" he shouted as he jogged to meet her.

A grin lit up her face as his name, broken and bloody, left her lips. She slammed into him with force, her arms around his neck.

Her entire body trembled. The wetness of her tears was cool against his skin. He kissed her hair and held her tightly to him, reassuring himself she was real and unharmed—while hopefully doing the same for her.

"God, that was awful. I thought you were..." She shook her head, still gripping him firmly, pulling fistfuls of his shirt into her hands.

"I know. I know. I thought you were hurt or worse..." Aiden couldn't bring himself to actually voice the rest.

He placed another kiss atop her head, trying to breathe her in, that familiar spring floral scent that was so much like home now. She was whole and in his arms. He could face whatever came next with her at his side.

"I had hoped we'd never experience anything like that," Andreas finally spoke up, his voice gruff.

Aiden and Theo finally broke apart but linked hands, unable to let the other go.

"What's next?" Theo asked, clearly as eager as the rest of them to put that nightmare behind them.

Andreas pulled his phone from his pocket with shaky hands and grimaced. "It appears we lost more time than expected within the forest. Bridget said they already finished filming in Ireland and are at the castle." He typed out a quick response before looking up at them again. "We need to move now so we can meet her and get the map."

Aiden reluctantly let go of Theo's hand and unsheathed his machetes. "Okay then, let's do what we came here for. The quicker we do it, the quicker we can go home."

Theo drew her weapons as well, a small smile gracing her lips. Looking almost proud, Andreas gave them both a nod. "Let's go."

A dirt path led them to the edge of the castle's property. From there, Aiden could get a better sense of the fortress they were up against. The castle was undoubtedly a mixture of Gothic and Renaissance architecture with towers and bastions, but the most impressive was the tall—fall off the path and die tall—drawbridge over a river. The structure had obviously seen better days as it rose into the night sky like a crooked tombstone—all strange angles, as if it had been cobbled together.

As they drew near the fortress, that now-familiar shriek cut through the night again, and this time it sounded from right above them. Aiden's head shot up, just in time to see a silhouette soar over them. It was enormous, making him think of pterodactyls. The thing swooped low.

Lighting from the production crew illuminated the animal, which turned out to be a griffin—a creature with the head and wings of an eagle, and the body, tail, and back legs of a lion. Spotlights set up all along the top of one of the castle walls lit up both the creature and the group of what had to be contestants standing along the top of the wall. They all seemed to be dancing around each other—as if the contestants needed to get past the beast.

"Griffins are endangered and protected by the council," Andreas finally spoke up, his eyes on the scene before them. "It won't hurt the contestants as long as they don't mess with its nest."

"Looks like Max wants them to do just that." Theo pointed to the shadow of a large nest atop a half-destroyed tower.

"That's exactly the plan," a new voice spoke up.

Everyone turned to find Bridget, a scroll in her hand.

"We don't have much time, but here." She handed Theo the scroll. "Theo and Aiden, you two need to enter through the tunnels on this map." Her gaze swung to Andreas. "Andreas and I will act as a distraction to keep Max off your trail for as long as we can. We can pretend we're here on official council business to stop the filming and protect the griffin."

"What's the task that he has them doing?" Aiden gestured toward where the contestants were trying to sneak around the birdlike creature.

"To get a feather from the griffin's nest. Utterly ridiculous." She rolled her eyes.

"Sounds like Max," Theo added.

Andreas stepped forward. "Then we need to move. Are we all clear on what to do?"

Everyone nodded.

The Guardian's mouth pressed into a grim line before he spoke again. "Before you go, Aiden, I need to tell you something that will aid you on your quest."

Nerves twisted in his stomach as he met the older vampire's intense stare. "I'm ready."

"Now that your magic has awakened, you can locate the Solis Occasum. It's almost as if you're a human metal detector, except your treasure is the chalice. Once inside the castle, focus on the cup, and it'll make itself known to you."

"How?" Aiden couldn't help but ask.

"You'll feel it. Trust your instincts to guide you." Andreas clapped him on the shoulder, before moving to Theo. "Theo, I want you both to be careful, okay?"

With the moonlight and lights from the television show, it was easy to see that Theo was holding back tears. She bit her lip as she faced her sire. "You have to be careful too, got it?"

A small smile wavered across the Guardian's lips before he pulled Theo into a quick hug. "We will meet again," was all he said before he and Bridget were off, jogging toward the castle.

Once they disappeared from view, Theo shook tension from her shoulders and unrolled the scroll between them. "It looks like we won't even have to use the drawbridge. The tunnel is out here." She pointed to a grassy knoll near where they stood. Thankfully, brush covered it.

"If I wasn't looking at the map, I wouldn't even know it was there." Aiden waited for Theo to fold up the parchment and put it in her pocket. The way through was an easy straight shot. The hardest part would be finding Max, or facing him in general. The guy was a disturbing genius.

"That's the point of secret tunnels." She laughed, gesturing for them to start walking.

Aiden grinned at her, loving that she always kept him on his toes with her snark. They moved in the shadows, careful to avoid the light provided by the production crew. Max evidently hadn't cleared this part for filming. Where the door was supposed to be, there was a ton of underbrush, which they had to scrabble through. They stifled curses as brambles cut them and branches scratched them.

Finally, Aiden's knuckles connected with a wooden door. "Here!" He moved quicker, pushing the remaining weeds and brush out of the way.

It took both Theo and Aiden to yank the door open. Clearly the thing hadn't been used for years. The putrid scent of rot and dampness hit them in a wave.

"Damn," Aiden grunted, covering his nose.

Theo followed suit while shaking her head. "We definitely did not come prepared for this."

Aiden peered deeper inside. It was not only rank, but cold and completely dark. He tugged the cell phone Andreas gave him from his jeans pocket and turned on the flashlight. "I feel like this entire experience is something we didn't prepare for." Which was really the understatement of the year. Here he was with magic and a vampire mate, trying to reclaim an enchanted chalice.

Theo nodded. "True."

The tunnel was suffocating, made even worse when they closed the door behind them. Aiden couldn't help but think they might be like trapped rats, but he kept that to himself. Instead, they moved through the passageway, careful to avoid fallen rocks and other debris. Theo swept through gracefully, of course, not even needing a flashlight. After what felt like forever, they came to another door.

"We should be in the basement hallway, and then we roam based on what you feel," Theo whispered.

"Got it."

Aiden opened the door as quietly as he could. It surprised him that it didn't need two people to do so. He looked down both dimly lit stone corridors before stepping fully out, Theo on his heels.

Taking the nearest set of stairs, they crept upward and into the actual castle and foyer.

The space was large and empty, a chill permeating everything within. Only one torch illuminated the room. A grand set of stairs stuck out from the side, candles lit on each step. The candles were the only sign that the crew had been there. Otherwise, everything else appeared dark and gloomy, and not in the fun gothic sort of way.

Aiden straightened as an unfamiliar pull went through his body upon looking at the flight of steps. He whipped his head around to Theo, who already understood what was happening.

She gave Aiden an encouraging nod, and he moved toward the steps with her at his back. Up they went until they emptied out into a darkened corridor. The buzzing in his blood intensified. Apparently things were about to get serious because the hallways were empty—everything as silent as the forest.

Stopping in front of one of the large closed wooden doors, Aiden knew that the very thing that brought him and Theo together waited behind it. It all but thrummed in his blood, calling to him. Just as Andreas said it would.

Wordlessly he pointed at the door. Theo gave him a thumbs-up before he opened it. As it swung open slowly, it made the loudest creak known to man. He drew his weapons up in front of his body, prepared to block an attack.

The stone-walled room had floor-to-ceiling windows set off by two closed enormous, moth-eaten, red curtains. Moonlight streamed in around the edges, and tons of candles glowed all throughout. Max stood hunched over a desk, which was one of the few pieces of furniture in the room. At their entrance, he whirled around, brows all the way to his hairline.

"Surprised to see us, huh?" Theo swaggered into the room.

Aiden loved that about her. He took his place next to her, still holding his weaponry.

Max tilted his head to the side in a creepy avian manner. "I am surprised, indeed. I can't believe you knew where to find us. After all, last you knew, we were in Ireland."

"We have our ways," Aiden said as he lifted a shoulder, going for nonchalance even though his heart began to thud painfully in his chest.

This was the showdown they'd been waiting for.

And all he could do was hope and pray—and fight his heart out—this wouldn't be a repeat of what happened to Cassidy.

The director chuckled. "Oh, I don't doubt that. I thought perhaps you might figure it out, but I had hoped the Forest of Nightmares would do my dirty work for me."

He moved away from the desk to reveal the golden, black, and red gemstone-bedecked Solis Occasum. The amount of power that radiated from it throbbed like a heartbeat.

Ignoring Max's comment, Theo forged ahead. "Where's Brandt?"

There was no doubt that where one was, the other wasn't too far behind.

Aiden and Theo were careful to be on constant alert, adjusting their stances so they didn't give any one part of the chamber their backs for too long. They had dealt with Max enough by now to know how sneaky he was and to what lengths he'd go to get what he wanted. The thought made Aiden's blood boil all over again as Cassidy's face played across his mind. Her death, his life being ruined, putting Theo in danger, it was all Max's fault.

Max chuckled and adjusted the lapels of his bloodred blazer. "Oh, Brandt?" he singsonged.

From the shadows emerged Brandt, looking a little worse for wear but still formidable. Behind him lay a door hidden by curtains, much like their tunnel door, that closed with a thud.

"Nosferatu wannabe," Aiden and Theo both snarled.

"It seems I'll finally get the joy of tearing you each apart." Brandt looked back and forth between them. "And I'll enjoy every moment of it."

"See? That's exactly the sort of reunion I'd hoped for." Max glided across the room to meet the vampire, turning to shoot them a gleeful, manic smile.

Aiden took a step closer, Theo right beside him.

"The Solis Occasum doesn't belong to you," he said, moving even closer, he and Theo trying to box Max and Brandt in.

Max lifted a finger like an evil genius. "Ah, see, that's where you're wrong. It actually does." He raised his chin. "And with Andreas's appearance outside battling the griffin, I can surmise you must know what you are now."

"A Guardian. And I've got a job to do."

Brandt hissed, but Max waved his hand to stay the older vampire. Cracking his neck from side to side, the director pierced them with a crazed look in his eyes, which had turned completely red. "Now. Shall we get this nasty bit over with? I hadn't expected it to happen so soon, but oh, what the hell."

"With pleasure," Theo growled.

Aiden was the first to strike, his sword cutting a strip of Max's blazer, but the vampire moved with threatening agility. Max climbed up the curtains like one of those possessed demons in horror films. The director *tsked* as he looked down at them. "See, now you've really made me angry, ruining my favorite jacket."

Brandt wasted no time retaliating by going after Theo. Sweat began to bead at Aiden's brow as an onslaught of memories of Cassidy played before his eyes. He wanted to interfere and help Theo, but he knew that he had to take on Max—while somehow making sure his mate survived. He had to trust her to fend for herself. It killed him inside, but he had to do it.

"Won't the council look down on you killing a fellow vampire?" Brandt called out to Theo.

"Don't care," she said.

Just then Max landed right in front of Aiden, his lips curled in a sneer. "Let's see what you got, fledgling."

"Gladly." Aiden parried and attempted to land a strike, but Max was quicker.

This was definitely not good.

If Max was this fast, then how in the world would Aiden manage to use his magic on him?

Grunts and hisses filled the room—Theo and Brandt going at it —while Aiden and Max danced around each other.

Finally, Aiden found an opening as soon as Max made his way to the chalice.

He stabbed at the vampire, and the sword managed to slice into his arm. Max howled. Then he was on Aiden. The vampire threw him to the ground, teeth snapping. He bit Aiden's bicep—the pain hotter than a brand.

But Aiden couldn't stop to think about it.

Or Theo.

Defeating Max meant they could live their lives happily, without looking over their shoulder.

"Time to put you in a trance." Max snickered.

"No!" Aiden yelled.

He tried to stab Max again, but the vampire had his arm with the weapon pinned. Gaze focused on Aiden, Max began to weave the vampire trance, forcing Aiden to reach for his own magic and focus with all his might.

It was difficult with his blood roaring in his ears, but he thought of Theo.

Always Theo.

"Duratus," he whispered.

The vampire stilled. Then he threw his head back in laughter. "You think that will work on me?"

That was an interesting development.

And not a good one either.

"No," Aiden grunted. "But this will." And then he reached for the stake hidden in his pants with his unpinned hand. He jabbed the weapon just below the director's ribs and shoved upward.

Max sputtered and then fell to the ground, his body facing the moonlight streaming in from the curtains.

Aiden pushed a twitching Max off him and sprang to his feet. He turned just as Brandt fell to the ground with a stake thrusting up from his chest. Theo stood over him, breathing heavily. She was bloody and torn, just as he was. She heaved a sigh, her chest rising and falling rapidly. Aiden rushed to her. Before wrapping her in his arms, he drew back and skimmed her up and down.

"There's a lot of blood here. Are you okay?" he asked.

She nodded, weariness weighing her down. "I'm fine. I had to use a lot of old vampire tricks against him. It took a lot out me."

They looked down at Brandt. It was probably the only time the vampire had ever been peaceful.

"How did you manage to take out Max?" she gestured behind them where the director still lay.

Thankfully, wonderfully dead.

"I couldn't use my magic on him."

"What do you mean?"

Aiden shrugged. "I'm not sure. I tried, and it didn't work. Then he acted like I was a child for even attempting it."

Theo ran her hand across her forehead. "Hmm...that's definitely something we'll have to ask Andreas about." She paused as her lips wobbled into a shaky smile. "But I'm so glad you're okay."

Not waiting a second longer, she tugged him closer in a hug. Aiden inhaled the scent of her perfume and smiled against her cheek.

"I'm just happy this is over." He shifted so that he could cradle her face in his hands as he grinned at her. "And I have something else to tell you. Something that can't wait a second longer."

Theo arched a worried brow, and Aiden kissed it before meeting her stare again. "You're my heart, you know that, Theo?

You're basically my heart walking around outside my chest," he admitted, pressing his lips to hers. After a long, tender moment, he pulled back. "I love you. So damn much it scares me."

Before he had thought of her as radiant. Now she looked effervescent.

She stood on her tiptoes, kissing his nose. "I love you, Aiden. It feels like I always have."

Someone cleared their throat, giving them both a start. When they turned, weapons ready, Andreas swept into the room. "I hate to interrupt." He took in the two dispatched vampires, and pride gleamed in his eyes. "But it looks like we need to get a move on."

"Thank God you're okay." Theo sighed before giving her sire a quick hug. "Where's Bridget?"

"Bridget is procuring our getaway van." He smirked. When his gaze landed on the chalice, he sobered. "I'll be better once we get this behind us." The Guardian walked over to the chalice and picked it up, his attention directed solely on Aiden. "You have a decision to make."

Andreas placed the Solis Occasum in Aiden's hands, and suddenly everything went quiet—the buzzing, the adrenaline, everything ceased to exist. He had the chalice, the very thing he'd wanted for so long. This cup was his to protect and cherish. Turning to Theo, he realized something, well, *someone* was more important than all of that.

"Theodora Nash, do you still want to be human?"

Theo's blue eyes widened as her hand flew to her chest. When she spoke, the words were cracked with emotion so thick he could barely understand her. "Yes, more than anything."

Aiden met Andreas's stare, the Guardian giving him an encouraging nod. But Aiden had no idea what to do next. He arched a brow. "So how does this work? Do I need to fill it with my blood or...?"

Suppressing a smile, Andreas came over to him, gesturing for him to open his palm. "No, you won't fill it. You'll only put a few drops of your blood in the Solis Occasum." He turned to Theo. "And then you'll drink. Are you sure you want this?"

She nodded vehemently, gaze locked on Aiden.

"Very well. Aiden, you may continue." Andreas stepped to the side.

"Theo, I hope you know I would've given you this regardless of killing Max tonight," Aiden whispered.

She wrapped her hand around his free one. "I know. And I would've done the same, but now..." She grinned brightly. "We don't have to worry about that."

Tugging her to his body, he kissed the top of her head. Andreas pulled out a pocketknife and brandished it in the air.

"Time for the next step. Aiden, your palm please."

He lifted his hand, and the Guardian wasted no time slicing through the meaty flesh, moving the chalice beneath to catch the blood.

Aiden hissed at the sharp pain, but this was worth it. It was all worth it to make Theo happy.

Ripping off part of his shirt sleeve, he tied a makeshift bandage on his hand as he held the Solis Occasum out to Theo.

Her eyes glittered in the moonlight, tears cutting ribbons down her cheeks. "Thank you," she whispered. She lifted the chalice to her lips and drank.

The air around Theo began to shimmer. Whatever he'd been expecting next, though, it certainly was not the blur that shoved past him and knocked her to the ground.

Max.

28

THEO

Gold glimmered before her eyes, and then it dissipated like dust motes, replaced instead by the visage of a feral Max. Who was definitely not dead, even with a stake protruding from his white dress shirt. She had no doubt that Aiden had driven the stake home correctly. Andreas would've shown him that in their training session.

Max's talons—yes, they were now talons—dug into her skin as he spun her to face a stricken Aiden and Andreas. "You thought you could kill me so easily? Not with the enchantments I've had placed on the Solis Occasum."

He kicked the chalice, causing Aiden to flinch as he inched closer to them.

"You can take that piece of garbage with you, seeing as I no longer need it." The huge, half-crazed smile on his face was one of someone couldn't wait to share a secret that revealed their brilliance. "The final piece of the puzzle is this one. I need the blood of someone who is a vampire halfway through the transitioning process to become a human, and then I can walk in the sun."

Just as Aiden moved to strike, Max's fangs pierced Theo's neck. And everything went black.

29

AIDEN

Aiden lunged forward with a speed that surprised even him, and his sword pierced Max's side, causing him to drop Theo. Thankfully Andreas was fast and was able to catch her.

Max just cackled, and then with that frightening speed of his, he jumped out of the window. Glass rained down on them as maniacal laughter echoed through the night.

Aiden's heart felt as though it stopped beating. He fell to his knees where Andreas held Theo. The Guardian gently transferred her to him. His fingers went to her neck, finding no pulse. Even as a vampire, she still had a pulse, albeit a light one. Struggling to force the words from his throat, he looked at Andreas, unable to stop all the guilt and anguish he felt over having failed twice from seeping into his gaze.

"She may not..." Andreas got a little choked up. "She may not be dead. We have to wait."

A huge part of him wanted desperately to ask Andreas if he could turn her back into a vampire. But he could never do that. Being a human again was all Theo had ever wanted, and he couldn't take that from her, certainly not for his own benefit. He refused to allow his own selfish needs to override her choice.

Face wet with his own tears, Aiden lifted Theo to his chest. "Please, Theo. You have to wake up, not just for me, but for you. You're finally going to be a human. *Please.*" His voice completely shattered on that last word, painting the entire room in the heartbreak he felt.

He kissed her forehead, cradled her tighter, and as he did, he felt a tiny hitch in her body, a gasp almost. Pulling her away from him, he was met with the most beautiful sight in the world—her eyes were wide open and staring back at him.

"Theodora!" Emotions flooded him, threatening to break the dam. His breath hitched as he tightened his grip on her.

"Aiden?" she croaked out as she sat up a little in his arms. Her gaze swung over to Andreas. "Am I...?"

"Human?" Andreas finished for her.

She nodded slowly, her head resting against Aiden's thunderous heartbeat. More tears streamed down his face. He'd never been so happy in his life. Theo was alive and okay!

Andreas pulled out his pocketknife, slicing open his own palm this time and holding it up to her. "Let's find out."

Theo gagged, turning her head away and into Aiden's shirt, and he felt her heart race against his.

"You're human again, holy shit!" Aiden cried out, this time not holding back from kissing her, letting her know just how much she meant to him.

She wrapped her arms tightly around his neck as she returned his kiss just as wildly. "I'm a human! We can have dates at the beach during the day, and I can eat pizza!"

His grin grew so wide it nearly hurt his cheeks. She might be human, but thankfully she was still his same Theodora.

Finally, she stood and turned to Andreas, opening her arms to hug him as well. "Thank you for everything," she whispered. "You're still like my vampire dad even if I'm not a vampire."

Andreas chuckled. Everyone rose from the floor, Theo only the slightest bit wobbly. Bending down to pick up the chalice, she handed it over to Aiden. "Max is gone, so now what?"

The Solis Occasum glowed in Aiden's grasp as he looked to Andreas for the answer. That was a hell of a good question, indeed. Now what? How would they ever manage to defeat a vampire that could walk in the sunlight? And was also apparently a little on the indestructible side?

Andreas pulled out a phone from his jacket pocket. "We call in a witch, that's what. Come on, we gotta meet Bridget out front."

Aiden didn't have to be told twice. They left, going into a courtyard within the confines of the castle. There they saw the crew swiftly wrapping up, packing off the remaining contestants into production vans to take them to a hotel. The griffin had been safely tranquilized and placed back with its nest, allowing everyone to get out of there without incident.

Their little group continued moving until they saw Bridget leaning against a van, arms crossed, a soft smile on her face. "You all look awful. Let's get out of here."

"That sounds heavenly," Theo said with a grin.

They all piled into the van without another word.

Within hours, they were tucked away in Andreas's underground lair again. He and Bridget had gone into planning mode, or as Andreas called it, Guardian mode, leaving Theo and Aiden to their own devices.

When Theo beckoned him into her room, he had zero regrets about not being included in the plan. He had his own plans to fulfill.

30

THEO

PEOPLE ALWAYS MADE A BIG DEAL ABOUT HOW WHEN A PERSON WAS turned into a vampire, everything was sharper, clearer. Theo noticed that to be the case, *then*. But now? With her hand in Aiden's as she led him into her room, it felt like the clearest thing she'd ever experienced in her life.

She'd just died and been reborn as a human, her heart beating a regular pace, although it did still speed up when around Aiden—that was to be expected. She loved him, after all, and now she needed to express that in a different way, needed to feel his skin against hers.

What they'd gone through had been terrifying, and she never wanted to see that type of pain on Aiden's face again. One day...one day, they were going to rid the world of Max's evil. One day. But right now? Right now, Theodora Nash was going to revel in being alive and being loved.

Gently tugging Aiden's hand, she led him over to the couch situated in the corner of the room. "Strip and then sit," she instructed, proud of her voice remaining steady despite practically vibrating with lust. She'd had sex with Aiden before, but this time felt different. This time she knew that he loved her.

And she loved him.

Undoubtedly.

Aiden arched one brow wickedly, his lips curved into her favorite smile—the kind that looked downright wolfish, like he might eat her up. Hell, she wanted him to go right ahead.

"Yes, ma'am," he answered, his voice a deep, rumbly timbre that hit her in all the right spots.

His shirt was the first thing to go, and he threw it with a flick into some corner of the room. Theo bit her lip at the muscle on display, alongside the sexy smattering of chest hair leading to her favorite part.

Her entire body flushed with all the things she wanted to do to him, but also with the amount of love she felt for him. The realization that this man was hers warmed her from the inside out. Everything about her felt as though she was on fire, a walking livewire.

Aiden's strong hands went to the waist of his jeans, unbuckling his belt, the fast slide of it giving Theo all kinds of goose bumps. Of course, he didn't miss a beat. He laid it to the side and wiggled his brows. "I'll leave this over here in case we want it later."

Yes, please.

And then he flicked open his jeans, tugging them down slowly to show off his black boxer briefs that looked like they were struggling to contain his length. Solid quads and calves flexed as he stepped out of the pool of denim, removing his socks.

"Damn, you're hot." Theo grinned, incredibly happy that this was her life. Her fingers flexed with the need to touch Aiden, but she couldn't—not yet. She wanted to tease him a little more, knowing it would pay off for them both in the end.

Aiden's gaze turned sharper, hungrier as he reached for the hem of his underwear, yanking those off too. She gulped as heat scorched her core. Her cheeks burned, and she drew her hands there, her mouth open as she studied a naked Aiden, a work of art, truly.

In two steps, he was in front of her, her face cradled in his hands. "You blush. I always thought you would if you were a human." His smile turned soft. "It's fucking sexy, Theodora."

She grinned back at him as he reached one hand to capture a strand of hair, wrapping it around his finger. His gaze lingered on her as he did so. Lust burned between them, but love, love was the undercurrent that kept them going strong.

Butterflies swooped in her stomach as she reached up to his scar, running her fingertips along the stark reminder of all he'd lost. His breath turned ragged as she stood on her tiptoes and pressed her lips where her fingers once were.

"Theo," Aiden whispered her name like a prayer as he released her tendril of hair. He stroked her cheek with the back of his knuckles, the touch sending a shiver down her spine. Then his lips were on hers, warm and smooth, kissing her like a man possessed.

She dug her hands into his hair, forgetting she was in charge of this little seduction. Instead she tried to get as close as she could. She moved against his erection, desperate for him to soothe the ache inside of her. After a breathy whimper fell from her mouth, he broke away, taking a step back before motioning to her clothes.

"Now it's your turn to strip...and I believe you said something about the couch?" He turned around to glance at the piece of furniture in question and then back at her. He looked perfectly disheveled and flushed. And she'd been the one to make him that way.

"Uh-huh," was her brilliant response. Her horniness had fried her brain.

First, Aiden grabbed a condom, thankfully thinking because she'd already forgotten they needed one. After putting it on, which was hot in its own right, he moved backward, not taking his eyes off her, his gaze expectant as he licked his lips. He plopped onto the couch, sitting there naked, with his perfect cock standing at attention. Theo knew she needed to get on with this, or she'd be spent before she even got the chance to ride him. She was already slick with need.

Never having been one for any type of seduction, she took her shirt off, revealing her balconette bra that pushed her boobs together in an incredible amount of cleavage. Aiden hissed at the sight, tightening his hands into the sofa. Theo bent down, giving him a show of her girls as she unsnapped the bra and oh-so-slowly peeled it off, followed by her pants and socks, shucking those as well, leaving her in her sky-blue lace boy shorts.

"Get that sexy ass over here," Aiden rasped.

Clad only in her underwear, Theo didn't hesitate to straddle him on the sofa.

Her hands went to the back of the furniture for leverage, Aiden grasping her waist. His mouth crashed down on hers as he ground his hard cock against her.

She smiled against his lips. "I was supposed to be the one teasing you."

Aiden rested his forehead against hers for a moment and grinned. "Mission accomplished, but you know I can't resist returning the favor." He moved one of his hands from her waist to dip between them so he could grip his length. He didn't take his eyes off her as he slid it over the front of her underwear, teasing her. Back and forth, he rubbed his cock over her as his other hand cupped her ass. He dropped his lips to her neck, kissing over her pulse.

Theo's breaths came in rough pants as she squirmed against him. His kisses went further south before landing on her breast, licking her aching buds. She rocked against his cock, loving the friction provided through the lace, and then he slid her underwear to the side, brushing his fingers over her clit in a slow, languid swipe. Her head fell back at the sensation, her grip tightening on the sofa.

"You're soaked, gorgeous," he whispered against her skin, the words hot like a brand. "Do you want to get off on my hand? Or my mouth? What about my cock?" he asked with one more hard thrust. She was about to explode, and he wasn't even inside her yet.

"I want you inside me, right now," she pleaded, maneuvering a little awkwardly to take off her underwear, not caring how it looked.

She resettled herself, slowly sliding down on Aiden's length, a moan falling from her lips at the same time a hoarse groan tumbled from his. A thousand sensations ran through her, all of them technicolor and vivid—it had been amazing when she was a vampire, but this? It was truly magnificent because she felt like herself for the first time in a long time.

"I'm going to let go of you, so I can thrust," Aiden instructed as he nibbled her lip.

Theo tightened her hold on the furniture, and Aiden gripped the sofa for purchase, driving up into her, slow and steady first, but Theo needed more, wanted it all. He brought his fingers between them, rubbing her sensitive bundle of nerves, which set her off, making her ride him harder and slower. He met her pace and he tugged her breasts closer to his mouth. He bit her nipple, applying the pressure she desperately craved, and then licked it until she pushed back slightly, giving them a new angle.

They looked down between them, Theo finding the sight sexy as hell, watching him slide in and out of her.

"I'm gonna move us, okay?" Aiden warned.

She nodded. "Yes," she moaned, and then he had her flipped over the arm of the couch, ass in the air. She grinned as her pulse thundered in her chest with sweet anticipation.

"Is this okay?" he asked, hands on her waist.

"Yes, it's okay. It's *always* okay." She wiggled her butt for emphasis.

And then the time for laughing was over. Aiden drove into her, Theo arching her back as she gripped the sofa, a wanton sound coming from her. He rubbed her clit with his thumb, while the other hand tweaked her nipple, his mouth on her neck.

"Do you like it when I fuck you hard, Theo?" he growled, pushing into her quicker.

"That's what you call hard?" she teased.

A dark chuckle let her know she was in for it, and then Aiden worked her hard enough that the sofa moved. It was perfection. "Oh, Aiden," she whimpered, feeling her orgasm on the brink.

"I want to hear you when you come, baby. I could get off on that alone. It's so sexy." Aiden grunted as he thrust into her, gently tugging her hair.

She came in an instant, fireworks and explosions setting off behind her eyelids and throughout her body as she clenched around his cock. Aiden followed right after, driving into her three more times, roaring his release. Theo collapsed onto the couch in a motionless heap, her limbs jelly, everything hot and filled with lightning. Aiden pulled away to take care of the condom.

She grabbed her underwear and shirt and fell back onto the couch, her eyes shut. "I could do that forever," Theo whispered to no one, thinking Aiden was still in the bathroom. After all, she was fully sexed up and blissed out.

"Then we should do it," came Aiden's reply right next to her.

Her eyes snapped open to see him standing before her, dressed in only his boxer briefs. Seeing the outline of his still-hard cock made her lick her lips. Somehow, she managed to sit up while feeling mortification hum through her veins, her face turning red. "What do you mean?"

Theo's heart pounded wildly in her chest as she awaited his response. She'd known she wanted a forever with Aiden before they ever had sex the first time, but it was cemented after everything they'd gone through in the Forest of Nightmares. This man was someone she wanted to wake up to each morning, to fall asleep and drool on his chest each night. Simply put, she wanted this man, *always*.

With a smile, Aiden kneeled before where she sat on the couch, his hands on her thighs. "I mean that one day, I'm going to ask you to marry me. Not today. I want you to enjoy being a human for a while, and I don't want you to feel pressured, but just know that I want to spend the rest of my days with you, Theo." He tugged at her bottom lip with his thumb. "And don't say anything now. It's just something I wanted you to know."

Tears clouded her vision, and she blinked them back—not because she was ashamed to cry, but because she needed to see this moment in its entirety. A grin curved her lips as love and happiness hummed in her chest as she nodded.

What he didn't know was that she would've said yes on the spot, but she also appreciated him being so considerate. She would need an adjustment period, that much was true, but there was no one else in the world she wanted to be with. Her heart always knew—in human or vampire form—it knew.

"I love you," she said as she leaned forward to press her lips to his.

"I love you too, gorgeous."

He moved so he sat next to her on the couch, pulling her into his lap as he kissed her hair, holding her tightly to his chest. She loved that she could hear his heartbeat steadily against her ear, knowing her own now matched. It also meant that despite everything they'd just gone through, they were alive.

Theo smiled, thinking back to how she had needed adrenaline to calm the guilt and rage—one thrill after another, after another. Now that rage was quiet. She would never forget her past because it made her who she was today. But now she was excited about carving out her future with Aiden.

EPILOGUE
THEO

ONE YEAR LATER

THE MOON CAST A THOUSAND LITTLE DIAMOND SPARKLES ON THE
surface of the water. Theo cuddled even closer to Aiden as they sat
on their towel, listening to the waves crash upon the shore. They
were both freckled and sunburned, smelling of sunscreen and
saltwater, having thoroughly been enjoying their honeymoon. It
had been a beautiful day, the best day. Theo couldn't help but smile
each time she looked down at her wedding ring sparkling on her
finger.

She knew Jonathan would be happy for her, glad she'd opened
her heart once more. Being a human again had been all Theo
dreamed of and more. She'd gorged on all kinds of food and had
practically lived outside during the day. She'd picked up gardening
and loved it.

"I love you," she whispered as she nuzzled her nose against
Aiden's neck.

He pressed a kiss to the top of her head, and she felt him smile
against her hair. "I love you more."

It was a game they played, knowing full well they both loved each other more than they ever thought possible.

A figure walking down the beach made them both sit straight up, tension running through Theo's body. Max still hadn't been found despite all Andreas's efforts.

Speaking of which...

Andreas paused right before them. Theo blew out a big, dramatic breath.

"I thought you were Max or something." She laughed, placing a hand over her racing heart. Not that she was chicken or anything, but damn, she'd had enough adventure to last a lifetime.

"Hey, Andy," Aiden started.

The vampire shook his head, although a smile tipped his lips upward. "We talked about this. *Andy* is not a nickname I approve of."

"But it sounds cool. It fits you."

"It most definitely does not."

The two bickered like son-in-law and father-in-law, and Theo thought it was adorable.

Theo cleared her throat, getting their attention. "Not that we aren't excited to see you, but what's going on? I never took you for a honeymoon crasher." She made sure to smile to let him know she wasn't upset by any stretch of the imagination.

Andreas motioned to someone in the darkness beside a palm tree. Or *someones*, rather, since two figures stepped forward from behind swaying palm trees. She recognized them instantly. How could she not? Prior to going on *Night Race*, she'd seen an episode or two of *Forever After*. It was Oliver and Autumn Gray, the vampires from the show.

Aiden and Theo stood up, shaking hands with the couple as Andreas handled introductions.

"So what are you guys doing here?" Aiden asked.

Oliver ran a hand over already mussed hair as he shot his wife a look. "Well..." A British accent filled the air. "Have you ever heard of a place called Fang Island?"

Theo's brows furrowed, and Aiden's lips twisted. Theo was the first to speak. "No, can't say that we have. Why?"

Autumn's eyes went wide as she looked to Andreas. He rubbed his hands together, a slight smile on his face. "Well, it appears there's another vampire reality show in the making, *Fang Island*. Let's just say...I'm pretty sure we found Max."

❥

Thank you for reading! Did you enjoy? Please add your review because nothing helps an author more and encourages readers to take a chance on a book than a review.

And don't miss book three of the *Vampire Reality Show* series coming soon, and find more from Ashley R. King at www. ashleyrking.com

Until then, read more Mystic Owl books with A MATTER OF TIME by Lizzy Gayle. Turn the page for a sneak peek!

You can also sign up for the City Owl Press newsletter to receive notice of all book releases!

SNEAK PEEK OF A MATTER OF TIME
BY LIZZY GAYLE

The hat was the best part. What kid didn't fancy playing the hero in the ten-gallon hat, pistols at his sides, spurs on his boots, ready to take on the outlaw? Doyle didn't have pistols, that would've required permission forms and red tape he didn't have time or patience for, but he did have the tan hat.

"What do you think, Lacey?" he asked, tipping the brim to the resort's costume designer.

He enjoyed making her smile. Maybe it was the blush that always came with it that did it. She was way out of his league, not to mention her relationship with Casey McGovern, the resort's captain. McGovern was the one who'd get credit for helming the maiden voyage of the Time Capsule Resort, or TCR, but he, Doyle, was the one who designed the actual mechanism that travelled through time, not to mention the cloaking device. Either invention would be enough to make history if it weren't for the fact the patents were owned by his employer, Bennet Systems, since they'd doled out the cash for his research.

Why did engineers never get the credit?

"Adorkable," Lacey said, tapping her chin as she studied Doyle's appearance. "The jeans fit perfectly. But are you sure you want to go for the rancher look and not more of a tinkerer? I have a bowler hat and three-piece suit that comes with a nifty stopwatch."

Doyle placed his hands on his hips, trying not to be offended. "This resort is about enacting our fantasies right? Not becoming our 1880's personas. Besides, I've been working out." He pumped a bicep for her, and smiled when she bit her bottom lip.

"There's my girl," McGovern's deep voice came from directly behind, crushing Doyle's fantasy into dust. "All hands in position for departure, Doyle. We want this trip running smoothly, especially with the Watcher on board."

Lacey crinkled her nose. "Is it just me or is the Watcher creepy? I get that they're here to make sure nothing happens to the timeline, but do they have to wear that weird black suit? It makes them look like they don't belong in any known time."

Not too pleased with having another person on board keeping an eye on them, Doyle grunted his agreement. Having Nicole Bennet of Bennet Systems around was enough pressure, never mind a representative of multiple governments, policing them all on what was billed as a luxury vacation.

"So?" McGovern pressed, hands on the slim hips of his own cowboy getup. "Get to work!"

Annoyed, Doyle thought better of snapping back and bit the inside of his cheek. Instead, he ignored McGovern, thanked Lacey for the duds, and went off in search of engineering, where he would sit and monitor the ride and equipment until they docked. They'd done practice runs, but this was the first time he'd seen so many people in the machine. It was the way he liked to think of the Time Capsule Resort, which some called a hybrid ship that didn't sail and some saw as a time machine that looked like a hotel on steroids. The whole thing was part and parcel of the mechanism in Doyle's brain. The amenities and window dressings existed to make it more comfortable to humans as far as he was concerned.

Built in a giant corkscrew shape, the only floors separated from the rest by elevator and stairs were the top and bottom, the "bridge" where McGovern worked in the former, and the day-to-day tech monitoring system on the latter near the exit/entrance. Lacey's costume shop lived on a higher portion of the corkscrew, above the equivalent of three floors worth of immersive magic courtesy of the designers.

Doyle strolled through the winding halls covered in dirt with various storefronts accurate to the late 1800's old west and tipped his hat when he spied a couple of women dressed to the hilt just like him. The older woman and the younger mirror image beside her, who could only be her daughter, both tittered at the attention, which added some swagger to Doyle's step. Lacey already had it in her head he was a nerd. It was an image he wanted to shatter, at least long enough to get laid. He'd thrown himself so hard into his work that he hadn't had time for much else, including his girlfriend, when he'd started the job. He pulled out of the relationship a mere three months later, citing his single-focus attention span. But as the work eased up and the interior design and marketing crews took over, he was able to lift his head out of the sand and rejoin the human race a bit. Which in his case meant playing video games, particularly wild west themed ones, out of excitement for the voyage, that and going to the gym.

Lost in his thoughts, Doyle slipped through the throngs of excited passengers, eyeing the door to engineering. Situated near the bottom of the spiral, it had been disguised as an old gold mine entrance with an OFF LIMITS sign. The passengers were only supposed to see the mirage created by Bennet Systems, which took the form of an old west town, complete with plenty of saloons and dance hall girls. Everyone on board was dressed the part, cosplay to the extreme. The idea was to be immersed in the setting. The real setting. It would change along with the costumes and scenery every voyage when they changed themes and time locales. They were starting with the initial trip to the wild west – Arizona circa 1888. They'd subsequently move on to 1920's Chicago, 1640's England, and so on.

Doyle didn't plan on joining them on all the excursions, but he wouldn't miss the first time people got to see his baby in action, even if they didn't realize it was his.

He reached for the hidden button that would allow him entrance as it opened and a woman slipped out, almost smacking into him. She had on one of the fancy dresses from Lacey's costume shop, but Doyle doubted her bright purple hair would blend in with the real wild west.

"Sorry," she said, averting her eyes and scurrying out of the way and off into the throngs of excited people.

Looked like Jones was already taking advantage of the scenery as far as the guests were concerned and they weren't even there yet. Still, he'd have to have a talk with the guy about letting patrons behind the scenes, even to impress the women.

Catching the door, Doyle entered the quiet space of the control room.

"You gonna be able to sit in those jeans, Wally?"

Doyle grimaced at Jones, his ass of an ass-istant. He hated his first name, Walter, but the second Jones found out what it was, he'd grabbed hold and wouldn't let go.

"How are the readings?" If he ignored the comment maybe it and Jones would go away.

"Ship shape. Get it?" Jones's eyes sparkled. His red kerchief and straw hat were more reminiscent of Huckleberry Finn than a cowboy, especially on his small frame.

Doyle shot him the side eye as he spun his chair toward the consul. Eight holo-screens displayed 3-D views of the perimeter of the machine from the inside out. The whole thing was basically a cylinder encased in super thin, nearly indestructible AC glass, so that when they parked themselves near the action, they'd feel like they were in the center while staying safely cloaked from view of the people in 1888. It was an assurance that the timeline would remain uncontaminated and satisfy the government Watcher sent along to keep an eye on things, not to mention Doyle's own conscience. That way when they took small groups on excursion into the Tucson of the old west, they'd remain inconspicuous among the bustling population.

As nervous as taking civilians back in time made him, if his design proved to be the marketing win for Bennet Systems's

Fantasy Resorts, he'd get credit for the tech and that meant unlimited opportunities for future funding.

Since this was the first real time machine ever invented, no one knew what would happen if things were altered during a previous time. Sure there were plenty of theories—not to mention plenty of science-fiction supposing various scenarios. But the reality was likely very different and not something Doyle cared to experiment with. During all the test runs, he had been absolutely careful, but he was one man, and the environment had been easy to control. Throwing so many people into the mix had not been his idea, but in order for Bennet Systems to pony up the money it took to develop the tech, he had to agree to their choice of use. It was better than the alternative—selling the design to the government, who would likely bury its existence and his accomplishment along with it all for covert use. Bennet Systems may not be perfect, but it was public and powerful, which helped calm his nerves about the Watcher on board.

McGovern's baritone blasted all around them. "Welcome aboard the Time Capsule Resort. I am your captain, Casey McGovern. As you are all aware this is a one of a kind voyage, not through space but through time. Now I know you all signed your waivers and passed your physicals, but when we hit the Go button, I need you to be in a seated position."

Doyle cringed at the words "Go button." He hated when people didn't call things their proper names. "It's a time destabilizer, asshat," he muttered, adjusting one of the gauges to his left. He'd been double checking the cloak all morning. While the time destabilizer was an interconnected array of neural nets throughout the machine, the cloak was an external piece, roughly the size and shape of a baseball bat and encased in metal. It was attached dead center to the bottom of the resort, where the whole thing was designed to hover eight feet in the air above the ground, just in case landing on a spot of ground had unforeseen timeline consequences. It also avoided the possibility of anyone walking into it by mistake.

The cloak always felt a little unprotected to Doyle, considering the absolute importance of it, but he'd been too busy fine tuning the neural network and had to delegate the job to Jones. When his triple check left him satisfied, Doyle tucked his hands behind his head and tilted his hat forward to cover his eyes. With his feet resting on the console, he leaned back in his chair to take a hard-earned break.

"Sleeping already?" Jones asked.

"Pushing the 'Go button' doesn't sound hard. I'm sure you can handle it."

By the sound of Jones's chuckle, Doyle figured he was down for the job. The truth was, Doyle didn't want his nerves to show and if his heavy boots, crossed legs, secured arms, and face weren't arranged just so, he'd probably be a bumbling mess. It was the old "I can't look" feeling as his heart stampeded in his ribcage.

"And we're off!" yelled McGovern. "*Yeeeehaw!*"

Doyle tensed as the tell-tale shift of balance almost convinced him to grab hold of the chair. But even as the world tilted, he stayed still in his position. His muscles were so taught that he'd probably be sore later, but no need for Jones to know that.

A quick peek proved the tech held up as the air around him swirled with bright pinks and golds. Something told him if he reached out and touched, it would feel like jelly, but the strange pressure and dizzying sensation kept him anchored in his seat. As they slowed to a halt in the late 1800's things began to shift back to normal, the glowing colors fading into nothing and the pull dipping low in his center of gravity, sort of like being sea sick. Doyle counted down to the gentle halt of the engine in his mind's eye.

3...2...1...

The world jerked and bobbed like a car sideswiped them, dumping Doyle from his chair. A horrible scraping sound vibrated from beneath followed by a crunch and another jolt. He gripped the edge of the console, righting his hat so he could see the problem and not just hear and feel it, like somehow that might make it better.

What he saw was chaos. All the screens showed furniture, objects, and people being tossed around like kernels in a popcorn machine. Jones lay on the floor bleeding from his head where he must have banged it against the edge of the console. Doyle swore under his breath and fell to his knees by his side, applying pressure with shaky hands even as the floating resort continued to bounce and sway before coming to a complete stop.

"Engineering to Medcenter," Doyle yelled into his wristband. "Man down. Jones is bleeding and unconscious."

A woman's voice crackled back at him, the sound in the background filling in the audible anarchy missing from the viewscreens. "Dr. Cantor here. Is there a pulse?"

Doyle watched Jones's chest rise and fall, felt a solid thump beneath scarlet fingers. "Yeah, doc. But there's a lot of blood."

"Shit. Fine. I'll send someone down there. I'd tell you to bring him up here, but navigating through all the turmoil is another issue. What the fuck happened down there?"

Doyle choked on the lump in his throat. What had happened? Everything had been fine on the test run not twenty-four hours prior.

"Not sure yet. We have to assess the damage. Just hurry up and get over here so I can start working on it. I'm not taking my hand off this wound until someone's here." He cut off the communication with a sharp tap on his wristband.

The second he hung up McGovern's voice exploded through. "What the hell happened to my ship?"

It's a fucking time machine, was what he wanted to say, but Doyle swallowed back the first thought that popped into his head.

"Jones is injured," he said instead. "I can't check yet. I need a medic to relieve me."

"Did you call one?" McGovern asked in patronizing way.

"Of course I did!" This time Doyle's temper got the best of him and he let it out.

"You need to check the instruments, Walter." McGovern's voice was low and even now, steady like he'd leaned in to speak only to him. "We need to protect one-hundred-twenty-seven patrons and crewmembers. I need you to Do. Your. Job."

Doyle licked his lips and nodded. McGovern was right. If they'd landed in the wrong time or worse, it could be bad. Very bad. But his assistant's life was just as important as those rich guests on the other level. Looking down at Jones, he remembered his first-aid training. *The head bleeds a lot, sometimes making the wound look worse than it is*, which meant he could probably let go so long as he wrapped the wound. He let go to take the red kerchief from Jones's neck and tied it around his head. It would do until a medic arrived.

"Right." Doyle stood back up and shoved the chair out of the way so he could read the smoking console. Warning lights flashed, and a worrisome high-pitched sound came from one of the control panels to his rear.

His fingers flew deftly over the controls, first checking the time destabilizer. When he saw it did in fact read 1888 he emptied his lungs of the breath he'd been holding then tipped up the hat to wipe sweat off his brow. Damn thing was hotter than he'd expected.

Next he checked navigation. They'd come in too low and off course by...*that can't be right*. They were miles south of Tucson, which put them right in the middle of a tree and near a field of Saguaro cacti. Doyle winced, picturing the collision from the outside. How had the nav gotten so messed up? He'd checked the coordinates himself just that morning. He'd ask Jones about it, but...

"Computer!" Doyle yelled. "Where is the nearest town?"

The soothing female voice answered, "Devil's Creek, population sixty-seven as of August 24, 1888."

Shaking himself, Doyle checked the cloaking device. His

muscles tensed again, his neck cramping. That couldn't be right either. His fingers flew as the doors behind him opened and two people came in, rushing to Jones's side. Doyle slammed his hands down on the console just as three more people entered the room.

Swinging around to face the new crowd, Doyle let out an exasperated groan. The heat boiling up the back of his neck threatened to explode out of his head like a volcano. McGovern and Nicole Bennet, his boss—two of his least favorite people. The man accompanying them fell immediately to Jones's side to help the medics as the other two glared daggers at him.

"Report," Nicole barked. Her demeanor clashed violently with the pastel and ruffles that covered her. Even under the circumstances it was hard for Doyle to keep his gaze off her heaving bosom tied into the corset like top.

He cleared his throat and decided to start with the good news. "The machine itself is intact."

McGovern visibly relaxed, looking almost ready to faint. Bennet's eyes stayed sharp.

"And?" she prompted.

"I can't get a reading on the cloak. Somehow the landing coordinates were way the hell off too. We're in a low populated area. But I checked them myself this morning."

"You should have triple checked them before departure," Bennet snapped.

Doyle pressed his lips together, not wanting to let out what he had in mind. Things like 'Navigation is not my job' and 'You should be asking how it happened'.

McGovern stepped between them. "It's okay. The time machine is ok, so we just press the Go button and head back, right?"

"It's a time destabilizer and there's no such thing as a Go button," Bennet corrected.

Doyle sat back in shock and sudden appreciation.

The man who'd come in with them stood as the others left with a still unconscious Jones. He was dressed as a gentleman, the kind who'd own a bank and get robbed in the old west. When he put an arm around Bennet's waist without being thrown over her shoulder, Doyle guessed it was her elusive boyfriend he'd heard whispers about, Dr. Jackson Meadows.

Meadows spoke. "We can't leave here until we verify that there are no other significant injuries among the passengers or crew and the timeline is intact. I've already had words with the Watcher on the way over here. It took all I had to convince them to let us handle this."

McGovern swallowed and his smile faded as Bennet nodded.

"Let's hope it's just a censor. Doyle, you'll have to go out and check it physically. I'll make an announcement to calm the masses. Luckily as far as we know, Jones was the worst hit. Until we have more information there will be no rumors about issues aboard. They are here to get the experience they paid for, and as far as the Watcher goes, the less they know, the better for everyone." Without another word Bennet swirled her large skirt around and swept from the room, Meadows in her wake.

McGovern looked at Doyle and shook his head. "You heard the boss. Get going, cowboy."

🦇

Don't stop now. Keep reading Mystic Owl books with your copy of A MATTER OF TIME by Lizzy Gayle.

And don't miss book three of the *Vampire Reality Show* series coming soon!

Don't miss book three of the *Vampire Reality Show* coming soon, and find more from Ashley R. King at www.ashleyrking.com

Until then, find more Mystic Owl books with A MATTER OF TIME by Lizzy Gayle

🦇

Arizona circa 1888 may be a fun place to visit, but the Time Capsule Fantasy Resort didn't mean to crash land there.

It's up to Walter Doyle, inventor of the new technology, to find and repair the missing cloaking device without altering the timeline. Easier said than done when he runs into a real-life, real-sexy Annie Oakley named Sadie. From the moment she points her shotgun at him, he's smitten.

All Sadie Rogers wants is to be left alone to mind her ranch and her son, something the men in town wouldn't be keen on if they found out her husband was dead. Keeping a low profile gets more complicated when the handsome Wally shows up on a hush-hush mission from Washington. When his top-secret contraption kills a man on Sadie's property, she hides the evidence. Though, she might be convinced to turn the thing over in exchange for Wally posing as her new fiancé to help save her ranch...

With sabotage afoot and a town full of corrupt cowboys and nosy neighbors, can Wally and Sadie find a way to solve both their problems? Maybe. But they'll create an even bigger one while trying—how to hold on to love that transcends time itself.

🦇

Please sign up for the City Owl Press newsletter for chances to win special subscriber-only contests and giveaways as well as receiving information on upcoming releases and special excerpts.

All reviews are **welcome** and **appreciated**. Please consider leaving one on your favorite social media and book buying sites.

Escape Your World. Get Lost in Ours! City Owl Press at www. cityowlpress.com.

ACKNOWLEDGMENTS

First and foremost, I always want to thank God for everything He's done for me. I wouldn't be here without Him, and I'm grateful for this life He's given me.

I'd also like to thank Jared, my precious husband, for his love and support. Thank you for loving me like you do, baby, and for helping me brainstorm ideas for this novel! I love you more than you will ever know!

To my editor, Heather McCorkle, thank you so much for taking a chance on my vampires and for helping me make these novels the very best they can be! It means more than you know. I am so grateful for this opportunity.

To Tina Moss and Yelena Casale, thank you for all you've done to make my dream of becoming a published author come true. It means the world, and I appreciate you both more than you know. You two are amazing.

Thank you to the incredible cover art designers at Miblart for creating the perfect cover for this novel—it's exactly as I imagined! Also, thank you to our amazing copy editor, Michele Moore, for all you did to get this novel in perfect shape. I appreciate you so much!

Christina Ramos, Gabrielle Ash, Vicki P., and Christie C., thank you all so much for taking the time to beta read this novel and help me work out the kinks in it. You all helped me SO much, and I am so grateful for each of you and your support. You all rock!

To Phil, TK, Brent, Melissa—thank you all for always believing in me no matter what. I love you more than you know!

Ginger, Lee, and Aaron, thank you for your support and encouragement on this journey. I love you more than you know!

Katherine Quinn, you beautiful soul. Thank you for being you. I am so grateful for you and your support, but most of all for our friendship which is so much more than just writer besties. You always make me laugh with the TikTok videos you send and just our texts, and I am thankful to be on this journey with you! I love you so much and I can't wait to get our house in Ireland lol!

A huge thank you to my amazing write or die twin, C. D'Angelo, for all of your ongoing support and encouragement—our friendship means the world to me, and I am beyond grateful for you. You never fail to make me smile, and our daily chats are the best. You are just one of the sweetest people and I am so lucky to know you! I can't wait to start our Twins band and to retire to Italy with you and our guys! I love you more than you know!

Thank you to Bonnie Ritch, for always believing in me and cheering me on. It means the world, and I am so thankful for you. I love you so freaking much!

Lori Taylor, for always reading my books and cheering me on (from day one). I'm so thankful to have you in my life and love you lots!

A huge thank you to the amazing City Owl authors for always being so supportive and amazing. I am so grateful to be a part of the flock.

A huge thank you to my ARC team, to all the amazing bookstagrammers who took a chance on this novel. I am so thankful for you and your time. You mean the world to me and are so appreciated!

Also a shout out to Colby Bettley, Kelly from @andkellyreads, Ashley from @owl_always_read_books, Cassandra Celia, Tiffani of @Tiffaniandherbooks, Rachel from @readingforamoment, Marcia from @itsabookthing2021, Stacie from @bookswithstacie, Michele from @lost_in_books82, Thuy from @tweezyreads, @vamplit, @ruthsdepp, Emily Hornburg, Starla DeKruyf, Anita Finn, Brittany

Sellers, Beth Merritt, Gerty Sue, Michelle Thompson, Candace Smith, Laura Ezell, Kelly Emery, and Lisa Fales for simply being amazing! I appreciate each of you more than you will ever know! Thank you to the incredible Sarah Norris for creating such stunning teasers for this novel!

To my readers—I am so incredibly grateful for you. Thank you for picking up my books. You have made this dream a reality, and I adore you for it.

ABOUT THE AUTHOR

ASHLEY R. KING is a middle school English teacher whose love of the written word began when her mom took her to the public library, letting her check out stacks of books taller than she was.

She loves swoony romances and is addicted to sweet tea. When she's not teaching or writing happily ever afters, she can be found hanging out with her husband, snuggled up with a book, travelling, or quoting obscure lines from her favorite movies and tv shows. She lives in a small town in Georgia with her favorite person in the world—her husband, and their sweet and chatty spoiled cat, Cleo.

www.ashleyrking.com

ABOUT THE PUBLISHER

City Owl Press is a cutting edge indie publishing company, bringing the world of romance and speculative fiction to discerning readers.

Escape Your World. Get Lost in Ours!

www.cityowlpress.com

facebook.com/YourCityOwlPress
twitter.com/cityowlpress
instagram.com/cityowlbooks
pinterest.com/cityowlpress

www.ingramcontent.com/pod-product-compliance
Lightning Source LLC
Chambersburg PA
CBHW020824260626
47169CB00003B/819